"Your m___
handsome ___ ___ ___ ___ with
construction..."

Wes sighed. His mother was a menace. "What did you say to that?"

Sarah patted his hand. "Don't worry. I told her how helpful you'd already been."

Wes stared down at her hand as he worked through that. Should he tell Sarah that he was almost certain he hadn't been the son his mother was trying to match her up with?

If he'd known he had to worry about both his brothers, he might have given up completely. In the ranking of handsome sons, how far down the list did he fall?

Then he realized that Sarah had assumed he was the handsome son.

And he immediately grew ten feet tall.

She was grinning at him, happy to be there in the conversation, but he knew the instant the feeling shifted to something else, to something more.

Possibility was there, shimmering in the air between them...

Dear Reader,

Beginnings can be scary, can't they? The first day of school, starting a new job or writing the first book in a new series... Those blank pages mean so many unknowns! Of course, they also mean so much exciting possibility. Here's a writing secret: I have the big pieces in mind when I start a series, but all the details that make people and places unforgettable fall into line as I go. Exciting *and* scary!

Let's explore Prospect, Colorado, together. In *The Cowboy Next Door*, Sarah Hearst returns to this small Western town because she and her sisters have inherited a run-down fishing lodge from their larger-than-life great-aunt. There are so many unknowns here, and Sarah desperately misses Sadie Hearst, who has always been her lifeline. Fortunately, Wes Armstrong is there to provide the answers she needs...as well as a few important questions of his own.

I hope you enjoy meeting the characters of Prospect. To find out more about my books and what's coming next, visit me at cherylharperbooks.com.

Cheryl

HEARTWARMING

The Cowboy Next Door

———

Cheryl Harper

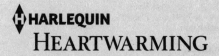

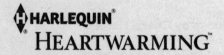

HARLEQUIN®
HEARTWARMING™

ISBN-13: 978-1-335-58486-1

The Cowboy Next Door

Copyright © 2023 by Cheryl Harper

Recycling programs for this product may not exist in your area.

For questions and comments about the quality of this book, please contact us at CustomerService@Harlequin.com.

Harlequin Enterprises ULC
22 Adelaide St. West, 41st Floor
Toronto, Ontario M5H 4E3, Canada
www.Harlequin.com

Printed in U.S.A.

Cheryl Harper discovered her love for books and words as a little girl, thanks to a mother who made countless library trips and an introduction to Laura Ingalls Wilder's Little House books. Whether the stories she reads are set in the prairie, the American West, Regency England or Earth a hundred years in the future, Cheryl enjoys strong characters who make her laugh. Now Cheryl spends her days searching for the right words while she stares out the window, and her dog, Jack, snoozes beside her. And she considers herself very lucky to do so.

For more information about Cheryl's books, visit her online at cherylharperbooks.com or follow her on Twitter, @cherylharperbks.

Books by Cheryl Harper

Harlequin Heartwarming

Veterans' Road

Winning the Veteran's Heart
Second Chance Love
Her Holiday Reunion
The Doctor and the Matchmaker
The Dalmatian Dilemma
A Soldier Saved

Otter Lake Ranger Station

Her Unexpected Hero
Her Heart's Bargain
Saving the Single Dad
Smoky Mountain Sweethearts

Visit the Author Profile page
at Harlequin.com for more titles.

CHAPTER ONE

SARAH HEARST WAS certain of a few things when she slipped into a cushy leather seat in the boardroom of Winthrop, Marshall, and Fine, attorneys at law.

First, her great-aunt Sadie had staged her final scene perfectly. Hiring the premiere law firm in Los Angeles came with perks, including a richly paneled conference room, efficient assistants who distributed coffee and water unobtrusively and the hush of hallowed old money that had never once managed to subdue the Hearsts.

Second, Sadie would have appreciated the size and energy of the crowd. The whole family had answered the summons to hear the reading of her will and the atmosphere was more low-key family reunion than true mourning. She had always called the people in the room her "favorite do-gooders, no-gooders and charming rapscallions" and loved every one of her four nephews—Sarah's dad included—and seventeen great-nieces and great-nephews even when they were "messier than a bag of nails."

The boardroom's view of the city was unimpeded on the beautiful late summer day, but inside, they might as well have been gathered around the island of Sadie's comfortable kitchen. Bluegrass music provided a backdrop for the various conversations. Instead of a publicity shot of a perfectly turned-out Sadie, TV chef and personality, a candid shot of her in her element, with flour dotting her red-and-white-gingham-check apron and a big grin on her face, filled the screen at the head of the table.

Sarah also knew without a doubt that some of the Hearsts would be surprised at Sadie's decisions. Her great-aunt had been unpredictable and relished every minute of watching people scurry to catch up with her. As a girl, Sarah had admired Sadie's over-the-top style; she'd come to understand the strategy behind Sadie's zigging when others expected her to zag after she'd started working her way up in the family business, the Cookie Queen Corporation.

"If they don't hurry up and get this started, the executor may need his own executor. None of us are getting any younger," her baby sister, Brooke, muttered. She smoothed her perfectly knotted blond updo and twitched a heel. "I've got to make my flight this afternoon. Paul's campaign manager is meeting us for dinner. This came at the worst time." Brooke and her husband were making plans to move into the mayor's mansion someday. Winning this election to the New York City Council was the critical first step.

"Too busy in New York to properly pay respects to Aunt Sadie," Sarah's middle sister, Jordan, said softly. She jostled Sarah as she crossed her arms with a huff.

Brooke and Jordan had been together for a full ride from the airport without an argument, so the cease-fire was clearly winding down.

Sarah didn't roll her eyes. She counted that a victory.

The lawyer executing Sadie's will, Howard Marshall, was both impressive and elderly, and the two qualities together meant he kept no schedule other than his own. Sadie had always done things as she liked and on her own time. This gathering would be no different. Fussing wouldn't change a thing, and Jordan's fidgeting suggested she agreed more with her younger sister than she'd ever want anyone to know.

As the peacemaker of the group, Sarah bit back the urge to shush her sisters, but if Brooke reminded her one more time how important it was that she get back to New York that evening, Sarah was going to...

"Thank you for joining us," Howard Marshall said as he opened the folder in front of him. "I'll be forwarding a copy of the letters Sadie left for each of you after this reading. Today we're here to cover the bequests Sarah Abigail Hearst outlined in her will." He cleared his throat, licked his finger and turned the page slowly. Hearing the lawyer call her great-aunt Sarah illuminated how clearly the world had changed. If Sadie were here, she'd smack him wherever she could reach, head or arm or chest, and remind him she only answered to Sadie. Being named after Sadie had always made Sarah proud. Today she was proud and heartbroken all over again that Sadie was really gone.

"Sadie did her own writing, so you will excuse the…" Howard sniffed. "Ahem, casual tone and hear these words in her voice, if you please."

Jordan bumped her shoulder again. "You okay?" she whispered.

Sarah nodded and wrapped her hand around Jordan's on one side and Brooke's on the other while they listened to Howard Marshall outline the bequests connected with the Cookie Queen Corporation, including the small corporate headquarters near Los Angeles, and the fortune Sadie had amassed over a lifetime as top baker, television chef and name brand for kitchen appliances and a line of Western wear.

A Los Angeles home and New York apartment and other large assets would be sold and the proceeds divided equally between Sadie's list of heirs after the final sale. Simple enough. There were keepsakes left to each member of the family, and Sadie hadn't made any rules on keeping, selling or trading. As always, her gifts were true gifts, no strings attached.

As the lawyer's reading slowed, Sarah felt the weight of her sisters' stares. Their names had been conspicuously absent from the list of keepsakes and special notes.

"The final items are rather…delicate. Thus, Sadie wanted to handle telling you herself." Howard Marshall lifted his chin in a sharp motion to give his assistant a signal. Behind him, Sadie's photo became a video.

"Well, now, if this isn't the sorriest bunch of rascals I ever saw gathered in one place. Not a solitary tear to be seen." Sadie tsked and shook her head. Sarah tried to guess when it had been recorded. Her aunt had never gone gray, thanks to the best salons money could reserve. Until the end, she'd preferred a red lip and dark mascara. She might have recorded this video last month or last century, honestly.

Sadie waggled her finger. "I better not see any tears when I gaze down from my comfy cloud at you all. I'm celebratin' today, and you better be, too. I'm guessing Howie's almost finished reading my will. Let's tie up business, shall we? Wilson, raise your hand."

Wilson Douglas, Sadie's chief financial officer, followed Sadie's order.

"Aw, put your hand down, Wil. Everyone at this table knows who you are." Sadie chuckled. "First. My four darling nephews will form a new board of directors, with Wilson Douglas serving as the fifth member. During my last contract negotiation with Wil, I included a clause about what should happen if I died before the end of said contract." She held her hands out as if to say, "and here's where we ended up."

"Wilson will step up to lead The Cookie Queen Corporation. His position is guaranteed for one year. At the end of that year, either Wil or the board of directors may make a change there, but he will continue to serve on the board for a period of at least five years. Nobody knows the business better than Wil. I trust him with my baby."

Sarah studied Wilson Douglas's face. He was not shocked. He and his boss must have discussed her plans for the board of directors in advance. His firm jaw indicated he was prepared to honor Sadie's wishes even if her family bucked the decision.

Sadie cupped a hand over her eyes. "Michael, you better be at this table."

Sarah watched her oldest cousin straighten in his seat. "I'm here." A flush covered his cheeks when he realized he was responding to a video. Michael was the first of all the great-nephews and as such, took his position as eldest seriously. Michael took everything seriously; he marched through the Cookie Queen headquarters as if he were the official hall monitor. His "management by walking around" had earned him his own nickname; Sadie compared him to a stray calf.

"Okay, my little dogie," Sadie said, "you've been gunning for the top spot for years. Here's your chance. You also have one year, serving under Wil, to learn the ins and outs of the job. At the end of your trial period, Wil decides whether to recommend you permanently as CEO or to toss you out on your ear." She waggled a finger a second time. "I believe you can do this, Mikey, but try not to incite a riot in my employees. I love them more than a bear loves honey."

Michael relaxed against his chair, and Sarah immediately understood that her own position at the company had changed and not in a good way. He was going to be her boss. Her cousin had never understood Sarah's role as the single person in the customer relations area. It wasn't about answering phones or resolving complaints; Sarah and Sadie had brainstormed ways to keep her connected to her fans. Sarah's job had been about building strong relationships through appearances, social media posts, special fan messages and big and small ways to draw people to Sadie Hearst for recipes, advice and entertainment.

When Sadie continued on without addressing her position within the business, Sarah started to worry.

"Everybody study that wall. Those are my mountains, remember?" On the video, Sadie pointed to the right. There in the boardroom, a large painting filled the wall exactly where Sadie had ordered it to be put, no doubt, showing soaring mountains covered in tall trees and with white-capped peaks.

Sarah noticed everyone in the room followed her great-aunt's directions and stared hard at the painting. They'd all learned not to ignore her wishes. Sarah didn't have to. She had the painting memorized. It had hung behind her great-aunt's desk in her messy office until today.

"Home. Where I grew up. Some of you might even remember before I was the Cookie Queen, when I was only a local talent on public broadcasting, that I lived in a place called Prospect. My daddy's fishing lodge, grandly

titled the Majestic Prospect Lodge, you recall? We used to get together during the summer, fish and swim and generally enjoy every
blessing Mother Nature has tucked away in
the prettiest locale in creation. Been a long
time since I've been there, but the memories
are sweet." Sadie cleared her throat. "Sarah,
Jordan and Brooke…well, you might have
hoped for something less troublesome, but
I know you'll figure out what to do. After
fifteen years, the Majestic may be nothing
but weathered wood and cobwebs, but it's all
yours. Renovate it and run it, sell it as quick
as you can or let the mountains claim it again
after the buildings turn to dust. You girls decide. But do it together and remember this
legacy we've built.

"We all had such good times there. When
I think of your mama, I picture her in the
old hammock by the lake, remember? Place
never was the same after she was gone, was
it? That lovely girl could bake like a dream,
too. I despair that not a sorry one of you children caught the bug, but those days sure were
special. I could never let the lodge go myself,
but it's a puzzle that needs a solution. You
girls were always my favorite troublemakers,

and that is saying quite a lot with this crowd. I couldn't trust the Majestic to anyone else."

Sadie cupped a hand over her ear. "What's that? Can't be complaints, not from this lot. A bunch of questions? Well, my time is up. I love you all. Don't forget to miss me but not too much."

The screen went dark.

Howard Marshall stacked his papers efficiently and waited. "May I answer any questions?"

Stunned silence filled the room. Not even Sarah could recover quickly enough to get her mouth in gear.

Eventually, Jordan asked, "Is there more information about the fishing lodge? A budget or…"

Sarah understood why Jordan trailed off. The questions were too big to chew unless they bit off small pieces at first.

The lawyer slid a second folder down the table. Heads turned as it slipped past to land in front of Sarah. "Instructions are here. There are funds to cover this year's taxes and any minor incidentals, but the rest of the funds will come after the sale of all other assets are final and distributed among the heirs. Nothing additional has been set aside for upkeep. The property manager in town has only secured the physical building, so the repairs may be extensive and all utilities will need to be restored before improvements begin." His lips were a tight line, as if he expected this to present a problem.

He could be right. Without upkeep, what state would the lodge be in after all this time?

The longer Sarah and her sisters took to decide about this remote piece of land they hadn't seen in years, the greater the threat of losing the lodge or their own savings to hold it.

"When should we expect to see the rest?" Brooke asked. "The funds…"

"The sales won't be rushed. Sadie had particular wishes." Howard Marshall sniffed. "My office will see to the disposition of any assets. Make sure your current address is on file with my assistant. We'll be in further contact when funds are ready to be disbursed." Howard Marshall stood. He didn't wave them toward the door, but his expression suggested he was ready for them to clear the boardroom. "If the new members of the board could remain, I have paperwork for you to sign."

Sarah and her sisters moved out into the

hallway and followed the silent pack of Hearsts to the elevator. They waited for the next car to go down.

"Well, Sarah, not sure how you managed to get the family land," Michael said, sidling up next to her. "You and Sadie spent a lot of time together at the end, I guess." He shoved his hands in his pockets and jingled his change.

The urge to return a snarky comment about worming his way into the top position burned, but Sarah shoved it down.

"Congratulations, Michael," Sarah said, holding on to her position as the peacemaker with a tight grip. "I know you'll do a great job as CFO." Did she, though? Maybe not. She was certain he expected her to say so and there would be trouble if she didn't. Since Sadie hadn't done anything to protect Sarah's job, making nice with the new boss seemed prudent.

"Sarah worked with Sadie, the same as you did," Jordan snapped, ready to step in front and go to war as usual.

"Not exactly like I did." Michael ran his hand down his tie. "I worked all the way up to the head of marketing. Sadie had to create the customer relations director role, which…" Michael tapped Sarah's shoulder. "That's marketing, isn't it?"

It was more than that but explaining it to him again would be a waste of time.

Jordan's exasperated gust of air was enough of an answer that Sarah let the whole thing go.

"Good thing your position isn't essential day to day," he said. "You'll have plenty of time to sort out the lodge. Not sure there's much of a decision, though. You three have the money to reopen it? Lack of experience wouldn't stop you from trying."

"What's it to you, cousin?" Jordan drawled.

"Nothing, I guess." Michael jingled his coins again. "I look forward to your decision on what to do with the lodge and Sadie's legacy in Prospect. Sarah, when you're back at your desk, let me know. I'm going to make a presentation to the new board, a realignment of staffing and duties that makes good sense now, and I'd like to include your position in my plans."

He walked away before she could demand any details.

"Does that mean you'll still have your job or…" Brooke asked, her forehead wrinkled in concern. It was a valid question. His tone made Sarah think she wouldn't survive any personnel changes.

"Let's stop at Lark's on the way to the airport," Brooke muttered. "We need to talk."

Since her sister was right and she'd finally stopped harping about not missing her flight back to New York, Sarah was happy to agree. They were seated around a cramped table with the pizza they'd ordered ahead of time before anyone spoke.

"How quickly do you think we can sell?" Brooke asked before she took a bite.

The fact that Jordan paused and chose not to fire back convinced Sarah that both of her sisters were on the same page. "We won't know until we see what shape it's in," she said. "Since my job is apparently…open-ended now, I'll head up to Prospect this weekend." She wiped her fingers on her napkin. "We could make it a girls' trip, go together and make the decision as one."

They hadn't successfully traveled together ever, but certainly not after the summer her mother had died. Sarah had spent every family trip in the middle of the backseat, the wall preventing her sisters from brawling and her father from turning the car around.

"It could be fun," she added.

Both of her sisters sucked in air, ready to explain how wrong she was, when her father pulled out the fourth seat at the table. He wrapped his arms around her before hugging Jordan and Brooke. "The Everything Pizza. My favorite." He immediately pulled the mushrooms off a slice and took a bite. "What's the plan?"

Sarah rubbed her temple. "We got here fifteen minutes before you, Dad. We're good, but we aren't that good."

He nodded and waved his hand to tell her to go on.

"I'm heading to Prospect. Brooke has to get home. Jordan…" Sarah raised her eyebrows.

"I've got a project to wrap up, but I could make it…next week? Do you want to wait that long?" she asked. "My guess is that the internet service in Prospect may not be up to running high-speed cybersecurity tests and tech firms want everything finished yesterday. My boss will complain if I extend this unexpected break." Jordan's guilty expression was so familiar that Sarah immediately winced. Her middle sister had always worried so much about doing enough that she overcompensated. Not joining Sarah weighed her down.

"No rush, I guess. Once the taxes are paid, you should have a year or so." Her father frowned. "But I'm not sure how many buyers there are for a run-down fishing lodge. It could take a while to get a decent price." Her father made a good point. Since he and his art supply store scraped by, he wasn't known for giving financial advice.

"But the proceeds from the sale of Sadie's assets will help if we have to hold it longer," Sarah said.

"Unless we need those for…life." Brooke closed her eyes before forcing a smile on her face. "Sarah, when you go, be sure to take some pictures. Then we can all see the place and decide on how to go about listing it for sale."

Jordan wanted to argue; the urge was written on her face, but it was a valid suggestion.

"What if we don't want to sell?" Jordan asked. "I mean, what if we can't agree?"

"Why would we want to keep a fishing lodge in a town in the mountains hours away from anywhere?" Brooke asked slowly and loudly. Before Jordan could reply, Brooke's cell phone rang. Brooke snatched it off the table and scowled down at the number on the display. "I have to take this." She was shaking her head as she stood and marched toward the door.

They watched Brooke pace in front of the window of Lark Street Pizza, the hole-in-the-wall pizza place that had kept their whole family alive after Beth Hearst had died and their father had moved them to this modest, albeit neighborly neighborhood. Leaving Denver had been hard, but Lark's had always hit the spot.

"That was Paul's number, I think." Jordan chewed her bottom lip. "It was definitely New York."

Sarah knew Jordan was worried about Brooke. They all were. Talking to her on the phone only kept her up to date with the big events in her youngest sister's life. Seeing the circles under her eyes and the way the fancy suit hung on her thinner frame was enough evidence to support their concern.

If it was Brooke's husband on the other end of the call, were they having trouble? What should she do about it?

"I'm going to run to the restroom so we can

hit the road," Jordan mumbled before walking away.

Sarah met her father's stare.

"Good thing Sadie lumped you three together, isn't it? No better way for her to leave chaos in her wake, and she loved chaos." He squeezed Sarah's hand. "You'll work it all out, Sarah. They'll follow you."

Sarah sipped her water and wondered if it was worth mentioning to her father that Brooke was losing too much weight and Jordan was shorter tempered than usual. His sunny disposition had always made him better at celebration than problem-solving. That was her job.

"Ever notice how often they disappear when the bill hits the table?" he asked with a grin. He plopped his credit card down and handed it and the bill back to the waiter. "Like they have honed a sixth sense about it somehow."

The tension headache forming in her temples was going to be a problem.

"Listen, don't worry about your job. We've got a board meeting planned for two weeks from Friday. We'll all sit down and discuss any major changes before they're set in stone." Her father squeezed her shoulder. "Try to enjoy this trip back to Prospect. Sadie was always one with ulterior motives. It wouldn't surprise me if she planned this for you to take a break and have the chance to revisit old haunts in Colorado."

While also saddling her with her sisters' futures, too. Maybe. Maybe not.

"Dad, why do you think Sadie didn't make a place for me? At the company. I work hard there." That worried Sarah more than this lodge problem. When she got to Prospect, the problem about what to do with their inheritance would be answered, no doubt.

But what about her career and her life and all the rest?

If she wasn't working for her aunt, then...

He sighed. "Hard to say. I wish she'd been the kind of person who made her plans clear, but there is one thing I am certain of." He bent his head to meet her stare. "My daughters are equal to whatever Sadie dreamed up for them. She knew that, too."

Sarah nodded to reassure him. He was right, of course. Finding another job wouldn't be difficult.

Finding anyone else like Sadie, though, would be impossible.

Stretching her neck slowly from side to side as she followed her father and sisters out of Lark's didn't do a lot to ease the headache. For now, all Sarah could do was take the next step: find her way back to Prospect.

CHAPTER TWO

THE THIRD TIME the pleasant GPS voice said "Recalculating," Sarah contemplated turning around in the middle of the two-lane highway and driving right back to the airport. Her reasonable two-hour drive had turned into more than four hours, thanks to the traffic snarl caused by an accident outside Denver, what had to have been sightseeing tourists in front of her for another half hour, then a missed turn and unexpected detour.

Sarah enjoyed driving. She'd booked the flight to Denver instead of making the trip from LA in her own car because two days driving to Prospect and then back would be longer than she planned to spend exploring Sadie's lodge and taking photos.

Could she take that much time off work? Obviously, yes. Her cousin and new boss had made sure to email her and reiterate that she could take however long she needed.

"That would give him more time to move someone else into my office, of course," Sarah muttered to herself while she made the careful U-turn in the middle of the road as the GPS woman suggested.

Prospect was close. It had to be. The GPS had run out of alternate routes, the sun was setting and there was absolutely no other traffic on the road anymore. If signs of life didn't appear around the next curve, Sarah would head back toward Denver to find a hotel. Starting fresh in the morning was beginning to sound both pleasant and inevitable.

She almost missed the sign in the growing shadows of the mountains.

Prospect. Est. 1873.

That was it. No Welcome!

Or Home of the Fighting Elk or whatever the local high school mascot might be.

Or even a nod to their most famous citizen, Sadie Hearst, the Colorado Cookie Queen.

There were no billboards leading into the town to advertise restaurants or points of interest.

As Sarah slowly drove, she was struck by how familiar Prospect felt even as nothing was quite the same as she remembered. Dark storefronts were set along a raised wooden sidewalk marked by hitching posts here and there for atmosphere. In the shadows of the setting sun, it was harder to make out all the details on the historic storefronts, but it was easy to identify the long, low livery stable that marked the beginning of the historic downtown; the squat, square old jail; the fancy, two-story bathhouse offering a shave and a haircut for two bits; and the lovely old movie theater. Parking spots slanted in to the sidewalk along the road, but the streets were empty.

Prospect's history as a silver boomtown was on display, and the town had leaned into that history to draw tourists when Sarah and her family had visited years ago, with modern businesses filling those preserved buildings. Were all the businesses closed now?

In the dusty corner of her memory, Sarah could visualize a bed-and-breakfast that had taken the pride of place right near the center of Prospect. When she was a kid, they'd watched a parade move down the main thoroughfare of town from the front porch of the B-and-B. Her plan was to stop there for the evening and pick up the keys to the lodge first thing in the morning.

She turned down the radio so she could see better and hunched forward over the steering wheel to peer through the windshield. As soon as she saw the white gingerbread trim of the old blue Victorian that sprawled from corner to corner of one of Prospect's short blocks, Sarah relaxed. The lights were on. The dim illumination from the windows highlighted the sign out front.

Bell House. Sarah frowned as she tried to remember if that had been the name the last time she visited Prospect.

The fact that the sign didn't mention anything about being a bed-and-breakfast or having rooms available caused Sarah to hesitate before pulling into one of the parking spots in front.

The urgent pressure to find food and a restroom, not necessarily in that order, convinced her to move quickly up the dark sidewalk and across the broad porch that wrapped around the building. Sarah paused, her hand raised to knock on the front door, when she noticed a ragged piece of paper stuck to the doorframe.

"If this door's shut, go over to the Mercantile," Sarah read out loud. An arrow pointed to the right, so Sarah walked to the edge of the porch to see a brightly lit building about three blocks away. Light spilled out of windows on two floors, and several cars dotted the street.

"Signs of life," Sarah said, relieved to know there were actual people still living in Prospect.

Ready to stretch her legs after being cramped into an airplane seat followed by hours on the road, she hurried down the sidewalk. If the Mercantile didn't have a public restroom, she was about to make an awkward introduction to the townspeople.

Her first riddle was the entrance to the Mercantile. She remembered trailing behind her father through the jumble of stacks and aisles inside the Mercantile. He'd been delighted to poke and dig through the assortment of merchandise inside. She remembered his grin when he bought a squirrel feeder that held an ear of corn and transformed into a spinning squirrel circus with the weight of one hungry squirrel; it might still be hanging up at their old house in Denver.

At some point since their last visit, the Mercantile had been renovated. The door opened into a foyer lined with pamphlets about things to do and see in the area. Then there were two doors, one on either side of the small room.

She read the hand-painted signs hanging over the opposing doors. "Hardware. Handmade." Sarah peeked through the door of Hardware and saw no one. She did the same on the Handmade side. It didn't matter that it was empty; the restroom sign caught her eye and she made her decision.

Prepared to make awkward conversation, Sarah hurried through Handmade, weaving her way through tables and displays set up with all kinds of crafting supplies, but she didn't have to speak until she stepped back outside the restroom, relieved and focused on the delicious smell wafting through the empty space.

"Come on upstairs," a man yelled from the top of the staircase. "We're about to eat." Sarah could only see boots, but she didn't have a lot of options at this point, short of opting for the car and starting all over the next day.

Sarah tried to devise something clever to say when whoever it was who had invited her upstairs realized that she wasn't who he expected. On her way, she almost stopped to study a small pillow with a beautiful columbine embroidered on the top. She needed a souvenir, but this might not be the time to shop for an embroidery kit to remember her trip by.

At the bottom of the steps, she took a deep breath and started to climb. Just before she reached the top, she could hear the jingle of the bells downstairs and heavy boots behind her. Blocking the entry to whatever gathering was happening was a bad idea, but she struggled to move, very aware that she'd be the center of attention when she stepped inside.

"Ma'am, I don't want to hurry you, but I am late for that function. Missing the first planning meeting for our Western Days festival can have consequences around here, mainly jobs you never asked for landing squarely in your lap."

Sarah turned to see a handsome man yank off his cowboy hat and smooth a hand through his dark hair. "I won't tell 'em you're out here if you don't want me to. I'm already in trouble, so I have to take the leap."

He held a hand out and let it hover near the small of her back to urge her to the side and then hurried through the door. Sarah followed him quietly inside as a woman standing at the head of the room said, "Well, finally, our mayor has arrived. You'd think he would be on time for the meeting and the vote."

The mayor, the man who'd convinced her to step inside, met Sarah's stare and raised his eyebrows to communicate that he'd expected every bit of that disapproval. Sarah shrugged her sympathy and smiled at his resigned sigh.

From her tone and the gavel in her hand, Sarah understood that the tall woman waving the cowboy forward was In Charge. She was all business, even if the flowing kimono-style jacket and beautiful scarf made her seem artistic and approachable.

Her eyes met Sarah's for an instant. They were curious but she had other matters to attend to.

"All in favor of Matt Armstrong, the handsomest mess you ever saw, serving as chairman for this year's Western Days, please say aye." Then she cupped her hand over her ear as if she needed to hear the loud chorus of ayes better. Sarah wasn't sure how many people were in the room, at least twenty, but when the woman added, "And against, say nay," there was only one voice in the room: a cowboy who tried to slip the gavel out of her hand before she could bang it.

When the audience hooted and clapped, Sarah realized it was a joke everyone in the room was in on. He must be Matt Armstrong.

"This will be an excellent lesson for my baby boy. Mateo is going to do big things for this centennial celebration." She leaned over to the table behind her and picked up an enormous three-ring binder. It was black, but even across the room, Sarah could read the label: Western Days.

"Come spring, we need to have the biggest weekend yet. Crowds are dwindling, but with new leadership—" she patted Matt's back "—and a few other tricks I got up my sleeve, we can make this centennial unforgettable."

The woman clapped her hands as if that was the final word on the topic.

Sarah wondered if Matt was really sick to his stomach or if his expression only made it seem that way as he stared at the binder.

Her friendly cowboy, also known as Prospect's mayor, had moved over to say something to Matt. Was it congratulations? His wicked grin convinced Sarah it was closer to amusement at the other man's predicament.

The loud clap must have been the sign that their business was done because people stood and started rearranging chairs and opening up tables that had been stacked against the wall. A couple of women removed covers from the food lining the bar. The small kitchen filled with volunteers who started setting up the potluck dishes and drinks.

Sarah was considering her choices while she watched the mayor move over to a group of men talking and laughing. They all smacked him on the shoulder or back.

"Miss, if you'd like some food, you better step up and grab a plate."

Sarah spotted an older man with one shoulder propped against the doorway. Gray dusted his temples, but the merriment behind his eyes helped Sarah relax a fraction. She also recognized his voice. He'd been the man at the top of the stairs who'd told her to come up.

"Food goes quick around here, but you can bet it'll be good." He bent forward as if he had a secret to share. "Do not skip the desserts because you think you can come back later. That is a rookie mistake. If you see it and you want it, you better go for it right now."

He held his hand out to hover near the small

of her back as the younger cowboy had done, not quite touching but offering guidance. Was that a cowboy thing?

"Thank you, but I can't crash. I was hoping to find whoever runs the bed-and-breakfast." Sarah grimaced. "Bell House? Is it still a B-and-B?"

The man tipped his head back. "Well, now. I didn't know Rose was expecting visitors." He studied the crowd. "She's over there in the kitchen. Gonna be a minute before we can untangle her. You better go ahead and make a plate. We'll get you all taken care of after we get a helping of Prue's meatballs, 'mkay?"

He patted her shoulder and motioned her forward.

Short of arguing with the first person who'd offered help and food at the same time, Sarah wasn't left with much choice.

She stepped up to the end of the line that was forming, picked up a plate and studied the dishes crowding the bar. As soon as she figured out the slow cooker must be the source of both the delicious barbecue smell and the meatballs, she had the beginning of a loose plan: eat first, worry about a bed after that.

CHAPTER THREE

WES ARMSTRONG WATCHED the beautiful blonde stranger who'd taken her place in the food line. Ignoring his mother's expression and the shenanigans his younger brothers always got up to at these town meetings took practice but he was good at multitasking. Every single one of his brothers was grown and successful, or should be, but when the eyes of the town were on them, they might as well have been in high school again.

"Pretty visitor, huh? Where did you meet her?" his mother said slyly as she bumped her elbow into his ribs.

Wes held out both hands. "She didn't come with me. Found her on the landing outside, trying to decide whether to come in or head for the hills."

His mother frowned but she was never discouraged for long. "Well, go introduce yourself properly. Make sure she feels welcome here." She raised her eyebrows expectantly.

"Mama, you don't know a thing about her except that you don't know a thing about her." Wes shook his head. "Are you so anxious to marry me off that you don't care any more than that?" He poked his bottom lip out. "Sad. I thought you loved me."

His mother sighed. "Five boys and not a single one of you serious. Fine. I admit, we should ask a few questions before we get you hitched, but I'm concerned, Wes. You don't leave Prospect, so whoever your special someone is will have to stumble into town somehow. I wanted you to have a head start with this stranger, as you are the oldest and my favorite at the moment, but you have to seize your chance. When Matt gets past the shock of being in charge of the festival, he'll swoop her up." She made a scooping motion. "Plain swoop her up."

Since Wes knew his brother had been seeing a weather reporter in Denver quietly for about a month, he wasn't worried about Matt or his swooping. She worked the morning shows, so Matt made it a habit to be in Denver in the afternoon when he could manage it.

Matt had threatened retaliation to make sure Wes didn't tell their mother, and Wes had agreed because having a bargaining chip against one of his brothers was always nice.

That didn't mean Wes would have no competition for the attention of a beautiful female. Travis, Clay and Grant could give Matt a run for his money if they decided to focus on a woman. However, Clay was stuck in Colorado Springs and the other two were wrapped up in their own troubles. That was why his mother had chosen him to harass first.

"Okay, if you won't approach her, I will. Somebody needs to find out why the sweet-looking stranger is in town." His mother brushed off her shoulders. "I know my duty."

Strategies and tactics were Prue Armstrong's two middle names. When he'd met her the first time, the night after his biological mom had been arrested in a drug bust and the social worker had introduced him to his new foster parents, she'd set him at ease immediately and then slowly but surely became the first woman in his life who'd never let him down.

So, when she swept across the floor, the light shawl-y thing flapping in the breeze she stirred up, Wes followed in her wake. Like the perfect host, she touched shoulders and hugged necks as she worked the room, before stopping at the end of the potluck dishes.

The blonde stranger plopped one of his mother's famous meatballs in her mouth as his mother said, "Welcome to Prospect. We sure are glad to have you. Rose didn't tell us she was expecting anyone to check in tonight."

Wes contained the unexpected grin that almost escaped as the stranger's brown eyes widened and she chewed furiously so that she could speak. Good table manners. She didn't want to talk with her mouth full.

After the stranger smiled warmly, she said, "I don't have a reservation. I had intended to be here earlier in the day. Traffic outside of Denver delayed me. I'm hoping there's a room available. I don't want to climb back into my car tonight just to make the same trip tomorrow."

His mother held out her hand. "I'm Prue Armstrong. Handmade is my store. Is that what brought you to Prospect? We do get a fair number of crafters, mainly because we've been named Colorado's best quilt shop."

Wes met his father's stare over the blonde's shoulder. It wouldn't do to roll his eyes, but his mother never failed to work that fact into a conversation. That honor had taken place more than ten years ago, when the Prospect Western Days event had drawn large crowds. Her shop still did well because she taught classes and people loved the idea of an authentic Western retreat, but it wasn't drawing people from Denver regularly.

"Or did you need a shovel?" his father asked dryly. "A saw? Hardware is my store. You may not have heard of it, but I'll be happy to tell you why you should have." He raised a hand to stage-whisper, "It's the only one for thirty miles."

Wes watched their visitor turn from one to the other and decided she was amused instead of worried about the dueling chamber of commerce taking place in front of her.

"Ignore my ex-husband. He always has to

say something." His mother pointed at the plate the blonde was holding. "My meatballs also deserve an award, don't they?"

Their visitor was nodding as his father said, "Nobody can argue with that, Prue."

His mother pursed her lips. "Thank you, Walt."

"Miss, if you'd like to take a seat at a table and enjoy your supper in relative silence, I'll be happy to make them leave you alone," Wes said, worried his parents would continue their conversation until the long potluck line behind them revolted. He pointed the way to urge her forward.

"Wait, before you go, I hope you'll tell us your name. We'll send Rose on over when she's ready to head back to the B-and-B." His mother followed behind Wes and the woman she'd been urging him to make a move on. Did she not see it would be impossible to flirt with his mother standing right next to him?

"Of course, I'm sorry. I was…"

The blonde considered her words. Was she wondering how to say "I was trying to break into the conversation you were having around me" without saying that? If she stayed for a while, Wes would warn her every day could be like this. She'd need to learn to step on the conversation if she had anything important to say.

"Enjoying my food. I'm Sarah." She held out her hand for his mother to shake. "Sarah Hearst. I'm here to take a look at the lodge."

Wes watched his mother shake her hand and wondered if Sarah noticed how the temperature dropped, conversation stilled and the room became noticeably quiet.

"Oh," his mother said softly. "A Hearst has come back to Prospect." The curious interest on her face faded away, leaving her impossible to read. "After all this time."

Sarah blinked slowly. The change in atmosphere had to be registering for her, too. "Yes, my great-aunt is Sadie Hearst. Was. She left the lodge to me and my sisters."

No one spoke.

Sarah cleared her throat. "We used to come to Prospect in the summer when we were young. Lots of great memories of the lodge and the lake."

His mother crossed her arms. "Been many

years since then. Lots of changes out there and here in Prospect."

Sarah nodded. "Right. We had no idea what Sadie's plans were, so we don't know much about what the Majestic is like these days." She held out her hands as if she was saying "and that's why I'm here."

"We sure missed Sadie around here," his mother said. "I hope you'll take some time to get to know Prospect before you make any final decisions on Sadie's lodge."

"Prue, let's get some food," his father said, one hand wrapped firmly around his mother's shoulder. "Leave our guest to enjoy hers. Wes can connect Miss Hearst and Rose. Tomorrow will be soon enough to talk more about… things."

His mother wanted to argue. She opened her mouth to do so, but thought better of it when his father met her stare. Her shoulders eased back down, she turned on a heel and let Walt lead her over to the line. There were a few intent, whispered words between the two, but eventually conversation began to trickle through the room again.

Sarah was biting her lip when he focused

on her again. "I never imagined we wouldn't be welcome in Prospect." The wrinkle between her brows showed her concern. "We loved it here once upon a time."

Wes inhaled. This was not the moment or place to discuss his mother's reaction. He wasn't sure he could explain it, but he had a feeling she expected the Hearsts to sell the land to the highest bidder.

It would be a logical decision.

It would also mean big changes to the town they all loved.

"You will not find anyone who loves Prospect more than my mother, except my father." He pulled out a chair. "Please, finish your food. I'll ask Rose to come over and walk you back to Bell House later."

Wes pointed toward the kitchen. "See the small woman dead center of the crowd in the kitchen? That's Rose. She'll look after you."

When Sarah moved closer to see where he was pointing, he realized she smelled like sunshine, a clean, warm scent that he wanted to remember.

"In the hat with the…orange blob on it?"

He raised his eyebrows, amused at her description. "I can't tell if that's a sign of how bad your eyes are or how sad your sports knowledge is, but that is a bronco. Rose's favorite team. Quite popular in these parts. I wouldn't use that tone regarding the team around anyone you want to impress."

Sarah pursed her lips. "Bronco. Right. I should have remembered that." Her lips twitched. "Don't tell anyone I said that."

Wes met her stare. "Our little secret." Her smile slipped away but she didn't put distance between them. It might be nice to share secrets with such a beautiful woman.

She cleared her throat. "Thank you. One more thing, if you have a second. I need to meet with the lawyer who has the keys and any account information for the lodge. My paperwork listed his name as Wesley Armstrong, but didn't have an address."

"Call me Wes, please." He offered her his hand. "At your service."

"You're the lawyer," Sarah said slowly before clasping his hand. The feel of her skin against his was nice, much more exciting than any handshake he'd had ever.

"I am. I am also the mayor of Prospect.

Prue and Walt are my parents. It's a small place, Prospect. Almost everyone likes it that way. We always know when someone new rolls into town." He forced himself to let go of her hand and was relieved. Conversation might be flowing in the room, but he had no doubt everyone was watching them out of the corner of their eye. "My office is at the Rocking A Ranch. Rose can point you on your way in the morning. You can't miss it."

He waited for Sarah's nod of understanding. After she'd taken her seat and picked up her plastic fork, he moved into the potluck line behind Matt.

"Mama changed directions on a dime over there, from warm welcome to poker face just like that," Matt said under his breath.

Wes agreed. "Yeah, it was something close-up, too."

"Glad I'm not the mayor," Matt sang under his breath. "I would not want to be negotiating with our mother on one side, insisting nothing changes in Prospect, and what has to be a large sum of money almost guaranteeing big developments on the other."

Matt had a point. Sarah Hearst's arrival

in town was going to bring some headaches. He watched her sip from a plastic cup and pretend not to be bothered to be the center of attention. Sticking close to her side might make it clearer how to navigate the situation.

"Being mayor around here might not be easy every day, but just wait until Western Days ramps up. We can compare jobs then." Wes chuckled at Matt's dramatic groan before he headed for the kitchen to tell Rose she was going to have a guest for the evening.

CHAPTER FOUR

As Sarah followed Rose Bell down the wooden sidewalk back to Bell House, she believed she could feel the eyes of the town on her back. A careful check over her left shoulder at the Mercantile should have convinced her she was imagining things. No one was outside the building. There were no faces in the bright windows. The prickle of awareness lingered. What was that old saying about a person's ear hurting when people were talking about them? Was that right? She had a feeling she wasn't recalling that superstition correctly, but if she had to guess, the potluck crowd was dissecting her right now.

The welcome she'd experienced had transitioned after Prue Armstrong had introduced herself. No one else had approached her while she'd been seated at the table, but the curious stares had been impossible to miss.

At least she still had the support of Prospect's mayor. Wes Armstrong trailed along behind her and Rose because he had insisted on seeing that she was comfortably settled for the night.

Was that because he was the mayor, a gentleman or secretly afraid that Sarah would slap a for sale sign up on the Majestic and head for home?

"How long are you planning to be in Prospect?" Rose asked as they walked up the sidewalk to the front steps of Bell House.

Sarah paused at her car to grab her suitcase from the trunk, wrestled with carrying it herself for a single instant before Wes was there to take it from her and hurried to catch up as Rose unlocked the front door.

They were the first words the quiet woman had spoken since she'd materialized like a ghost at Sarah's elbow. If Wes hadn't identified the B-and-B owner by her cap, Sarah would have been concerned by her silent presence. Rose didn't introduce herself. She didn't even do the "holding out a hand to indicate a direction" like the cowboys had done. Her invitation had been a jerk of her chin toward the stairs.

Instead of asking questions, Sarah had decided to take Rose's body language as instruction to stand, throw away her plate and follow the woman out into the night.

Her relief when Wes followed them out was overwhelming. How she'd gotten so attached to him from one brief conversation should concern her, but he was still the most welcoming person she'd met in town.

It was nice that Rose's sweet voice lowered the apparition vibe a notch. Bell House's host paused with her hand on the doorknob and waited for the answer to her question.

"I'm not sure how long exactly. My sister Jordan is planning to join me, but I don't know when she can get away. If it's soon, I'll stay here. It's nice to have a chance to explore Prospect again. We enjoyed our summers here." Sarah set her bag down in front of the short counter that divided the entryway of Bell House while Rose waited for her computer to start up.

"Did you?" Rose murmured. She didn't face Sarah so there was no additional clue to gather from her face. "Did you miss us as much as Sadie did all those years?"

"Uh, well…" Sarah cleared her throat. "It has been too long since we visited. Definitely.

Sadie never stopped loving this place. She made sure we all understood Prospect meant home to her." Sarah was beginning to wonder how much of her chilly reception was due to inheriting the Majestic and how much was the result of hurt feelings because Sadie had moved away.

"Interesting. All that time, she was missing us but never visited. I assumed Sadie would remember how to get home." Rose sniffed. "I have the Liberty Room open for you for two nights. Should I extend the reservation?"

"Um…" Sarah evaluated her options as she stared around the empty foyer. "If you're expecting a big crush, I guess so."

"Fine. Four nights." Rose clicked and clacked before pulling an actual key ring out of the drawer under the computer. No key cards at Bell House. "Breakfast is served in the dining room at seven." She slid the key across the counter. "No visitors after dark. If you leave and the door is locked when you come back, check in down at the Mercantile. They'll know where I am."

Sarah picked up the key. The urge to ask how long breakfast would be available was there on the tip of her tongue, but it felt like pushing her luck. She didn't want to have to get back on the road that night, although the idea of inspecting the lodge to see if there were any acceptable rooms for her and Jordan was now something she wanted to do at first light. Even if she had to evict a bear, it might be easier than warming up Rose Bell.

"Okay. Well, good night?" Sarah asked. She'd never stayed in a bed-and-breakfast before but it seemed like an occasion where the owner might ideally give a lodger a tour of locations like the dining room and possibly the bathroom. Or perhaps at least point her toward her room?

Rose nodded.

Wes had moved to the bottom of the stairs. Sarah took that as a sign that the Liberty Room was on the second floor. That's where bedrooms were, right? As she climbed, she scanned the photos that lined the staircase and ignored the urge to ask questions about the people in them. Maybe Rose would be chattier in the morning.

Since Bell House's hostess had watched them leave from her spot behind the counter without a "good night," or even a wordless wave, Sarah had her doubts.

The first door on the left at the top of the stairs had an enormous wreath bedecked in extravagant red-white-and-blue ribbons.

"If that doesn't scream liberty, then what does?" Sarah muttered as she dug the key out of her pocket and tried it in the door.

Wes's chuckle reassured her.

The knob turned easily, revealing a comfortable room decorated in dark wood antiques and flags. So many flags. "It could definitely be worse." Sarah made a mental note to discover the names of the rest of the rooms. Assuming the decor matched as literally as it did for the Liberty Room, she could reserve the one that would amuse or annoy her sister the most ahead of her visit.

That was the kind of thoughtful older sister she was.

Wes set her bag down and moved closer to speak in a low voice next to her ear. "Anything we say will be repeated word for word for town-wide broadcast, so I'll say good night here. We can talk in the morning out at the ranch?"

At close range, Sarah realized his eyes were green but there were gold flecks. Hazel? Had she ever seen hazel eyes at this range?

Then she realized he was waiting for an answer, so she nodded. "Thank you for the help tonight."

She didn't want him to leave.

"Anytime." Wes squeezed her arm before stepping back. "Good night, Sarah."

She smiled and moved to close the door behind him. The thump of his boots heading down to the door filled her with a strange hollow spot, as if her best friend were leaving.

Sarah rubbed her temples to eliminate some of the tension that had built over her long drive and delicious but uncomfortable potluck supper.

Then she noticed the black-and-white photograph of a large bell with a crack in the side took center stage over the bed.

"The Liberty Bell. Are the rooms all named after famous bells?" Sarah frowned. Were there any other famous bells? Did jingle bells count? "I am too tired for this mystery tonight."

She pulled out clean jeans and a T-shirt for the next day before deciding she needed to investigate the bathroom situation. With her toothbrush and toothpaste clutched in one hand, she ventured out into the hallway, prepared to find Rose hovering somewhere nearby, silent but there in her Broncos hat.

Instead, the hall was quiet and empty. The wreath on the room next to hers was festooned with the Union Jack. Sarah puzzled over that as she brushed her teeth in the bathroom opposite. "British bells..." The shock of the icy water as she washed her face made it easier to think. "Big Ben? Is that a bell?"

She was still shaking her head as she slid into the comfortable bed. There would be time to answer all those questions in the morning. Falling asleep in unfamiliar beds had always been a struggle, but her final thoughts before she slept were to wonder how long it had been since Bell House was redecorated and whether Wes Armstrong was single.

MORNING LIGHT WOKE Sarah slowly, and the smell of bacon and coffee made it easy enough to sit up in bed. Breakfast was the most important meal of the day, mainly because it was her favorite. She hurried to dress, muttered a quick wish that Rose had woken up ready to chitchat and hurried downstairs.

"Good morning," Sarah said brightly as she found Rose seated at the dining table, her plate filled with yummy breakfast goodness. "Something smells delicious."

Rose had already donned her Broncos hat. She stared at Sarah over her mug. "If you'd like, you can serve yourself. Everything's on the stove."

Not exactly welcome, but Sarah didn't let it slow her down. She hummed happily as she piled scrambled eggs and bacon on her plate before grabbing toast to go with it. After she filled her coffee cup, she joined Rose at the table.

"How is your room?" Rose asked. It didn't sound painful exactly, but there wasn't much warmth of hospitality, either.

"So comfortable, thank you." Sarah decided to make sure she was finished with her food before she started asking questions, in case the atmosphere took a turn for the worse. "The photos on the stairs, are those all relatives, Rose?" Miss Bell? Ms. Bell? Mrs. Bell? Madam? Rose was the best choice. Probably.

Rose nodded. "Yes, my family has been here in Prospect for many generations, along with the Armstrongs." She sipped her coffee. "They came in as part of the silver rush. Quite a story. Armstrongs, Bells, lots of families in Prospect put down strong roots here. We like our roots."

Sarah agreed. "I grew up in Denver, but we moved to Los Angeles when I was a teenager, so I miss that close connection to a place."

Rose nodded. "Never did understand people who left Prospect, never to return."

Ah, it was easier to read into that comment. Sadie had left and never moved back.

"Life takes interesting turns, doesn't it?" Sarah pretended she missed the undertone. "Sadie never planned to leave. She never planned on building a successful corporation, doing something she absolutely loved. She kept a painting over her desk of these mountains. Prospect was her home, even when she died. That's why she asked me, her favorite niece, and my sisters to decide what to do with the lodge. It was too important to leave it up to someone who didn't know her and where she'd come from." She hoped that was true. It was what she'd tried to convince herself of over the course of the long travel day. Did it make up for the fact that Sadie hadn't secured a place for her inside that company, one that would be protected against the profit-and-loss statement? Eventually, it might.

"Interesting." Rose sipped again.

Sarah gave her time to add to the comment. When it seemed clear there was nothing more coming, she decided not to press her luck on the first morning. "Can you steer me in the direction of the Rocking A?"

Rose motioned with her thumb. "Head on out of town that-a way. You'll see a sign at about five miles showing you to the ranch."

Instead of asking any other questions that would result in less than satisfactory answers, Sarah stood. "Great. I'll put my dishes in the dishwasher?" She waited for Rose to agree or disagree, but one narrowed eye was her answer.

By process of elimination, she figured out where the dishwasher was, rinsed her dishes just in case and slid them in. The kitchen was rustic. Worn wood floors and moldings, apple-themed wallpaper and an old-fashioned pitcher with wildflowers in the center of the small table brought to mind past family dinners and celebrations. It was comfortable. So was the bedroom. Sarah wondered if Rose Bell's attitude normally matched the furnishings at Bell House. Was she putting on the unfriendly vibe specifically for Sarah?

If that was true, it could be thawed with enough work. She'd had to do the same thing when Sadie had brought her into the Cookie Queen offices. The people who had put hours into the business from the ground up had expected a spoiled heir. Sarah might be the spoiled relation, but she'd always done her best to pull her weight. Her coworkers had eventually warmed up. Rose could, too.

On her way back through the dining room, she stopped. "When you have the time, I'd like to hear any stories you know about your relatives." She motioned at the staircase in case Rose had forgotten about her interest in the photos. "And I'm so interested in seeing the rest of the rooms here."

Rose nodded. Was that a softening of her lips? Hard to say, but Sarah resolved not to worry overmuch about that as she trotted up the stairs. She wasn't in town to make friends. All she had to do was take some photos of the lodge. If Jordan made it in time, they could discuss their options. If not, she'd head home. The idea of repeating the long journey to finalize whatever they decided to do with the lodge made her instantly tired, but Sarah pushed it away.

For now, she had enough challenges ahead. She had to find the Rocking A and the handsome lawyer-slash-mayor who was also the son of the woman who unofficially led Prospect. Sarah paused at the door as she wondered if Prue would also be at the Rocking A.

Not that it mattered. This morning, she intended to find out everything she needed to know about the business affairs of the lodge. If Prue Armstrong was there, Sarah would nod politely and then take charge of the meeting. She'd done it a thousand times before.

Besides, this time, she'd also get to see Wes Armstrong again.

CHAPTER FIVE

THE THIRD TIME Wes walked out of the barn to check for new arrivals at the Rocking A, he realized he was going to waste the entire morning unless Sarah Hearst appeared soon. Normally, he'd hear a car coming down the gravel drive long before it stopped in front of the house, but today he was worried he'd miss her arrival. How? The lane ended at the wide opening where the ranch trucks lined up. It wasn't like she could drive past it.

Wes knew the anticipation was silly.

That didn't mean he could brush it off.

As often as he lectured himself that he could go in and sit at his desk to review the ranch accounts, he knew he'd accomplish… nothing at all.

"What's got you rattled this morning?" his brother Travis asked from the stall he'd been clearing out. They'd decided to make one of the stalls storage, so they could free up space in the house. It was a simple task on paper that turned into a lot of hard work in reality. "You're wearing a rut between here and the door, you're doing so much pacing."

"It's nothing." Wes wouldn't have answered truthfully even if he could put his finger on what it was about Sarah Hearst that was provoking his restlessness. Clients came to the house now and then. Most of his law business was related to negotiating and preparing sales of assets or drawing up wills, that sort of thing, nothing that knocked him off his game.

Travis grunted as he walked past with two thirteen-inch saddles that they hadn't used in years.

"You going to get rid of those?" Wes asked. "They're in pretty good shape. Might be able to sell 'em if you clean 'em up."

Travis shook his head. "Might need them."

Wes watched his brother and tried to gauge whether Travis wanted to talk about the previous week's visit from the family services caseworker or continue to work in silence.

When Travis returned to the stall, he must have noticed Wes's hesitation. "What?" He didn't stop moving. He hadn't stopped moving ever since he'd come home. At first, Wes believed life in the army would mean some adjustment would be required before Travis settled back into the rhythm of ranch life, but it had been months and his brother showed no signs of resting.

"Has your caseworker given you a date for the follow-up visit?" Wes asked. The long list of changes she'd "suggested" be made to the house itself before welcoming fosters would take time to address.

The Armstrongs and Rocking A had made them a family, but the house was showing signs of all that hard work and time.

Travis straightened and yanked his hat off to ruffle sweaty hair. "First week of November." He stressed the last word carefully. "Clay is hoping to tie up work in Colorado Springs next week. Then we'll start renovations. I'll get as much cleared out of the bedrooms as I can, but they're all occupied right now."

Wes gathered the trash that had piled up in the stall and jammed it down in the wheelbarrow Travis had dragged in for that purpose.

Wes had two jobs as the oldest Armstrong: keep the ranch going and take care of his family. Travis's dream of fostering kids at the ranch fell under both job descriptions. Finding the money for the necessary renovations from the ranch's accounts was Wes's job. He'd figure it out.

Each of his brothers had goals, passions that drove them.

For the youngest, Matt, it was animals. The kid had never met an animal he couldn't connect with. That charm also extended to people. Becoming a veterinarian made the best of both.

Clay made things with his hands. Drawing houses and then making them come true had been his dream forever.

Grant lived for the rodeo. Training horses and sometimes riders had been his calling and he'd been the best. Grant's sudden return home last week was proof that something bad had happened, but none of them had wanted to push for answers. Instead, they'd all opted to give him space, and rely on him telling them about it when he was ready.

That left Travis. Of the five foster kids Prue and Walt had brought to Prospect, Travis had struggled the most with leaving his old life for the new one. His determination to provide a safe place for a new generation made sense. Wes admired it. He would do whatever he could to help.

That was his calling. Wes had been the first to arrive at the Rocking A, and he'd taken his job as big brother seriously.

"We know what's got me preoccupied. Want to share your problems, Wes?" Travis asked as he turned to pick up a shovel to clear out old hay and other debris.

"Just waiting for a client to show." Wes propped a shoulder against the gate. "Doesn't make sense to get into something I'll have to put aside."

Travis nodded and scooped a shovel into the wheelbarrow. "Right. Does the fact that it's a very pretty client explain why you keep moving outside to see if she's here yet?"

Wes exhaled loudly. "I sure hope not. Wouldn't be anything but bad news to be getting interested in a Hearst. The last Hearst was born in Prospect but had no trouble leaving for good. No way is this one staying in Prospect for long."

Travis raised an eyebrow.

"Nobody said you had to marry her. People date for fun. F. U. N. Ever heard of fun, Wes?"

"Nope. Never heard of it," Wes drawled.

Travis's rusty chuckle almost covered the sound, but Wes forced himself not to jerk upright when he heard the crunch of tires on gravel.

Not that it mattered. Travis knew he wanted to stand to attention immediately. "Better go see who it is!" His brother's fake excitement would have garnered a punch to the arm when they were teenagers and liked to battle over every word either one of them uttered, but they'd both matured. A little. Travis's quiet laughter echoed in Wes's ears as he hurried down the barn's main aisle.

In the shaded doorway of the barn, he watched Sarah Hearst park an expensive rental next to his truck. How long would it take for her to notice him watching her? As she scanned her surroundings, he wondered if she'd experienced the same instant connection with him the night before.

Then he realized how creepy it might appear for him to linger there in the shadows and headed outside. "Morning. Did you have any trouble finding the place?"

She shook her head, a long ponytail trailing over her shoulder as she shut the car door. "No, Rose's directions worked." She motioned with her thumb over her shoulder and added, "Can't miss it."

Wes nodded. The Bells had never been known as big talkers, any of them, but Rose Bell might win the prize for the most unique. Only a few subjects animated Rose: her favorite football team, their players, their record and their chances to win a championship.

He wasn't about to tell Sarah about the earful he'd already gotten from his mother during a very early, prebreakfast phone call. His mother had been speaking to Rose and researching the latest news about the Hearst family. Sarah, the oldest of three sisters, worked for the Cookie Queen Corporation in Los Angeles. She'd graduated from a prestigious university with an MBA and, from a deep dive into her social media, she appeared as single as Wes was. His mother never missed an opportunity to bring up his lack of a wife.

Sarah had two sisters. From his stop in at Bell House last night, he knew one of them was on her way to Prospect, too. ETA undetermined currently.

"If they reopen the Majestic, Mama, won't Prospect be better off?" he'd asked, in an effort to shut down the gossip train.

Her snort had been a clear answer. "Those Hearsts don't have the cash or the interest in running a fishing camp in the middle of nowhere. They'll sell it. They'll sell it to some… developer who'll tear the old place down. We don't know who will move in out there, Wes."

He knew her concern about large-scale developers was valid. The companies who'd reached out with offers to buy the place since he'd been overseeing it for Sadie were big players. They'd have big plans.

The lodge had only been completely closed for about fifteen years, but before that, the Majestic Prospect Lodge brought in a steady trickle of tourists. They did a little shopping, ate in the restaurant and basically kept Prospect gently afloat. After the lodge closed, businesses in town had to cut back hours and some closed, but life went on.

In his mind, he'd pictured a return to that kind of business, but he realized his mother might be closer to reality. No one pursued an unlisted property like Sadie's to run a small fishing lodge on it.

"Let's sit down in my office. I've pulled the files I have on the lodge." Wes opened the screen door of the house and they entered.

Wes could see she was studying the large living room. Dark paneling needed to be up-dated, but neither he nor his brothers had been capable of taking on any extra jobs before now. The caseworker's impending final inspection had given them a hard deadline to meet.

Family pictures lined the walls, years of him and his brothers. When Prue and Walt had divorced and his mother had moved into town, she'd mentioned taking her photos with her, but no one had been in a hurry to make that happen.

He and his brothers were waiting for his parents to realize the divorce had been the mistake, not the wedding.

"Your ranch is beautiful, or what I've seen of it. That drive in is so pretty. How many cows do you have?" Sarah asked as she sat across from him.

"The number changes, depending on where we are in calving or taking them to the sale barn, but I aim to stay under three hundred head." Wes wondered how much information she wanted on ranching, herd sizes and acreage available. Her polite request could turn into a lecture if he let himself go.

"Wow, that's a lot of work." She licked her lips. "It almost sounds like I have a clue about what we're discussing, doesn't it?"

Wes chuckled. The way she shook her head, as if she'd embarrassed herself, was cute.

"It is a lot. If that was a guess, it was solid. That's about the limit of what I can oversee myself. My brother Travis is going to take over, now that he's back, so..." He had to leave it open-ended. The urge to expand the cattle was there. Especially since Travis was making long-term plans to stay there so the ranch could take on more livestock, but Wes was afraid to commit at this point.

He reached behind him to grab the folders he'd stacked up and the set of keys. He slid them across the glossy surface of the desk. "I guess you and your sisters have discussed what you'd like to do with the Majestic already."

"We just found out this week that we're the owners," Sarah said, "but none of us know anything about fishing lodges. As the oldest, I was elected to find out."

Wes covered his chest with his hands. "As the oldest, I understand how that works." They shared a commiserating grin. "Did you and Sadie ever discuss what she wanted to do with the place? It's not like her to leave it in limbo for so long." The grief on her face was clear.

Wes imagined being faced with a situation like this, one where she'd want Sadie's opinion the most, was a constant reminder that she was gone.

"Not really. Sadie had offers to sell, but was never interested," he said. "Seems like someone with business experience could run the Majestic. She might need some help now and then, but neighbors around here are helpful." Wes didn't want to push too hard, but he knew reopening the lodge was the desired outcome. Testing the waters made sense.

"Someone's been investigating the Hearsts, I see." Sarah wrinkled her nose. "I know Cookie Queen business, sure, but I'd have the same challenge Sadie did. My life? It's in LA. So is Jordan's. And Brooke? Asking her to leave New York for a day is annoying. No way she's going to do business here."

Wes nodded. Everything she said made perfect sense.

Sarah sighed. "I'm understanding more and more why Sadie left us this problem to solve. No answer feels right. I'm not sure how the finances are set up with the lodge, but please bill me for your time while we're figuring our way through this."

Wes decided to focus on the fact that selling wasn't the clear winner. That would give them something to work with.

"Happy to oblige. The top folder contains the bank statements, organized by year, and the receipts for all the tax payments I've made on Sadie's behalf." He watched Sarah flip through the paperwork quickly, eyes scanning and moving from one page to the next. He had no idea if she was good at her job, but she absorbed the information quickly.

"What happened when you needed more funds? Who did you contact?" Sarah asked.

"Sadie was easy to get a hold of by leaving a message at her office. She never hesitated to make sure the lodge was covered, even if overseeing all the staffing from Los Angeles was too much after her manager left Prospect." Wes leaned back. "I filed yearly reports there, too. Summaries of any communication, including letters from companies interested in purchasing the land, or incidents involving the lodge. Those are in the bottom file. You will see there was never much to report after the lodge closed for good."

Sarah did the same thorough review of the paperwork in the second folder and then she reached for the keys. "No other sets available?"

"No," Wes said, "when the last manager left, Sadie asked me to have all the locks changed and to keep two sets here. They're both on that ring." He held up his hands. "You have full control."

Sarah nodded and removed one set of keys to slide back to him. "Please hold on to these."

Wes nodded.

"Can you continue to manage the lodge's affairs while we're working through this?" Sarah asked before she bit her top lip. "If not, can you recommend anyone else who is qualified?"

"Sadie negotiated a yearly contract, so you're set for the rest of the year. In December, if the lodge is still yours, we can discuss how to move forward. Does that work?" Wes asked.

Sarah relaxed against her seat. "Yes. That's great. I wouldn't want to navigate this with someone who didn't know the history or the town."

That seemed encouraging. Were the Hearsts including the town's interests as they evaluated what to do with the lodge? That was a very Sadie thing to do, in his opinion.

"Smart thinking," Wes said.

Sarah nodded. "Rose gave me the impression that she didn't think much of the fact that Sadie moved away."

"Well," Wes said slowly, "it's a pretty tight-knit community. Doesn't change much. Folks like and respect that."

"Okay," Sarah said and made the "continue" motion with her right hand. "Surely there's more to it than that."

Wes could hear his mother's voice in his head, telling him he was supposed to be getting information about the Hearsts, not giving it away.

"Having a Hearst pop back up after all this time can only mean one thing." He shrugged. "Something is about to change. Your reception here is based on that fact. I've been the mayor for ten years without a single challenger. This house? Not a piece of furniture has moved ever that I can remember. Bell House is repainted every five years or so, but always the same color." Did she understand where he was going?

Sarah stared hard out the window. Wes loved the view of pasture that stretched out to where the foothills started rising up. It was another thing that didn't change much. Sometimes it was covered in snow, but all through the seasons, the Rocking A endured.

Eventually, she nodded. "Okay. Change can be scary. I understand that. A little. There's not much I can do to reassure them, is there?"

Wes sighed. "Not if you're planning to make a change out at the lodge."

Sarah picked up her files and started to stand. "I better get on with figuring that out, then."

"Why don't I take you over there? The building's pretty sturdy still, but it's been empty for a while. Might be good to have company if you're planning to explore." It would also be nice to see her expression as she toured the place. He could point out how simple it would be to polish the place and reopen it. "Simple" could be a matter of interpretation.

"Today, I'd like to go by myself, but I might take you up on that. I want to see the land

and meet the neighbors, too." Sarah shook her head. "In my head, we inherited the building, but talking to you about Prospect, seeing your ranch, brings back memories of when we'd stay over the summer. The lake, the old ghost town? Am I remembering that right? Sadie would never let us explore there."

Wes nodded. "If you want to go out to the ghost town, you'll definitely need a horse or an ATV. There's no good path for your car."

Sarah bit her lip. Was this turning into a harder job than she expected? If they were set on selling, would it be necessary to go to all that trouble to explore the ghost town or see the entire property?

"Your neighbors? That's easy." Wes tapped his chest. "The Rocking A is your neighbor."

Sarah brushed hair behind her ear. "Right."

Wes followed her back out to where she'd parked. "When you have time to review everything, I'll be happy to answer any questions." He'd been anxious for her arrival, but now that she was leaving, he was hunting for things to say to extend her stay. What was going on with him?

"Thanks, Wes. Is it okay to call you Wes?"

Sarah wrinkled her nose. "I should have asked that first, right?"

Her cheeks lit with pink, as if she was embarrassed by a faux pas. Why did he find that so charming?

"Of course you can, Sarah." He tipped his head down when she nodded. "We're neighbors and no one stands on formalities in Prospect." Besides that, now that he'd heard his name on her lips, he was prepared to conjure up opportunities to have her do it again.

Sarah waved through the window as she reversed and headed for the highway. As Wes watched her go, he realized Sarah had confirmed most of his mother's assumptions that morning but he didn't have much new information to pass along.

That didn't bother him. He'd have the opportunity to track down Sarah again soon.

CHAPTER SIX

"GOOD THING I paid for the extra car insurance." Sarah muttered a curse as her rental's tires fell into a large, unavoidable pothole in the rough drive leading up to the lodge and the whole thing groaned as if it were making an unfavorable comment on her driving skills. At least, she *hoped* this drive ended at the Majestic.

Nothing was as familiar as she'd expected. The faded sign on the highway had been hard to read, but the outline of the fish was promising. It seemed a much longer drive through the trees than she remembered, but the scenery was still gorgeous. Closer to the highway, rolling pasture matched the view she'd seen from Wes's window. Here the grass was overgrown, tall enough to sway in the breeze. As the lane curved, pines sprang up and created a sort of tunnel. The trees had seemed enormous when she was a kid, and still made an impressive entrance. Peeks through the leaves revealed sparkling water with a backdrop of the mountains rising up behind.

As she maneuvered around another dip in the road and eased across a low-water bridge, Sarah said, "I have to be getting close." The narrow road opened up to a clearing. A small stream heading for Key Lake bisected it, leaving room for parking on one side and the sprawling Majestic Prospect Lodge on the other. The wood siding had become dry and gray with time. The flower beds that Sadie had planned and tended before her cooking show took off and her career demanded a move to Los Angeles were empty with a few ragged sticks poking up. An overgrown hedge hid most of the wide windows that made up the front of the lodge. At some point, they'd all been boarded up anyway.

Sarah parked near the bridge that crossed over the stream, switched off the ignition and sat quietly to absorb the clash of what she remembered against the way the lodge had aged. Her memories were of warmth and welcome; none of that remained.

Warm brown siding had faded.

Beautiful landscaping had died.

And Sadie was gone.

Sadness swamped her. Was there any point in getting out of the car? Holding on to this place would not only be expensive, but it would also hurt. She should tell Jordan and Brooke that there wasn't anything here to save. They'd list it quickly and sell it to fund new, exciting things which Sadie would have loved.

Before she could convince herself to give up without even getting out of the car, her phone rang. She dug around in her purse and pulled it out, surprised at how strong the cell service was this far from town.

"Hey, Jordan," Sarah said brightly, determined to keep everything positive, "I didn't expect to hear from you this soon. Did you get your project finished?"

"Not quite, but you sound weird. What's wrong?" Jordan asked.

Sarah frowned. "I don't sound weird. I sound perky."

"That's weird. What's wrong?" Jordan repeated.

"I was doing my best to shield my baby sisters from any extra hardship as good big sisters do, but no," Sarah drawled, determined to keep this light.

"Uh-huh, shielding." Jordan wasn't convinced. "Like that time we were staying there on the lake and a snake slithered across the path in front of you? Was it shielding when you practically climbed on top of my head so the snake would get me first?"

"Rattlesnakes are scary. That was a valid reaction."

"It was a garter snake, my brave big sister," Jordan said.

"Okay." Sarah slid out of the car. "But I don't appreciate you reminding me of that snake as I'm about to walk around all this overgrown grass and into a boarded-up building. It's rude."

"I can't save you, but you can show me. Put the camera on. I want to see."

After Sarah did so, she met her sister's stare. "Are you sure? It's so different, kind of sad."

Jordan nodded firmly. "Yes. Show me."

Sarah felt relieved that Jordan had called when she did. Doing this with her company would be so much easier. She pointed the phone so that her sister could see the front of the lodge.

"Oh," Jordan said, "honestly, that's not as bad as I expected. Someone has made sure it's secure, no vandalism. It's all cosmetic repairs as far as I can see."

Sarah blinked at Jordan's reasonable tone. It did not match the sinking feeling that had filled her gut when she'd parked. "It's definitely not the same place, though. Nothing of Sadie is left here." As she said it aloud, Sarah realized that was what she'd been looking for. She'd wanted to find Sadie waiting for her outside as she always did when they made the drive from Denver.

"Yeah, I get that. I miss her so much, and I never spent every day working with her the way you did. It has to be hard. Almost like losing Mom again." Jordan held her arms up to the screen. "Here's the promise of a hug. When I make it to Prospect, I'll squeeze you so hard."

Sarah chuckled.

"Take me down to the lake. I can see sparkles now and then."

Sarah stared at the expanse of rough parking lot that filled the clearing. Along the edges, the heavy growth of pines had kept the grass in that area under control. "Okay, but if a snake gets me, I will know it was all your fault."

"And so will I. Can you imagine Brooke tiptoeing through this forest in her designer heels?" Jordan asked. "She's become fully citified at this point."

Jordan's tone would have been appropriate if Brooke had been lost at sea instead of living the life she'd always planned. "May I suggest that your suburban apartment twenty minutes from downtown LA might not be all that superior a position?"

"No, you may not," Jordan replied immediately. "Besides, it's only twenty minutes with no traffic. How often does that happen?"

Sarah shook her head as she stepped over a fallen tree and ignored the shivery sensation of something fanged lying in wait. The ground sloped down as she stepped out of the shade into the sunlight and Key Lake spread out in front of her. Walking into the bright sunshine had changed everything.

The water was calm and clear; the landscape here was the same as the last time

Sarah had run screaming into the cold water after Jordan and Brooke.

"Wow," Jordan said breathlessly. "This water is like no other water I've seen. I sort of thought I'd imagined it, but it's real."

Gentle waves lapped on the shore, and the water stretched out to meet the mountains rising in the distance. It was so clear as to sparkle like crystal, and Sarah knew if she dipped her toe in, it would be deliciously cold.

"Why hasn't someone snapped this place up?" Jordan asked. "To reopen the lodge or build the most spectacular vacation home the world has ever seen?"

Her question was valid. Sarah wasn't sure how much land sold for on average in Colorado, but if the right person with the right budget saw this place, it would be a treasure they'd happily pay for.

"The summer I worked here, before Sadie moved away, this lake was busy, not overcrowded but the marina did well." Jordan sighed. "I hated selling bait and gasoline so much, but I loved this view."

Sarah didn't want to dwell too long on Jordan's summer of exile. They'd all lived through it once, and her younger sister had learned hard lessons about skipping school and drinking with "friends" who didn't have her best interests at heart. "Where to next?"

If she didn't keep moving, she would sit down at the water's edge and get stuck in the past.

"Do you have the keys? Let's go inside." Jordan was the bossy one. She'd always been the bossy one. That was why she and Brooke argued instead of talked. Brooke would understand Sarah's emotional reaction, and then Sarah would have had to negotiate a truce that worked for all three of them.

"When are you coming?" Sarah asked as she carefully retraced her steps to the parking lot. She crossed the bridge and unlocked the double doors leading into the lodge's lobby. The lock worked easily. As she surveyed the shadowy gloom of the once grand space, she groaned. "Why does this feel like the beginning of a horror movie where the first person to visit in years mysteriously vanishes and a pack of teenagers has to solve the mystery as they are picked off one by one?"

"Because you watch too many scary movies," Jordan said. "Do you have a flashlight?"

That would have been an excellent thing to have brought, Sarah thought to herself.

"I do not, but the phone…" She pulled her phone closer to the crack of light around the door to locate the built-in flashlight and test whether she could make a call and turn on the light at the same time. "Are you still there?"

"Yes," Jordan said dryly. "Good job finding the world's smallest flashlight."

"It's what I have on hand. When you get here, bring a bigger one. Bring every flashlight you can buy because there is no way I'm stepping into the hallways of this place without illumination and backup." Sarah aimed her light at where she remembered the guest rooms started and shivered.

"Okay, what about the kitchen?" Jordan suggested. "Go back that direction."

"Why?" Sarah asked as she headed that way.

"If all the appliances are still there and working, that's a major value to us or whoever reopens this place." Jordan's practicality was nice.

If only she were the one doing the inspection.

"You're pretty careful to make sure to list

both options," Sarah said as she tested the waters with Jordan.

"Brooke wants to sell. Immediately," Jordan said. "I just… There might be a better choice, you know?"

Sarah wondered if that meant Jordan didn't want to sell or she only wanted to keep Brooke from having her way too easily. Asking would lead to more conversation than Sarah wanted to have about the friction between her sisters at this point, so she kept walking.

The small dining room opposite the guest rooms was…less dark, somehow. Light seeped in around the edges of the broad boarded-up windows that would have a view of the large deck and the lake. Tables and chairs were scattered across the floor, as if the last manager had walked out one day and never come back.

"Lots of good stuff here. I bet the kitchen's in okay shape," Jordan said. "Hey, wait, swing the light back to the right."

Since her tone was excited, not a warning of a nasty varmint lurking in the corner, Sarah followed orders. "It's a portrait of Sadie." She moved closer to see better. It was an early publicity shot, from when her local public broadcasting station had taped her show from Prospect. Sadie was young and full of life. Sarah surveyed the other framed pieces surrounding the shot: news stories about appearances Sadie had made, a clipping from the week her first cookbook had hit the bestseller list, book covers and a poster advertising her first national Colorado Cookie Queen show.

Pride and bittersweet memories flooded Sarah's heart; they crowded out loss and sadness. Sadie was still here. They'd just had to find her. If they held on to the Majestic, could they bring her back so to speak, fill the place with enough Sadie that visitors and family alike could get to know their great-aunt through the place she'd loved?

Sarah had tried not to do too much thinking that way because the smart thing for all of them was to sell. Brooke already knew that; Sarah needed to be practical, too.

When she saw the date on the bestseller list, she realized it was from the same summer Jordan had been sent to Prospect.

Jordan had been the last one to visit the lodge out of the three of them.

Before Sarah could mention that, a loud

crash echoed from the kitchen and Sarah didn't hesitate. She marched right back through the dining room, the lobby and out the front doors where she stopped to lock them quickly. Jordan's squawks were an accompaniment until Sarah was back across the bridge and safely inside the car.

Over the racing of her heart and heavy breaths, Sarah heard Jordan say, "What was that? I thought you knocked something over."

"No." Sarah shook her head wildly. "*Something* knocked something over. It wasn't me. It was something *else* alive in that building with me and I am not going back in there alone and you can't make me."

Jordan sighed. "I can't blame you. I've been worrying about you and this lodge ever since you left. I need to be in Prospect, not here. I'll talk to my boss and leave tomorrow. I'll stop about halfway the first night, and meet you in town at…"

"Bell House. I was hoping we could get out of the B-and-B and find rooms here that we could use because the reception from folks is extremely frosty here in Prospect, but now…" Sarah firmed her lips. "That's a no."

"Frosty specifically to us? Or strangers in general?" Jordan asked.

Sarah considered the question. "Both? Maybe? I don't know. There's some hard feelings that Sadie left and never came home again. Before they knew who I was, they were friendly, included me in the potluck I crashed. The town has changed; it's quieter now. I wonder if they wanted Sadie to do more here."

"Well, no matter what happens, we're going to make another change. They'll have to get over that." Jordan nodded. "I'm not a huge fan of change myself. Remember when Dad told us we were leaving Denver?"

"You hid inside Mom's pottery studio for two days. As if we didn't know where to find you." It had been a couple of months after their mother died. No one was thinking straight and no one was ready to let go of everything familiar...except for their father who couldn't stay.

Sarah had been forced to step up then. She'd learned a lot about working through fear at that point.

Not fear of whatever hid in the shadows of

the lodge's kitchen, but she could be patient when it was a fear of change.

The fact that Sadie had followed them to California as soon as she could had made everything easier.

Sadie had always used her career as the reason for that move, and Sarah had always believed her and been impressed with how her great-aunt had grown a love of cooking into stardom, but…

What if the reason Sadie had left Prospect and not returned was because they'd needed her where she was…in LA or New York, running the Cookie Queen Corporation for her gaggle of nieces and nephews?

Would Sadie have been happier to come home instead?

Sarah gripped the steering wheel.

"I'm a little better with change than I was then. We all are." Jordan smiled brightly. "I said a little."

Sarah laughed. "You are. Are you sure you can leave? What about the project? What will your boss say?"

Jordan rubbed her forehead. "I could use

the break. Driving to Prospect will be perfect."

Sarah noticed Jordan had skipped the question about her boss's opinion.

Jordan had daydreamed more than once about leaving her corporate job and creating her own business. This inheritance would give her freedom to try to make that dream come true. Sarah envied her sister for being that far along. That was something she'd have to consider if her position with the Cookie Queen Corporation disappeared. Figuring out what she'd do next would take a careful evaluation of her skills and the risks she was willing to take.

"What are you going to do for two days in Prospect without me? You should go back to Denver and find some shopping or something," Jordan said.

Sarah rejected the notion. "There are still things I can do here. I got all the paperwork from the lawyer in Prospect who has been overseeing the lodge. I can contact real estate agents to see if anyone is interested in taking a look at the lodge and helping us estimate the value of the property and proposing a strategy to sell it. I want to take a closer look at the letters from developers, too."

"So, Sadie had good options to sell the place but didn't," Jordan said softly.

As if she was bothered by that fact, too.

Sarah met Jordan's stare. "Yeah. There's a lot to discuss here."

In the back of her mind, Wes's comments about needing a horse to check out the rest of the land around the lodge had been percolating. After seeing the state of the road, she understood better. He had a barn. That barn was on a ranch. Surely he had a horse she could borrow. Sadie had made sure to get all three of them up on horses when they'd visited.

Would she remember how to ride? Would any good cowboy loan a horse to a city slicker who wasn't even sure she could stay in the saddle anymore?

There was no doubt in her mind that Wes Armstrong was a good cowboy. The mayor-slash-lawyer-slash-head-of-the-Rocking-A struck her as one of those guys who could do anything they had to do and do it confidently.

Could he be persuaded to show her the boundaries of the land and call an ambulance if she fell off his loaned horse? She could still be moving forward with their plan for the property while she waited for Jordan, and she wouldn't break anything.

Bones, possibly, but not the horse.

Why didn't she mention Wes Armstrong, their nearest neighbor, horses or riding with a good cowboy to her sister?

For some reason, Sarah wanted this plan to rope Wes into accompanying her for a ride to be hers.

Only hers.

"That's a solid idea—just don't go back inside the Majestic by yourself. Wait for me." Jordan frowned. "But if the murderer was coming after you, he's slow. You could probably defend yourself. Are you sure you don't want to—"

"I'm not going back in there, Jordan." Sarah started the car. "Bring flashlights. Bear spray. Defensive weapons of any sort. Then I'll go in with you."

Her sister's laughter as she hung up felt good. Sarah was relieved as she navigated the long rough drive back to the road. Having a plan, even if she didn't have all the answers, was a step in the right direction.

And if part of that plan included more time with Wes Armstrong, she had something to look forward to.

CHAPTER SEVEN

FRIDAY NIGHTS WERE busy in Prospect, but the street through town was packed as Wes hunted for a parking spot near the Mercantile. Shop after shop was lit up. He was lucky to grab the last empty parking spot in front of the Prospect Picture Show, the town's movie theater, but there was no traffic to slow down his crossing the street to pass Ace High, Prospect's only full-service restaurant. Cars lined the street in each direction. As mayor, he should be pleased to see local businesses doing well. As his mother's oldest son, he wondered if she'd had any influence about whatever might be happening there.

Wes entered the Mercantile, hung a hard left and headed for the hardware store and his father first. As expected, his dad was seated behind the cash register, his boots propped on the counter in front of him. He glanced up from the seed catalog he'd been perusing as Wes approached. "Well, now, if it isn't my favorite son."

Wes grinned as he always did when Walt said that. Did it matter that Walt had five favorite sons? Only now and then. Most of the time, Wes was happy enough to share the title.

"Any idea what's happening tonight? A special showing at the Picture Show or some fancy new fare at the Ace?" Wes bent to rest his elbows on the scarred wood top that had served as the only counter in the hardware store for as long as he could remember.

Before Walt had retired from running the ranch, he'd depended on a few part-time employees to keep the store open. But after Wes's parents had divorced, Walt seemed perfectly happy to prop himself up behind the cash register. Those part-timers handled the lumber and feed orders that came through the loading area while Walt jawed with customers and occasionally rang up sales and even less often put out inventory.

When Wes and his brothers had built the foyer to split the place in two, a requirement of the divorce settlement, they'd been afraid their parents would never speak again. Instead, they got along better than ever as neighbors.

Almost like two people in love, in fact. Sharing the Mercantile kept them close but not too close.

"Big crowd?" Walt closed the catalog and plopped it on the counter. "Word of the new arrival and the reception she received at the Western Days planning meeting roused some interest, I expect."

Wes studied the door to his mother's shop. "So that's it? No plotting going on behind the scenes?"

"Wouldn't surprise me if Prue put out a call to come to town tonight." Walt shrugged. "I always appreciated your mama's strategic mind, but she's not the only mastermind in the family."

"What do you mean, Dad?" Wes asked obediently.

"Have I ever told you the story of how the Hearsts came to own that piece of property?" Walt asked, his voice deepening as it always did when he was preparing to launch a tale.

Wes interjected. "Your granddad needed funds to rebuild the herd that was destroyed by summer drought and record-breaking snow, so he agreed to sell the spot there closest to the logging trail that became the highway along with nice access to Key Lake." He knew the story, but he had no idea why his father had brought it up. "Sadie's father had inherited money…or something? So he threw it all in to open the vacation spot. And the Majestic Prospect Lodge has been a good neighbor ever since."

"Well, sure if you want to strip all the poetry and music from the tale, that'll do, I guess. You hit the high notes. Let's get that land back." Walt held out his arms as if he'd proposed the simplest thing in the world. "We buy it. The Hearsts go home. The Rocking A is complete again and we have extra pasture to increase the herd size like you been talking ever since Travis moved back." He brushed his hands together as if it were a nice, neat solution.

"And, as the cherry on top," Walt continued, "we make Prudence Armstrong happy. Everybody loves a hero."

Wes tipped his head back to study the hand-planed boards that made up the ceiling of the Mercantile. Throughout the years, most of the places in Prospect had been up-dated with new paint, electrical and plumbing and better building materials, but at the surface, they retained the rough edges of the old boomtown where they could. The narrow buildings had been expanded and converted without erasing the bones where possible.

"You're immediately running figures in your head, ain't you?" Walt asked, exasperation in his voice. "Can't even ruminate on the brilliance of the plan without shooting holes all through it."

Wes rubbed his forehead. "It's not that I don't like your idea. I just..." He knew the ranch's finances. He'd seen the list of renovations necessary for things to work out.

And he had a fair guess how much it would cost to buy the Majestic and the land attached.

The numbers didn't add up.

Before he explained the situation without going into details he'd promised himself he'd handle so his father could enjoy his retirement, the connecting door opened and his mother strolled in. "I knew you were close. I can always tell when my boys are near." She pressed a kiss to Wes's cheek and nodded at Walt. "Hard at work, I see."

Walt threaded his fingers over his stomach.

"You said I couldn't do it, that I couldn't slow down, but look at me now. I was reading a seed catalog and minding my own business when Wes came in askin' what you were up to."

"Did you have the inside scoop, Walt?" Prue asked with a raised eyebrow. "You were always pretty good at untangling my threads."

Their eyes locked and Wes had the sensation that they were communicating telepathically somehow. It still happened even after their divorce.

"Should I leave the two of you alone to… whatever this is?" Wes asked dryly.

Prue cleared her throat. "Sarah Hearst is over at the restaurant. You should drop in and say hello."

Wes met his father's stare.

"At this point, Sarah knows there have been offers from developers. She may even have some idea how much the Majestic and the land around it are worth." Wes wanted to make it clear to his mother that change was coming, one way or another. "I suggested someone with her background would have no problem running a lodge, and she explained that her life is in LA, Mom. Just like Sadie's."

The Hearsts would eventually get over the pain of letting a piece of Sadie go. Selling was the right decision for them, even if it wasn't for Prospect.

His mother tangled her fingers together. "I confess, I might have had a small grudge against Sadie Hearst. She was a true celebrity, but to just let the Majestic close when it wasn't easy anymore?"

"She also refused to sell it despite what had to be nice offers," Wes said.

His mother nodded. "Now we've got to make sure this new Hearst generation understands what the Majestic means to Prospect. Welcoming Sarah would have been smarter than…what I did. I let old emotions take over."

Wes blinked as he replayed her words. "Are you saying you made a mistake?"

His mother poked his ribs. "Don't tell anybody I said that." Her lips were twitching as she wrapped an arm around his waist. "Convey to Sarah how welcome she is here. I might have encouraged a few other people to do the same when they see her. If they love it enough, maybe they'll never leave us."

"And if that fails, think about my suggestion, Wes," Walt added. "If the Hearsts have to sell, see if you can't influence our visitor to sell it to you."

Prue tilted her head to the side. "You're thinking of buying the land for the Rocking A?" Her brilliant grin caused another sinking in Wes's midsection. Of course she loved the plan. "That's smart, Walt."

His father straightened in his chair.

"Now we've got two chances to save the Majestic and Prospect." His mother patted his arm.

To her, winning was a foregone conclusion. All that remained was choosing the right path to victory.

Resigned, Wes bussed his mother's cheek and then headed for the restaurant.

The mouthwatering promise of fried chicken wafting through the air as he stepped through the Ace's swinging doors lifted Wes's spirits. Seriously, how bad could life be when there was chicken like that in the world?

The way people greeted him as he paused inside the Ace was nice, too. Mark Russell, the retired army vet who'd taken over Sam's rural mail route, shook his hand after he picked up his to-go order. Two of his mother's quilting group were paying their bills and managed to pinch his cheeks on the way out the door.

Almost everyone in the place smiled at him, waved or both.

Only one customer remained facing away, her blond ponytail draped over her shoulder as she stared, engrossed, at something on the table in front of her.

Winding his way through the tables took no time, so he was standing next to hers before he knew how he intended to start the conversation.

If he had more experience running covert ops, he would think faster on his feet. As it was, he had to fall back on what he knew.

Any man approaching a beautiful woman like Sarah Hearst would be smart to keep it simple. Anything else might lead to embarrassment, disaster or both.

CHAPTER EIGHT

"I SHOULD HAVE guessed from the lack of parking out front that it was fried chicken night at the Ace."

Sarah glanced up from the paperwork she'd brought along to occupy her time while she waited.

Wes Armstrong was standing next to her booth. It took her a minute for his words to register. "It's not always this busy, huh? I was afraid I was the draw. I'm glad to know it's the food." All heads had swiveled to watch her walk across the dining room, but she hadn't been able to catch a single person staring since she'd sat down.

"Honestly, I'm guessing it's both." Wes pointed at the seat across from her. "Do you mind if I join you? Not too many empty spots."

Sarah waved her hand magnanimously but still noticed three empty booths along the back wall. "Certainly. I could use the company and a few answers, too." She tapped the folders. "I've been doing my homework."

Wes yanked his cowboy hat off and set it on the seat next to him. "Yeah? How did the visit out to the lodge go? Better or worse than you expected?"

What an excellent question. It was hard to answer.

"Yes?" Sarah said uncertainly.

His lips curled slowly into an amused smile. "Hmm, that's perfectly clear."

The curve of his lips.

The drawl.

The fried chicken perfume in the air.

It was devastating.

Sarah realized she'd been staring for too long when he raised his eyebrows. "Would you care to elaborate?"

"Sure." Before Sarah could follow her thoughts back to the proper starting point, the friendly waiter who'd introduced herself as Faye paused next to the table with two large plates.

"Here we are," Faye said. She expertly maneuvered around Sarah's drink and papers. Sarah leaned back to study a plate piled with two pieces of chicken and all the "fixins" in front of her.

Since she hadn't eaten since the B-and-B's hearty breakfast, Sarah had worried she hadn't ordered enough food. The mound of mashed potatoes reassured her that she would not leave hungry.

"Since you aren't much of a fish fan, I figured you'd be going for the chicken, Wes." Faye waved at the young girl who was carrying pitchers of tea around the dining room to bring him a glass.

Before Wes could confirm or deny, Faye hustled back toward the kitchen.

"One of those places where everyone knows your name…and your food preferences, I see." Sarah motioned at his plate. "Was she right?" There was no menu at the Ace High. There were options; tonight Faye had asked her "chicken or fish?" Ordering couldn't get much simpler.

Brooke would have died if she'd seen the basket of corn bread muffins that landed in the middle of the table between Sarah and Wes. Carbs were Enemy Number One for her youngest sister, but Sarah was squirming with happiness as she picked up her knife to butter her first warm muffin.

"Faye and I dated for about three hours one summer when we were kids. She also dated Travis at one point and Matt's dated just about every single woman in town. I've lost count how often Faye joined us for dinner at the Rocking A." Wes shrugged. "Besides, the fried chicken can't be beat." He winked at her and took a large sip of his now full tea glass.

The way he mentioned this old relationship, so casually, as if it were the temperature outside...

Weird.

Very weird. No hard feelings? Were they both still single? In a town this small, there couldn't be a large dating pool, could there?

Even stranger, why did she care? Sarah was only in town for days. Had to be nosiness, so nipping that in the bud made the best sense.

"My visit to the lodge was nice in some ways. I remembered so much of the place, even if it seems not quite what it once was. I was happy to see old clippings and posters up about Sadie, too." She stopped to take a bite of Mashed Potato Mountain and had to close her eyes to absorb the burst of flavor.

When she opened her eyes, Wes was giving her the grin again. The dangerous one.

"Good?" he asked.

As if he didn't know it was heaven.

"Very good. All the food here has been excellent. Sadie always promised the fresh air here would cure whatever ails a person, but I'm thinking the cooking must help, too. Living in LA means you can get any cuisine under the sun, but what can top a buttery mashed potato?" Sarah studied her options on the plate. Eat all the potatoes first or save some for last? "I didn't realize how much I wanted to find Sadie here until I saw that poster on the wall."

"It must have been hard to see what's changed, though." Wes managed to make headway through the pile of fixins while never losing his focus on her. A man who could eat and make conversation at the same time…she'd thought those had gone extinct.

"It was. You've done a fantastic job of keeping the place secure." Sarah decided not to mention the serial-killer-and-or-raccoon infestation that had taken over the kitchen. Her idea was to ask him to go with her on the next tour. He might hesitate if he thought his life was in danger. "But seeing the empty flower beds and how much things have grown reminded me of how long we've been away, how long Sadie had been gone from the lodge. I also spent too much time thinking about a future without her. Harder than I expected."

He nodded. "I can imagine. The good condition of the buildings may help to sell the place, if that's what you want, but clearing out the memories will be tough."

Faye skidded to a stop next to the table again to refill Sarah's glass. "You two discussing the Majestic? When we heard you were in town, Sarah, we sure were excited about the idea of the lodge reopening. Days on the lake haven't been the same without stopping in at the marina for some of Sadie's cowboy cookies."

Before she could answer, Faye waved a hand at the kitchen and hustled away.

Sarah frowned down at her plate at the reminder that the people who were still in Prospect also had fond memories of the Majestic and Sadie.

Then she realized she'd been the one to drop the conversational ball when she put her chicken down. Wes's head was tilted to the side as if he was waiting for her to return to their conversation.

"It's weird." Sarah rested her elbow on the table. "Sadie was our world. I mean, we shared her with fans, but that's not the same as what she meant here in Prospect. Of course they missed her when she moved away."

Wes said, "Sadie was one of those people who leave a hole when they go, no matter how it happens. That's part of the reason everyone here is so invested in what you plan to do with the Majestic."

"I hadn't even considered what we'd do with any of Sadie's memorabilia. There's so much to take care of here. I wish we'd had a chance to talk to her about what she wanted before…" Sarah shook her head and sipped her tea.

They both concentrated on their meals while Sarah got control of her emotions again.

Grief had surprised her. Losing Sadie had knocked her sideways, of course, but the sadness overwhelmed her sometimes, like a rogue wave on the ocean that she couldn't see coming. Taking charge of the situation had been Sadie's method with everything, especially business. When in doubt, full speed ahead had been her great-aunt's philosophy. Imitating Sadie's gumption was her only choice here.

"I guess I can thank your mother for the stories like Faye's?" Sarah motioned toward the server who was clearing another table.

His sheepish nod lifted her spirits.

"That explains why the young lady at the hostess stand made sure to tell me that the Ace High was originally one of four saloons during Prospect's silver boomtown days, named for the high-dollar poker games and very fine liquor it served. During Prohibition, good food replaced the liquor and nowadays, the fried chicken and beer on tap keep customers coming." Sarah shook her head again. "I guess everyone is working with the sales pitches they have."

Sarah had to admire the tactic. Prue Armstrong had called in reinforcements, and their stories were making Sarah think twice about the logic of selling quickly and moving on.

It was a strategy worthy of Sadie Hearst.

"Selling the Majestic is the easy decision in some ways," Wes said, "but it will hurt, too." He reached across the table to squeeze her hand. "A lot of people care about what happens to the lodge next."

"Does your mother want to run the Majestic, too? I mean, if we could somehow come up with a wagonload of money to restore the place and reopen it, the next headache would be finding someone here to manage the business." Sarah buttered a muffin to take her mind off the hurdles of reopening.

"The thing about my mother is," Wes said as he leaned closer, "I would not put it past her. Though I'm not sure that's the best solution to your problem."

"No, it seems there's one really simple solution here, at least for the Hearsts," Sarah said as she cleared her throat. "You mentioned Sadie had offers. I was surprised at how persistent some of them were."

She'd pulled out the last offer to buy Sadie's land from the stack Wes had given her. "Henry Milbank from Platinum Partners contacted you last year to ask for a meeting with Sadie to discuss a purchase offer." Sarah studied Wes's face. She wanted to see his reaction. "Did you meet?"

"I tried to get them together. Milbank insisted." He motioned at the stack of correspondence he'd included in the file. "He offered to fly us both out to LA to make it easier for Sadie, but it never came together."

"Sadie didn't want to sell?" Why hadn't Sadie ever mentioned these offers, at least to Sarah?

He shook his head slowly. "Sadie refused to meet. 'Sell that place? Over my dead body.' One email response. Seven words. It should be in the file as well, but if it isn't, I can find another from an earlier request. She got two or three letters every year, and none of them intrigued her enough to find out more."

Sarah definitely wanted to know more, but Wes shrugged. "I don't know what his offer was, whether it would have been high or low, but it doesn't seem that the amount of money on offer would have swayed her."

Wes was right. Sadie had never been impressed by money, or not as long as Sarah had known her. Building the Cookie Queen Corporation had been about doing what she loved, not record-breaking profits, much to some of Sadie's advisers' despair. The Western wear line had never made much money, but designing each piece and making sure it sparkled with rhinestones had thrilled Sadie.

Sarah slowly flipped through the previous years of reports, scanning the letterhead on each piece of correspondence as she went. "Do you know anything about these other companies?"

When he hesitated, Sarah glanced up.

"Platinum is the most persistent." Wes tapped the letter she'd pulled out of the file. "Unfortunately, Henry is persistent in every way. When I don't answer his calls quickly enough, he shows up in Prospect or out at the Rocking A. He tried to get through the security at the Cookie Queen headquarters, but Sadie's security team there was too good, stopped him at the elevator."

"I believe that's called a motivated buyer in the real estate business." Those were the buyers who had the best offers and money readily available, right? "When we found out Sadie had left us the Majestic, we weren't sure anyone would be interested in buying a fishing lodge. It seems like that worry was for nothing."

Wes braced his chin on his hand. "Buyers are easy to find, yes."

Sarah waited patiently for the rest.

Eventually, he added, "Sadie isn't here to

speak for herself, but I think the problem is finding buyers who would use that place the same way Sadie would. That's what Prospect needs the most, someone who cares about the place like Sadie did."

Sarah considered that. His logic was sound. Did the perfect solution exist? She needed to discuss this with Jordan and Brooke soon.

"My sister called. She's on her way, should be here the day after tomorrow. I'd like to go inside with her." For backup, obviously. "There's so much to discuss."

He nodded. "Solid plan. They don't build places like that lodge anymore, great timbers all the way through, but it's better to have company." He rolled his straw wrapper into a tight ball. "If you need to kill some time while you wait for Jordan, you could head over to the Mercantile. My mother's usually doing a demonstration. This week I think it's quilting."

Quilting.

That brought back more memories from their summer visits.

Instead of following that bittersweet path, she said, "A quilting workshop could be fun. I shouldn't press my luck, though. Your mom's already not a fan. If I sew my quilt to my jeans, I'll never recover."

They shared a smile at that. As the moment stretched out, it was harder to turn away.

Sarah cleared her throat as Faye reached between them to remove their dishes. "Do we need dessert tonight, folks?" She waved a hand. "Never mind. I'll bring them to-go, my treat. Gotta make sure Sarah's sweet on Prospect, don't we?" She hurried away before Sarah could argue.

Wes's grin convinced her he could read some of the thoughts bouncing around her brain. Faye's energy was hard to match. If Sarah spent much more time in town, she'd need to get faster, build her stamina.

That reminded her of the loose plan she had to go exploring.

"I was hoping…" Why did this seem so much more awkward than she expected? He was kind of an employee of…her family's? Of Sadie's? Of the estate? If he didn't want to show her around, he could hire someone and charge her for it.

He raised his eyebrows. "You want me to teach you to quilt? I can, but it might kill my mother from the shock."

"Can't have that. I prefer all the impromptu sales pitches over the cold shoulders." Sarah nodded. "I was thinking that it would be good to take a look at all of the property." She bit her lip. "To make a more informed decision."

He waited. "I don't hear a request."

She sighed. "I used to ride horses. When we visited. Sadie always wanted the three of us to be cowgirls. None of us managed to perfect every Western survival skill, but I did enjoy getting in the saddle."

"Horse or an ATV. Riding's the best way to see what's what. But I have both." The corner of his mouth curved up.

Ever since she'd considered borrowing a horse, she hadn't been able to get the idea out of her head. "The horse. I think."

"Excellent choice." Wes paused. "But I have conditions."

She leaned forward eagerly. Conditions were smart. Any good cowboy would lay out ground rules here. That made sense.

"I'll be your shadow. It's a big place. I'd be as nervous as a prize turkey a week before Thanksgiving while you were out riding alone and if anything happened…" Wes extended his hand to shake.

"As nervous as all that, huh?" Sarah said as she slipped her hand into his.

She knew immediately it was a mistake to touch Wes Armstrong. At the potluck, she'd decided the sizzle of connection had been nerves; it made sense to be so aware of him when she was surrounded by strangers.

A hand was a hand was a hand. Right?

But his skin, his firm grip…it was different. Some of the noise of the Ace High's dining room faded.

"Have pity on my nerves, won't you?" he asked.

How long were they frozen like that before Faye paused beside their table with their desserts and shot a glance at their hands, still clasped together? Pulling back was easy enough, but the warmth of his touch stayed with Sarah.

"Thanks, Wes. Do you have time tomorrow?" Sarah straightened her spine. It was important to get back to business.

"Don't want to wait for your sister?" he asked.

The memory of the way Jordan had squealed when anyone steered her toward a barn made it easier to answer. "No, I want to go out with you as soon as possible."

He pursed his lips and Sarah realized there was more than one way to interpret her answer.

"Tomorrow. Meet me in the Rocking A barn about nine? I should be done with the morning chores at that point." Wes picked up his hat as he waited for her answer.

The kaleidoscope of butterflies that took flight as her idea to meet him, to go out riding alone with him fell into place, was surprising, but the bubble of excitement made her think of Sadie.

Her great-aunt would be thrilled to see Sarah back in the saddle.

Adding in a handsome cowboy would have sent Sadie into fits of delight.

For the first time, Sarah knew that Sadie Hearst was beaming down at her from whatever fluffy cloud she'd landed on.

Not a tear in sight.

CHAPTER NINE

THE NEXT MORNING, Wes stared hard at Grant's door and wondered what his reception would be if he were to wake his brother up to ask him to saddle a horse for Sarah. It wasn't necessary. He and Travis had managed to get by fine without Grant while he'd been riding the rodeo circuit. Wes would saddle his mother's horse for Sarah and make sure he carried enough apples in his pockets to lure the cantankerous mare back to the job when she spotted greener grass along the way.

Lady was the perfect horse for his mother. Each just as strong-willed as the other. Knowing how to talk to them was important.

It wasn't that he doubted Sarah's ability to ride, but he wasn't sure she'd made much time for practice in LA. He turned toward the kitchen. He had time for one more cup of coffee before he started pacing up and down the aisle of the barn with his ears perked up to hear tires on gravel again.

He skidded to a stop at the sight of Grant at the table, hands curled around a mug. Before he gathered himself, Grant glanced up. "Morning."

Wes was excited to have an opportunity for an actual conversation with his brother, but he still didn't know what had caused this unannounced visit. "Morning. Any more of that coffee left?"

Grant nodded. "I made some eggs, too." His loud slurp would never pass muster if his mother were running the kitchen, but she only made special appearances ever since she'd claimed her cozy little apartment in town.

"So," Wes said as he tried to decide where he was taking the conversation, "what have you got planned today?"

There. That was fairly nonconfrontational.

"Same as yesterday. Get an early start on tomorrow's to-do list, do as little as possible until I get tired of doing that and then take a nap. I believe it's called a vacation," Grant drawled. "Why?"

Since his to-do list also included staying out late and…and now making breakfast, Wes wondered what it would take to change his priorities. "Travis could use some help organizing the barn."

Grant nodded. "The two of you can handle it. I know you've been helping him with his plans to create the Rocking A Home for Wayward Boys, Part Two, every chance you get." He slurped again to punctuate the sentence.

The irritation that welled up made it hard to decide which part of Grant's response to address first.

"It was a pretty good home, and since you were one of the first group of lucky wayward boys to find a family, I'd think you might be interested in contributing." Wes dumped the last eggs in the pan on his plate.

"Still wayward. Not sure all the positive life lessons took. Hate to infect the new crop."

Wes yanked out a chair to sit opposite Grant.

"I don't hear you denying that it's home. When you needed it, you had a place to land. All Travis wants is to do the same." Wes didn't glare at Grant. It was hard, but he wouldn't push. Yet. He'd had plenty of time to learn how to maneuver his brothers when they were teenagers ready to fight at the drop of a hat.

Now and then, that wild streak boiled to the surface again. He could see it in Grant's eyes.

"I'm glad he's doing it, Wes," Grant said. "Just not sure I need to be involved."

That cooled some of Wes's ire.

"You could exercise the horses, clear their stalls, while he cleans out the junk we've piled up." Horses were Grant's thing. Out of all of them, Grant had the touch.

"To make room for more junk?" Grant asked. "I had to clear out five different sets of sports awards, comic books and hobby stuff before I could find my bed when I got here. This place could use a good airing out. Too much clutter and history."

"We've got a little over a month to accomplish just that. Clay will be happy to have an extra pair of hands when he starts renovations, too. You used to be pretty good with a hammer."

Grant didn't argue.

That was new.

"What will you be doing?" he asked. "Barking orders?"

Wes clamped his mouth shut to stop the angry response that wanted out. Beginning the day on a sour note wouldn't help either of them.

"Sarah Hearst wants to see the whole stretch of Sadie's property today." Wes shrugged as if it were nothing, no need to spend any time discussing. "We're going to take some horses out."

Grant nodded slowly.

Wes concentrated on the eggs in front of him.

"Think you'll get useful information today?" Grant asked. "Mom was not impressed with your results when I saw her yesterday at the store."

"What were you doing in town?" Wes asked, surprised. Why hadn't he noticed when Grant left the house?

"Mom called while you were *meeting with a beautiful woman in your office.* Her excuse to get me moving was bringing down the quilt boxes from storage at the Mercantile." Grant rolled his eyes as if seeing through her request was child's play. "Imagine my surprise when I found out you were both preoccupied with the same person." Grant smiled slowly. "I wouldn't ask me to take Sarah out on a horse, either. Once she saw me ride, you'd never stand a chance."

The urge to slug Grant had to be squashed, but he thought the gleam in his brother's eyes was proof that he knew the impulse Wes was fighting.

And the fact that it was normal, like dealing with the old Grant, made it easier to handle. This new Grant was too angry. Old Grant might have been annoying, but Wes would welcome him back.

"I was gonna put her on Lady. Mom won't mind. You have a better suggestion?" Wes asked, determined to keep the peace. His brother was talking. It was new enough that Wes would accept whatever he could get.

"You've got a couple of beautiful mares out there. Done any training?" Grant asked.

"Not much." Wes raised his eyebrows. "Another place your help would come in handy. If you're here long enough this time, you could get them shaped up."

Grant nodded. "At least there's one thing I can do better than you." Emptying his mug, he stood and put his dishes in the dishwasher. "I'll do both. I'll go out and lend Travis a hand. I'll start working with your

horses. Eventually, it'll be like I never left."
He propped his hands on the sink to stare out
the window.

Wes wanted to know why that sounded so
final, even defeated, but he could hear Sarah
driving in.

"Am I allowed to introduce myself to the
future town wrecker or should I stay here
until y'all are out of the barn?" Grant asked.

"Don't call her the future town wrecker to
her face. She already has a good idea of what
Mom thinks." Wes didn't hang around to see
if his brother was going to follow him or not.

This time, Sarah had parked near the barn.
When he crossed the yard in front of the
house, her car was empty. Wes paused in the
shadow of the barn to see Sarah up on her
tiptoes, peeking through a stall.

"Beautiful, isn't she?" a male voice asked;
someone was with Sarah.

Wes glanced at Grant, who'd come up along-
side him and knew the voice wasn't his.

Grant's lips were twitching. "I believe disaster has befallen you. That's our dear sweet-
talking brother Matt in the stall." He stifled
a chuckle.

When Sarah's gaze met his, joy lighting

her face, Wes felt the bolt of attraction land in the center of his chest.

"Hey, I ran into Matt. He's showing me the ranch's newest member. He said she doesn't have a name yet." Sarah's voice was soft and excited, the perfect sound for the arrival of a baby and one he hadn't heard on the Rocking A in a long while. When had the place become nothing more than all business?

He vaguely remembered the joy and excitement of new foals.

Grant stepped forward and held out his hand. "I'm Grant. Brother four out of five here."

Sarah's open grin was beautiful. Wes could tell that even Grant relaxed with her there.

"So we have the town mayor, the veterinarian...is this family filled with the most eligible bachelors in Colorado or is it limited to Prospect?" Sarah asked.

"We also have a soldier determined to become a foster dad and a builder who can create anything you dream up." Grant held his hands out. "Then there's me. Has-been."

Matt groaned theatrically and Wes was glad he was there. Without Matt, they all descended into awkward, angry silence too often. "Rodeo star. Magic with horses. And still, so humble."

Wes spoke up. "I've been warned about letting you spend too much time with any of my brothers. Two of them together is definitely overkill. Let's get the horses saddled up."

Curiosity lit Sarah's eyes. She wanted to know more about his brothers, and Wes didn't blame her. If he was certain she'd been intrigued by him instead of Matt or Grant, he might have taken it as a sign of something. What? He wasn't sure, but it probably had to do with why he had had trouble sleeping because he was ready to take Sarah out on a ride.

"Let me introduce you to Lady. She's an older horse but she still enjoys a mosey around the lake. Should be perfect for a beautiful day like today." He realized his voice had taken on the tone of those guided tours of the stars' homes even before Matt bugged his eyes out at him behind Sarah's back. Wes cleared his throat. "She's my mother's horse."

Sarah stopped in her tracks. "Okay, introduce me to Lady but only if you promise me one thing." She held her hand up as if she was asking him to take a solemn vow. "Your mother can never know Lady and I hung out like this."

"I have a better idea." Wes bent his head to murmur in her ear, "I'll let *you* spring that information on my mother when the time is right. I'm not saying she could stand to be surprised now and then, but actually, I am *definitely* saying that." He waited for her to nod her agreement. "When she's being contrary about something, you casually sprinkle into the conversation how you and Lady had a beautiful day together and watch her face. Tomorrow or ten years from now, that's at your discretion."

Sarah grinned. "I like this. You've given me two gifts in one."

Wes opened the stall door and smiled at Matt who had mouthed "Ten years?" with an exaggerated expression of surprise. It was weird to even suggest Sarah Hearst would still be around in a decade, but it had rolled off his tongue. There was no sense in calling more attention to it by stumbling over it now.

Lady immediately sauntered up to him to sniff the pocket of his shirt. "We've always joked that Lady has to be part golden retriever. She'd sleep at the foot of the bed if anybody had a bed big enough." Wes ran his hand down over her neck and patted when she whiffled a happy breath into his shoulder.

Sarah didn't pause. "Hey, pretty girl." She did the same motion on the other side of Lady's neck and laughed when Lady turned to check out her face and hair. No fear. That put her in good stead compared to most of the women Matt brought home.

Wes handed Sarah the carrots Lady knew he was hiding. "Get to know her. I'll put on her saddle."

As he worked, he could hear a soft, sweet murmur and Lady's responses. Whatever Sarah did in LA, she'd learned something about horses during her time in Prospect. Sadie had done them both that favor.

One of his mother's soft spots was Lady. Bonding with her horse would earn Sarah points if she were hanging around Prospect for long.

"She's dressed and ready to ride." Wes took the reins and led Lady out of the stall. "Mounting block outside." He was going to ignore his brothers if there was any way possible.

"Since I'm helping in the barn this morning, even though Travis has not yet made his appearance," Grant said sweetly, "I'll saddle up Arrow for you, big brother."

Wes faked a smile. "Thank you, little brother."

"I can do this without the block," Sarah said. "Give me a bounce if I need it, okay?"

Intrigued, Wes stepped back to let her move to Lady's side. He watched her closely, ready to step in at any minute. It would take a meteor crashing and a full bucket of grain to make Lady jolt, but life had all kinds of unexpected twists.

"Okay, pretty girl, do you want to go for a ride today?" Sarah murmured as she gathered the reins, snugging them close, before threading her fingers widely into the horse's mane. Sarah straightened the stirrup and put her left foot in. No cowboy boots, but sturdy hiking boots. No cowboy hat to keep the sun off her face, but she yanked a baseball cap out of her back pocket and tugged it on, pulling her ponytail through the hole to swing freely.

Sarah had taken the time to plan ahead. She was also confident enough in her knowledge to step out, but not arrogant enough to get herself hurt. Smart. Confident. Real.

Everyone who met Sarah would know that she was beautiful, but seeing her like this, teasing his brothers, loving a horse and showing genuine riding skill? His heart might be in danger. He needed to focus.

Sarah clapped the saddle with her right hand. "Ready, Lady?"

Lady's ears twitched.

"I'm taking that as a yes." Sarah smiled at him over her shoulder. "Here I go."

Wes carefully placed his hands on her hips. "When you put your right leg over, try to land gently in the saddle, not hit with a plop." Lady would be okay either way, but the horse might hold a grudge.

"Right. Got it." Sarah bounced once on her right leg and completed a swift, graceful mount to land in the seat.

Disgruntled that he hadn't had a chance to help her more, Wes shrugged. "Well, that was very nearly flawless, as if you've done it every day of your life."

Sarah patted Lady's neck. "Thanks mostly to a pro like Lady."

"Let's go for a turn or two, here in the paddock, before we head out. To make sure you're comfortable." He leaned against the fence post as he watched Sarah and Lady walk in broad circles. It was clear Sarah needed to relax a bit, and he could see the moment that Lady turned her head and told Sarah the same thing. Before he could translate, Sarah nodded. "I hear you, girl. I trust you." She rolled her head on her shoulders and shook out her arms to reset.

"She looks good up there. Like she was meant to be riding." Grant was standing at the fence line, holding Arrow's reins. "Since I'm the expert, I should know. Want me to tell her that?"

Wes frowned at his brother. "I do not. I will tell her that—thank you very much."

Grant sniffed. "Fine. You don't want her to like me. I get it."

Wes took Arrow's reins and swung up into the saddle. "It's fine if she likes you."

Grant pursed his lips. "You just want her to like you more." Then he grinned.

The difference in his brother's face was good. It was reassuring. Grant outside in the bright sunshine, some of the fatigue and tension wiped away, and this teasing... Wes was hopeful that whatever had a hold of his brother might be chased off at some point.

"Have a nice ride," Grant called over to Sarah who had convinced Lady to trot.

Wes joined them. "The thing about Lady is that she'll go far but she won't go fast. That might be her top speed that you've accomplished right here."

"Good." Sarah nodded. "Neither of us is up to a gallop this morning. I appreciate that about her."

Wes tipped his head toward the lake in the distance. "Ready to head for the lodge?"

Sarah inhaled slowly. "I am, but let's take the scenic route. I don't want this ride to end too soon."

He knew the feeling. She was clearly so happy to be back on the horse. It was a beautiful day. That's all she meant.

Right?

He wanted to ask if his company had anything to do with her satisfaction, but then he'd be admitting something he wasn't ready to admit even to himself.

As he led Sarah to the pasture closest to Sadie's land, he told himself to slow down. It was a nice ride with a beautiful woman, but she had no plans to stay in Prospect, not really.

This ride wasn't about getting to know an exciting woman. Wes's job was to keep the ranch going and take care of his family. Finding a way to buy Sadie Hearst's land would do both.

He hadn't been born on the Rocking A, but this was his home. Sarah Hearst was temporary; the land, this ranch…they were permanent. He owed it to himself and his family to put the two of them back together again.

CHAPTER TEN

SARAH INHALED THE scent of fresh mountain air slowly as she watched Wes maneuver a gate, so they could pass through. She was pleased at how well she and Lady were getting along after a meandering detour through what must have been a nice patch of breakfast grass and a negotiation over carrots. Wes had patiently put Lady back on track, but there was no doubt that the horse was humoring him. Figuring out how to open that gate on horseback would have required a math degree, Lady's good will and some serious stretching. But Wes handled it with ease.

She'd bet nothing rattled him.

"You aren't going to close the gate?" she asked as he resumed the tour, heading directly toward the clear water of Key Lake. Lady seemed to approve of this destination; she picked up her pace a fraction.

"Did you see how much trouble it was to

get it open?" He shook his head. "No, ma'am. I'll close it on the way back."

Did she want to ask what would happen if all the horses in one pasture ran into the other pasture? Or what about the cattle she could see in the distance? Would they make a break for freedom through the open gate?

Obviously, she *wanted* to ask, but she wasn't certain why. If either scenario happened, she would be no help.

Instead, she contented herself with the knowledge that he was the expert here. If it happened, he'd have no one to blame but himself and he'd be able to clean up the mess, too. The more time she spent with Wes, the more she trusted him to handle whatever came next.

It had been a long time since she'd met someone and instantly believed he could be trusted, but Wes Armstrong appeared strong, solid, unshakable.

Like a man who would step up when tough times came instead of packing up and running away.

He took on extra jobs and carried more than his weight because his family needed him. What would it be like to have someone like him in her life, someone who understood her own position so well?

"Okay, I have to ask. He called you big brother. Are you all twins somehow because…" Sarah had studied their faces and there might be some difference in age, a few months or even a year, but there was almost no way the three men could be more than three years apart.

"Of a sort," he drawled.

She wasn't sure he was going to continue with his story. That would be disappointing but she couldn't explain why.

If she was only making conversation to fill the time, it would be as easy to ride in silence.

It wasn't even uncomfortable silence. This was the perfect ride she'd imagined.

"We were all adopted. Pretty close to the same age, even though we didn't arrive here at the Rocking A at the same time." Wes shrugged. "Matt was two years behind us in school, but the rest of us graduated together. Thanks to that small difference, Matt claimed to be the baby of the family and abuses his position every chance he gets. We were too old for the matchy-matchy twin thing, but it's kinda hard to distinguish our fashion personalities when we're all wearing jeans and boots, you know?"

Sarah smiled. He expected her to.

"That's..." She wasn't sure how to fill in the blank. Nothing felt right. "What a remarkable story."

He wrinkled his nose. "Didn't start out too well for any of us, but I've still got my fingers crossed for a happy ending. I'm the oldest because I got here first. Grant was the last one in. He's always been a little...different about the Rocking A because of it."

Sarah studied his face to try to discern what that might mean, but his lips were a tight line. She decided not to chase down that rabbit trail.

"It doesn't surprise me that Matt's the baby of the family. Must be the charm. I guess the baby in every family likes to take advantage when they can," Sarah said. "My youngest sister will go out of her way to introduce herself as just that. Doesn't matter what kind of group, either. Did anyone ask, Brooke? Noooooo." She hoped her dramatization of Brooke's sometimes annoying habit translated. When Wes laughed, she was sure it had landed correctly. "Being the oldest comes with so much responsibility, doesn't it?"

He took his cowboy hat off and ruffled his hair. "It does. Some days too much."

Was he talking about today?

"I appreciate you taking this time out of your day, Wes."

When his head snapped up, Sarah wondered if she'd done something wrong. Lady was still ambling along calmly as if she'd never even heard of time or hours in the day.

Sarah tilted her head up to catch more of the breeze. "I'm not sure how a guy who is the mayor of a town and a lawyer and the oldest brother and running a ranch has a few hours on a Saturday for a favor. Do you never sleep?"

"Well, now, my mother really runs Prospect. Being the mayor consists of showing up at meetings and following her direction," Wes drawled.

"Why isn't she the mayor?" Sarah asked, intimidated all over again by Prue Armstrong.

"Good question. She prefers to be the power behind the throne. Over and over, I just seem to get elected," he said dryly.

Sarah laughed. "And law school because…"

"I loved school, mostly." He motioned to the left where Sarah could see a path that wound down toward the water. "After high school, my parents were dead certain we were all going to college, although none of us believed it was necessary. Grant flat refused. He's always been the rogue, wanting to go left if the rest of us went right. He loaded up a truck and headed for Wyoming to try his hand at rodeo. Travis always dreamed of being the hero. He sweet-talked my parents into approving his joining the army instead. The way my mother carried on after he left makes me wonder how he managed it. That summer, after Grant and Travis left and before Clay and I went to school, was tough. Mom was so worried about them, and my parents couldn't agree on what color the sky was. The rest of us were happy to fall in line. College was easy enough."

"So the three…" Sarah waited for him to confirm her math. "The three of you returned home after graduation?"

"Yes, we have an architect, a veterinarian and a lawyer, plenty of extra school to make our parents happy. I loved studying, classes and homework." He rolled his eyes. "You ever met a cowboy nerd?"

"I can't say I haven't anymore, can I?"

He shook his head sadly. "No, ma'am."

They were quiet as the horses sipped around the edges of the lake.

"It's so hard to believe that this spot is here, as beautiful as it is, and it isn't overrun with people every single weekend," Sarah said as Lady tossed her head.

Wes pointed to where the lodge was hidden behind the trees. "You remember when I showed you the fence that marked the property line between the Rocking A and your land?"

Sarah nodded even though she wanted to argue that it was Sadie's land.

Calling it hers changed the way she felt about the Majestic and she hadn't quite decided what that meant.

"Good valuable pasture. That's how a rancher sees this stretch we've covered. If you take care of it right, it'll last forever." He nodded at the lake. "But a developer will see that lake, and the person's vision will immediately be clouded by dollar signs."

That made sense to Sarah, the difference between making a life and turning a profit. Long-term goals versus short-term thinking.

"From here, we're riding up into the foothills." Wes directed the horses toward the lodge. "Not much wrong with seeing dollar signs, except it'll mean expansion. And depending on who and how that's done, it will change Prospect, too."

As they passed in front of the lodge, Sarah realized that all the ground she'd covered by foot the day before... It was a dot compared to the whole acreage. The Majestic Prospect Lodge, the old fishing lodge that Sadie's father had built, was how she thought of the property but that was because that's how she'd always known it.

"You sure you don't want to step inside?" Wes asked as he paused on the edge of the clearing in front of the Majestic.

Sarah shook her head. "No, I think I'll wait on Jordan. So many memories. She's pretty good at annoying me out of any sad slump I might fall into because of that."

Wes laughed. "Yeah, if sisters are as good as brothers are at that, I understand. Getting any one of my brothers to be honest about feelings takes torture and truth serum, but they will all do whatever they can to lift my spirits, even if it's start a fight."

Sarah was amused at how similar their experiences were. The baby of the family always acted like the baby, and these people they'd grown up with knew exactly how to handle the ups and downs with them.

That made it simpler to understand the Armstrongs.

It also encouraged the attraction to Wes that she'd been fighting unsuccessfully.

"Do you think that's what all these companies want? The ones who were contacting Sadie? They want to build something big here, a large resort or waterpark instead of a vacation home for people who will rarely cause a ripple in Prospect."

Wes nodded. "It stands to reason. As you said, this lake is special. Right now, it's one of those hidden gems. The locals know about it and enjoy it. If a developer or corporation comes in, they'll knock down the old lodge and build something larger, more imposing, that won't fit in as neatly with the surroundings. They'll invest, sure. They'll advertise. And they'll do their best to bring along other businesses who can fill out Main Street with shopping and restaurants for their visitors."

As much as Sarah enjoyed vacations, and nature, for that matter, she understood why the people who called Prospect home might not love that kind of change. "More places to eat and shop and work? It wouldn't be all bad."

"No, it wouldn't, but it wouldn't be home, either." He seemed to be studying her after he said it until she turned away.

"Right." Sarah bit her lip as she considered his words. "There may be no route to win over Prospect."

"Did some thinking about the offers last night?" Wes asked.

She had.

She'd also thought about calling Brooke to talk over the situation with her youngest sister. Jordan was on the road and she'd be arriving tomorrow. Brooke was depending on Sarah to keep her involved. "When we heard Sadie had left us this place, selling was the only choice that made sense. What do we know about fishing, running a lodge or even Prospect?"

"That's only a problem if you can't learn," Wes drawled. "Or you don't want to learn."

Sarah snorted. "Of course we could learn. We would be successful at running a fishing lodge, I bet. I've spent years learning all elements of a business at Sadie's feet, and she did well for herself. Jordan has been successful in corporate cybersecurity. I have no idea what that means, but I expect setting up a reservation system would be elementary for her, and Brooke…" It was hard to describe Brooke's career. Was she in politics? Her husband was. Was she a socialite? That suggested money which they didn't have all that much of anymore, if the rumors were true. "She's good at a lot of things."

Of the three of them, Brooke would be a natural running a hotel. She'd been managing things and people without them knowing she was pulling their strings for most of her life.

When Wes didn't respond, Sarah had to wonder who she was trying to convince. Was she making a case for the Hearsts reopening the Majestic themselves? If he'd maneuvered her into that, it was a neat trick. Sadie would have been impressed.

Sarah loved how the pasture rose in gentle inclines, but she could see the hills ahead steepening, heading to the mountains. "So, we're back to square one—we can't afford to renovate the place, and selling it will most likely destroy the Majestic and maybe Prospect. I now understand Sadie's non-decision regarding the place better."

Wes nodded. "Did you ever visit on Western Days weekend?"

She hadn't. She should investigate this big festival weekend so she knew more about Prospect's history. So far she'd crashed a meeting about it, and now Wes was asking.

"Prospect used to swarm with people, tourists and kids and grandkids who returned to town in a sort of homecoming, and the whole town got into the act. Lately, attendance has been dwindling. It's an exciting time, but it doesn't last forever. Otherwise, long summer weekends used to fill the town with visitors to support the local businesses, thanks to the lake, but life for the people who called the place home didn't change much beyond those exceptions."

Sarah nodded. "I can see how that would work…and be fun." It was hard to imagine the town absorbing a crowd like that now.

"The night you arrived, that was a typical weekday night. Quiet. Businesses closed. Everyone here would welcome some new energy, I think, as long as it didn't destroy what we have."

She and Wes rode along until she could make out the remnants of wood buildings. "Is this the ghost town? Sadie mentioned it but she would never let us come out this far. Was it also called Prospect?"

"No, the ghost town was named after the first miner to strike silver, Sullivan's Post. He and the early prospectors set up here so they could access the lake, but this clearing limited the size of the town. Sullivan's Post exploded in population early on." Wes motioned to a tree with enough green grass and shade for the horses. Then he slid out of the saddle and moved over to help her dismount. After the feeling returned to her thighs, Sarah realized it felt good to stand and walk.

She also understood that her thighs were going to remind her of her first horse ride in decades for at least a week every time she took a step.

"Don't know that we should take a chance on any of the buildings, but you can still see the layout of the town." Wes pointed out the buildings on either side. They walked slowly along the broken wooden sidewalk. "Sullivan's Post had a small general store, a saloon and a jail. My dad would love to tell you stories about the place. They may or may not be true, but they've been handed down through his family like heirlooms. My brothers and I wasted full days here growing up. We explored every inch of this place. It's a miracle we weren't injured or worse. Grant switched sides from sheriff to outlaw in his imagination, depending on whether he was in trouble at home."

Sarah watched his face as he surveyed the town. Being responsible for all the Rocking A business had to be a big job but there was no doubt that Wes loved his home and everything that made up the ranch.

"It's beautiful." Disturbing the silence seemed wrong, but she wanted to make it clear she understood how he felt and why.

Wes stopped in his tracks, so Sarah followed. "Beautiful? Ramshackle buildings held up by dirt and faith?" His head tilted to the side. "Wouldn't have been my first description."

Sarah sighed. "So literal. What I see is hope and resilience. Imagining how hard the people worked to carve out a home in these mountains."

"Taking a chance on luck. Never knowing

what might happen? It was a scary way to live." Wes's amused frown convinced Sarah that he was humoring her. That was fine. She could work with that.

"It's about what humans do to find community and what they'll sacrifice in order to go on." She tapped his shoulder. "The reason you don't see it is because it's a part of you, your family. Being an Armstrong means something because of this ghost town and because of Prospect and because you're the mayor when you really only want to run your ranch. You're a special guy and this is a special place." She paused because something else was making sense to her. "Whatever you build, make, save is going to endure, too. Because the community will."

Sarah realized Sadie had said something similar to her before. When Sarah had asked why the painting of the mountains hung behind her desk, Sadie had told her that she liked to know that no matter what sort of ups and downs the day might bring, home was still there, still waiting. She could always go back.

"Maybe you understand it better than I did," Wes said quietly. "But I do have it running in my veins, for sure. I got here late, but something about being chosen and included here makes it twice as special."

Sarah didn't have a story to match his, but she believed she understood what he meant. The family she'd been born into was good. She loved her dad and her sisters and she'd believed Sadie was something special.

But being chosen and accepted for who you were instead of growing to fit the circumstances you'd been given was something else.

"I love the country," Sarah said softly.

Wes stopped to pick a wildflower that had sprung up between the old boards of what seemed to be the steps to one of the weathered buildings. "I can tell." He offered it to her. "Do not sniff this. There's no telling what sort of critter is attached and I'm handing it to you in a moment of romance and chivalry. I cannot be responsible for what happens after."

Sarah laughed. "Truly a moment where it's the thought that counts."

"The thought is the only part of this that really counts." Wes's grin was beautiful, too, but Sarah was not going to say that aloud. She certainly did not want to have to explain what that softening did to the firm lines of his handsome face.

That stunning smile made an attractive but reserved man into a guy she'd do silly things for, if only to convince him to smile over and over.

"That's probably true of most gifts, but certainly about a weed in a ghost town." Wes shook his head. "You know, my mother wanted me to make sure to get to know the sweet blonde stranger who'd appeared in our town. She's desperate to get me and every one of us married off, and as you can probably imagine, prospects in Prospect are somewhat sparse."

"But then, in a dramatic twist of fate, the blonde was revealed to be an enemy of the town." Sarah added the "dun, dun, dun" of a shocking mystery reveal. "And now she'd do anything to save you from my clutches?"

Wes tilted his head to the side. "Well, I don't know about that, but I do believe I've changed my mind about her advice. Getting to know you is tempting."

Sarah raised her eyebrows. Coming up with a flirty answer escaped her. She cleared her throat.

"So, the reason you don't need to spend time with my brothers any more than necessary is that every single one of them can do this flirting thing without it descending into awkward silence." He motioned between them. "It should be abundantly clear at this juncture that I cannot."

Sarah grinned even as her cheeks heated with a mix of pleasure and embarrassment. It was nice to hear him come out and say he was flirting. It would definitely save her time staring up at the ceiling of the Liberty Room wondering if he'd meant to be friendly or something more.

Something more was nice.

"You might have more success if I were better at it. For years, I've done everything I could to contribute to the Cookie Queen Corporation. I had a goal and I can become intense about goals. Focused. When that happens, I let other things pass by, you know?"

He nodded. "I get that."

They resumed walking.

"Have you ever thought about restoring this?" she asked. "You could run horseback tours from the ranch. Tourists would enjoy it, I think." She was ready to return the conversation to what she knew. Building a business and creating a base of customers. Struck by inspiration, she grabbed his arm. "Oh, you could have actors dress up as ghosts and make spooky sounds." Would that scare the horses? It might rattle the tourists.

"Not our ghost town anymore. This isn't Rocking A land. If anyone were to do that, it would have to be the owners of the Prospect Lodge." Wes led her back to Lady.

Right. And those owners were out-of-towners who didn't know the history and certainly couldn't run horseback tours.

"Someone with a little experience, who decided to renovate and reopen the lodge, could negotiate a deal with the Rocking A to provide their horses and even tour guides," Wes said. "Grant trains horses and if I could get him on board, he'd be the kind of guy tourists would love. A real cowboy with a flair for the show." He gathered Lady's reins to hand to Sarah. He didn't hesitate when she put her foot in the stirrup; he wrapped his hands over her hips to give her a boost.

Like they'd done it a million times already.

"I should make sure the real estate agent knows that's a possibility when I find one,"

Sarah said quietly. The longer she stayed in Prospect, the harder it was to convince herself that selling was the only right answer.

If she wasn't almost certain that Brooke needed to sell, Sarah might start working on convincing Jordan that they could do… something else. The size of the job was so intimidating, though. They'd have to find contractors and live through the renovation. Sadie's funds would come through eventually, but in the meantime, Sarah should be in the job market hunting for the right position somewhere outside Cookie Queen

Wes rode silently for a while. "Selling is the smart answer. Sadie obviously understood how life twists and turns. Maybe she did love Prospect, but she'd have to know that it would be difficult for anyone to take on a project like restoration of the lodge, much less doing anything else with all the land around it."

Sarah nodded. Sadie had understood that. He was right. Her great-aunt had been practical in business.

But it had never stopped her from dreaming big.

Sometimes, she'd gambled on those too-big ideas, too, because she loved them.

When her local cooking show had started gathering fans, no one was doing cooking shows like that. She'd loved to bake and she'd had the personality, the ability to tell a story, which made even making the cowboy cookies that were always for sale at the marina an entertaining ride. That passion and personality had led to one opportunity after another, so dreaming big was rewarded, but she'd never once taken a risk that she wasn't prepared to lose big on.

"Selling to a developer or finding a buyer who wants to reopen the lodge are options. There could be a third choice," Wes said as he worked to close the gate between the fields, "but it's not going to be the most profitable. I do think it would be the best decision for Prospect."

Sarah straightened in her saddle. Something in his tone made her think this was important to him.

"I'm all ears, Wes. We don't want to harm Prospect. Of course not. Whatever folks think of Sadie, she loved her hometown. Part of my goal is to honor her legacy."

Wes pointed at the barn she could see in the distance. "Well, I've heard the story of why that Armstrong had to sell off a piece of the Rocking A. I also recall the story of how the first Armstrongs struck silver after traveling here from Tennessee. They bought land and together they built this place and handed it down through generations. Selling off a piece to survive is one of those scars, you know?"

Sarah wasn't sure where he was going.

"I can understand that."

Wes halted at the top of a small rise. From there, she could see more of the ranch house and the drive leading back to town.

"If you decide to sell, we'd like to buy back the land." Wes watched her carefully. "You understand what it's like to be the oldest and to love your family even when they drive you to cuss on a regular basis. My dad and four brothers… That's six grown men who will be on the Rocking A some or all of the time. That house ain't big enough for half that number."

Sarah understood. If she tried to house Jordan and Brooke in the same square footage, there might be enough physical rooms for all three of them but there would definitely not be enough breathing space.

"I can see that, too." Sarah nodded. "If

you'll draw up some kind of offer, I'll take it to my sisters. We would be happy to consider it and make a decision that Prospect approves of if we can."

Wes grimaced. "I'm firmly wading in the waters of conflict of interest at this point. You can tell me to take a long walk off a short dock if you like. Being the buyer and the lawyer advising you on the sale is never a solid arrangement, but I'm putting on my lawyer hat for a minute. You're my client. You owe it to yourself to find out about these other offers, too. If money is the deciding factor, well…" He shrugged.

Sarah studied his face as she waited. She thought he was warning her that his offer would be smaller than the ones they'd already received. That made sense. He had a full ranch to run.

"Right. That's good advice." Sarah touched his shoulder. "Don't worry too much about the conflict of interest stuff. I've spent years in business, and you've got two other hard negotiators to convince besides me. One of them is so practical she clips coupons and has the prices of her groceries memorized to be sure she's getting the best deal on her milk. The other one? None of that, but she likes nice things and prefers to own them instead of admiring them from afar."

His shoulders slumped. "I don't hear a lot of sentimental attachment or determination to support the greater good. That was my only hope."

Sarah wrinkled her nose. "Sorry. That's what I bring to the table. When you need an advocate, I'm your girl. I am easily overruled, but I have a couple of favors I can cash in to make my sisters take your offer seriously, at least. Make it the best you can and I'll do what I can to sell it."

They resumed their ride back to the barn.

"Just like that. You're so easily convinced to join my side?" he asked.

His face didn't betray suspicion, but Sarah could hear the doubt in his voice.

That was another reaction she understood perfectly.

"Sadie was smart, Wes. Not just book smart, but she had that people-sense, you know? Where she could read someone within two minutes of conversation and nail their personality perfectly. I don't know that I'll ever be as good as she was, but I want to be."

She inhaled slowly, mainly to enjoy the freedom and the sweetness of being outside and on a horse and talking with Wes. It was a perfect moment. "I trust you. I like you. I've always loved Prospect, even though I let it fade in my memory because I thought it was all about Sadie. When she was around, she was all you could see, one of those bright lights that made everything shine, you know?"

His eyes were serious as he nodded. "Yeah, I know someone like that."

"But I'm here now, and there's an echo of Sadie everywhere, which I love, but today, being with you, out here, it's like…" How could she say it so that he'd understand?

"Like you can see how Prospect and this place made Sadie? Like there was always an echo of Prospect in her wherever she went," he said slowly.

Something fluttered in Sarah's chest as she realized he'd stated what she was feeling perfectly. "That's it."

He nodded. "I do think that's how the community feels, too, like there's something special about Prospect. That's why you see people who aren't anxious to change it."

That made sense to Sarah.

"Take off your lawyer hat and put the rancher one back on. Draw up an offer. On behalf of my sisters, we look forward to seeing it." Sarah pointed at him. "But I'm also going to see if I can find a real estate agent to advise us. It's not because of the conflict of interest, but the sheer aggravation of answering all my sisters' questions if I don't, you know?"

His chuckle made her sit straighter in the saddle. It was nice. Imagining another horse ride with Wes, across to the lake on a sunny day, with no urgent business, no big questions to solve, was sweet. Sarah would love to do that.

But if they sold the lodge, there'd be no reason to hang around Prospect or even visit.

There was almost no way Sarah could imagine both of her sisters wanting to hold on to the lodge, not when it would require funds they didn't have and mean forgoing the sale and money they could all use.

Daydreaming about leisurely rides with handsome cowboys would only get her in trouble when it was time to go home.

This didn't feel like their first ride together or their last.

Seeing Wes in the saddle was right. Riding beside him stirred memories of falling in love with horses as a girl and clapping for the cowboys who rode in Prospect's Independence Day parades. It also made her think of being on horseback and seeing the seasons change on the ranch and at the Majestic and never growing tired of it. "Come for a ride any time, Sarah," Wes said.

Was he experiencing the same strange connection? Like they were meant to ride together?

"When we visited Prospect years ago, there was always a parade through the middle of town on the Fourth of July. Did you ever ride in one?" she asked. She could picture a younger, lanky Wes riding with his brothers. Was that a memory or her imagination?

He sighed. "Every single year, without fail. We still do. My mother loves to wear her Western finest and wave."

His long-suffering tone made her laugh, but it was easy to wonder what might have happened if she and Wes had met sooner and become friends or…

Or what? Their paths were so far apart. Would anything have really changed? It was almost impossible to imagine her life or his being any different than they were right here.

Doing her best to shake the sadness that settled over her, Sarah followed Wes back into the paddock and dismounted. She insisted on making sure Lady got all the brushing and treats a grand dame deserved, and loaded herself back in her rental car to return to Bell House. She needed her files, a solid cell connection and time to start making some headway. When Jordan arrived, Sarah wanted to have a solid plan in place.

Even if she'd rather spend more time talking with Wes, riding with Wes, laughing with Wes and commiserating over being the oldest with troublesome younger siblings with Wes.

Being practical about this budding attraction would save her some heartbreak eventually.

CHAPTER ELEVEN

No MATTER HOW he moved the numbers around or shaved the budgets or set up phases to delay parts of his brothers' projects, Wes wasn't substantially increasing his offer for Sadie Hearst's land. That was going to be a problem, so he'd called a family meeting. This was a tool that he couldn't use often. The rarity of the meeting increased the perception of its importance and his chances of everyone rearranging their schedules to make it work.

This time, he'd hit the jackpot and his entire family had shown up. Hinting that this particular occasion was related to the arrival of Sarah Hearst and what she intended to do about the lodge property had even convinced his mother to return to the ranch. As an added bonus, she'd insisted on preparing a family meal. She was bustling around her kitchen, as she had every day around this time when Wes and his brothers made it in from school.

Today, she was also muttering about the up-keep of her pots and pans and where all her serving spoons had disappeared to.

"Okay, spatulas, boys. Where are you hiding spatulas?" Prue spun around, her hands on her hips. "If I'd known this kitchen was going to turn into the Bermuda Triangle of kitchen gadgets, I would have insisted on carrying everything away with me."

Instead of fussing, Walt reached into the dishwasher and pulled out three spatulas. "You never did concern yourself with putting away dishes, did you, Prue?"

"The chef doesn't wash dishes. Everyone knows that." Her precise delivery suggested she was getting a bit irritated with the entire process. "Soon as I find something to put the meat loaf on, dinner's ready."

Walt chuckled. "How about you just put it on the table?" He grabbed two oven mitts and carefully settled the meat loaf in its pan on a stack of kitchen towels dead center on the table. "We're eating family style."

"If that was my mother's dining table, we'd be fighting, Walt. Since it's your mother's, I'll allow it." Prue handed off dishes, like it was an assembly line until everything was on the table, before taking her seat.

"Mama, not much could convince me to leave the subdivision I'm nearly finished building in Colorado Springs in the middle of the afternoon to head for Prospect." Clay was seated in his usual spot, both hands open as if he was ready to receive the bounty that had come his way. "Your meat loaf is near the top of that list."

She patted his arm. "Good to know, baby. You don't come home near often enough. I'll see if I can't stir up more meat loaf now and then."

Travis grumbled, "Could we put together a list of favorites, Mom? I wouldn't mind seeing your lasagna on the table, either."

Matt added, "I would like to suggest baked goods. That chocolate sheet cake you made? I could go for that."

She tilted her head to the side. "You boys are always here, I mean, there's no point to enticing you home or anything with a stew or a batch of brownies."

Matt patted his stomach. "We're still growing boys."

Clay snorted. "Better watch out, doc. Too

much cake might upset the weather reporter. That forecast would call for rain."

Wes crossed his arms over his chest and watched Matt threaten Clay with a dark glare as their mother narrowed her eyes. If Clay spilled the news about Matt's love life, he'd lose his tiny advantage over his younger brother.

Wes interrupted Matt's grumbles. "Thank you for showing up tonight. Everybody's heard about the Majestic, right?" He waited for Clay to nod. Since he was farther away from Prospect, it took a little longer for his mother to spread the news to him but Wes trusted her efficiency. Even with customers during the week, she would have found plenty of time to make phone calls from behind the counter of Handmade.

"Any movement on my plan?" his dad asked while he buttered one of the fluffy biscuits that were Prue's pride and joy.

Everyone seated at the table swiveled in Wes's direction.

"Some of you," Wes said as he leveled a look at Matt and Grant, "know that Sarah Hearst asked me to show her the land around the property. She's waiting on one of her sisters to arrive in town. Dad's idea was to buy the land back, return it to the Rocking A. Simple. Neat." He knew it was the solution that would make everyone happy. "What I'm not sure that everyone knows is that we've got a few different drains on the ranch's funds coming up."

Wes propped his elbows on the table because this was news he hated to deliver. "No matter how I work the numbers, my best guess is that we can only afford to offer the Hearsts about a quarter of what their acreage is worth."

Prue waved a hand. "They should be happy to return it to us."

Wes thought about reasoning with his mother, and knew that every man at the table was doing the same. But none of them would have settled for so much less than what the property was worth.

When the silence registered, Prue glanced around the table. "Okay, I take your point. All of them! You don't have to all think so loudly at once! The Hearsts aren't fools, but we need to make the best offer we've got. Then we can start pulling at heartstrings. Who knows if we can close the gap, but it's worth a shot."

She shrugged and scooped up a bite of green beans as if she'd settled the matter for herself.

Travis cleared his throat. "I realize the renovations Clay and I've discussed to get this place ready to take on fosters are taking a big bite out of the funds available. Renovating the kitchen and living room, adding on two bedrooms and then another cabin at some point. What if we…start smaller?"

Clay frowned. "How?"

Travis shrugged. "Instead of removing the paneling in here, we could paint it to lighten it up. We were talking about new bunk beds and desks, but we might be able to find used furniture."

Wes hated the disappointment in Travis's voice. As if he was seeing his dream shrinking before his eyes.

"We definitely could, but I don't see how any of that makes a substantial difference in the total number," Clay said. "If we knock off the cabin, that's a start, but all the minor changes to the house itself will benefit everyone. They're updates this place has needed for a long time."

He met Wes's eye. Of the five of them, Wes

and Clay were most often aligned. Clay was fully on board to support Travis in his plan, so committed that he was going to use his vacation time to oversee the renovations himself. Since his firm was growing quickly in Colorado Springs, it was a sacrifice to step out right now.

"Clay's right, Travis. We can economize, but to get where we'd need to go to match the other offers, we'd need something substantial. Some of these plans will have to wait." Worse, he couldn't predict how long the delay would be.

Wes knew it was the only solution but he didn't like it. He was still hoping he was missing something.

Matt swallowed his last bite of meat loaf. "Lack of space is a problem. I get it. We can postpone my getting a proper office and treatment rooms. For folks who need me to see their dogs or cats, I can find a place in town to rent and set up shop that way. The problem will be splitting my time there and here, or rather, on my large animals visits. I'll be around less to help out with the ranch but now that Grant is home, that should be fine. Easy."

He held out his hands as if it was simple and changing his plans was no worry.

His father frowned. "I don't want any of you who've desired to be here at the Rocking A to lose a spot, not even for a second."

"If I find the right storefront, I can sleep in the back for as long as we need." Matt leaned in. "I want these renovations. I want these fosters, too, Dad. And if this gets me out of swinging a hammer, even better."

Walt rubbed his forehead. "Everything I've got is rolled up in the ranch already, but maybe it's time to think of selling the store."

The loud chorus of shouted denial was immediate. Prue was loudest of all. "We aren't selling a thing, Walt Armstrong. I am telling you, those heartstrings are gonna help us make up the difference."

"Mama, we might be talking hundreds of thousands of dollars. Those three women have their own dreams and a file filled with corporations who will jump at the chance to meet with them about that property." Wes wrapped his arm around her shoulders. He hated delivering bad news. Hated it worse when he had to deliver it to his mother. "They'd be fools to let their feelings lead to a loss that big."

"Or they could be women who follow their hearts." Prue sniffed. "Money matters. I can't say it doesn't, but if we find something that matters more to them, we aren't without hope here."

"Like what?" Wes asked, desperate to believe she could give them any kind of answer. He hated letting his family down.

"Matt. He's our secret weapon. He can sweet-talk Sarah, convince her to fall in love and stay here in Prospect." His mother grinned as she watched them all blink. "For the important problems, we gotta get outside the box here."

Matt made a show of glancing down at himself. "You can see me, can't you? You aren't supposed to volunteer me for things when I'm in the room, much less…like that. You aren't serious, Mama. You wouldn't want me to string Sarah along to get your hands on a piece of land." His tone was certain, but his expression wasn't quite as convinced. Prue Armstrong could be ruthless, but that was a new level for her.

"I'm not saying trick her. You fall for her. She falls for you. You both stay here in Prospect. The land returns to the ranch. Soon enough, we have two new generations building the place up, Travis's boys and my first set of grandbabies."

"A set of grandbabies?" Matt asked. Was he sweating? "How many are in a set?" He glanced wildly around the table. "I'm just a baby myself."

Tempted to dwell on the injustice of the fact that his mother was choosing Matt to woo and win Sarah Hearst instead of…anyone else at the table, Wes held up his hands. "Hold on. No one needs to be making any sacrifices on the matrimonial altar, not yet anyway." He opened the laptop he'd picked up at the last minute. "What we're going to do is write a letter, explaining how much this purchase would mean to us and to this ranch."

The silence that descended felt like victory for half a second.

Then Grant drawled slowly, "A letter? Are we going to put a stamp on it and send it via the North Pole, too? Santa can wrap up the lodge and put it in your stocking after he slides down the chimney."

His mother tilted her head to the side. "Now, I have seen that on those home selling and buying shows. When there are multiple buyers, a nice letter can sometimes make a difference." She patted Wes's hand, but it didn't feel like a "good job" pat.

This was more like "I know you can't charm her by yourself so we better give this a shot" instead. Before his mother could elect Matt to deliver the letter, Wes said, "I want to make sure I've got all the details down. Heartstrings, yes. We're going directly to the heartstrings, but we're also going to build the strongest offer we possibly can. So Sarah and her sisters know about the plans we're making for the future here, I'll include them in the letter."

Grant sighed. "I wish I could save us from the letter experiment—" he shook his head "—but I have a feeling Wes has his mind made up. Instead, I'd like to throw in all the winnings I have left from the circuit. I had this idea that I'd someday need a retirement plan. Since I expected that to be several decades in the future, you'll understand why it's so small." He rubbed a hand across his lips. "But it's yours."

Everyone stared at him for a long moment.

Wes wanted to refuse the money. This wasn't about building the ranch at the expense of anyone's future, but about expanding to incorporate them all. Grant hadn't said what his retirement idea might be, but giving up his nest egg now would mean it would be delayed, perhaps indefinitely.

Grant had been the one who'd chafed at the restrictions of life on the Rocking A. Was he resigning himself to always struggle against those restrictions or had his feelings changed?

Before Wes could find the words to express that, his father said, "Let's go with what we've got for now." He interrupted when Grant started to argue. "Now, now, everybody at this table knows how ranching goes. A smart person keeps some funds in reserve." Wes met his father's stare and nodded. That had been the top of his list as he was budgeting, how far to extend the ranch's finances in order to still be able to grab an opportunity like this one. His father was making sure Wes understood that the longevity of the family and the ranch itself was top priority, even if they couldn't take advantage of a sale to regain this land that might never come again.

"Travis, we have to go for both opportunities, the land and renovating to make this a place for another generation of kids who need it." Wes knew his brother hated the idea of presenting himself as needy. He wasn't, but if the ranch was going to provide a home for the foster kids he wanted to shelter, then all of them would have to stretch beyond their normal boundaries here.

"Honestly," his mother said, "this place needs the renovations for the people who already live here. I've been saying so for years. Decades! You all deserve a nice place to come to."

Wes watched his parents do that mental communication thing. Was this something they'd fought about before the divorce?

"I can help." Clay cleared his throat. "We can talk about the renovations we'll be making, and how we're containing costs to stretch every dollar here and there."

Wes scratched his chin as he considered that.

Finally he nodded. "Okay. I can't see how that would do anything but help. Are you planning to stay in town for a while?"

Clay shifted in his seat. "I had planned to run back to Colorado Springs as fast as I could." He motioned to the archway. "But that was before I saw this kitchen and the living room again. This place needs a facelift soon."

"Just don't skimp on the kitchen," his father muttered.

His father scowled while his mother blinked her eyelashes innocently. "Did you tell him to say that, Prue?"

"He's got eyes, Walt!" His mother flapped her hands. "I didn't ask him to say it but he might have heard me say the same to anyone who'd listen. If you'd ever agreed to make improvements, even small ones, we wouldn't be in this mess right now." She crossed her arms over her chest.

Wes and his brothers were turning from their mother to their father as if they were serving volleys across a net, half worried that they'd stop playing and start fighting, and the other, half curious if this would be the day that the truth spilled out about their divorce.

When he'd left for his sophomore year of college, his parents were married.

By the time he made it home at Christmas, they were separated and divorce was on the horizon.

If their divorce had merely been over money and renovations, Wes was going to lose his temper. Loudly.

Walt finally huffed. "Can't argue with that."

Then he stood up from the table and walked out of the kitchen. They listened to his boots thump across the wood floors until the front door opened and closed.

His mother looked resigned. "You boys do the best you can, okay?" Then she left, too. The front door closed more softly behind her.

"I refuse to believe they couldn't get along because of money," Matt said. He fanned himself with his hand.

"Are you still sweating over the courting option?" Grant asked.

"No, I'm not sweating," Matt said as he fanned more broadly. "Why do you ask?"

Grant grunted. "If Mom had seen Wes and Sarah Hearst in the barn, she'd have put him up to bat instead." He thumped Wes's shoulder. "What if a birdie dropped her a hint?"

Since that was too close to what he'd been asking himself, Wes knew it was time to move on. Quickly.

"I've already outlined the details of the budget we've allotted for the upgrades, the new cabin, as well as improvements to the barn for Matt's vet practice." Wes scanned the document he'd laid out quickly. "If you guys can think of anything else, hit me with it."

Clay helped himself to the bowl of green beans. "Listen, the letter is an idea. I say go for it, but nothing beats the personal angle. If you can manage it, we bring the sisters here to meet with all of us. It's a whole lot harder to say no face-to-face. Letters, proposals, sound offers with legitimate dollar figures can stand on their own. If we're going to attempt a Hail Mary pass, we should go for the connection."

Clay was right. The strength of his offer came from his family, what the land meant to them. Sarah had already proven she understood that. The only chance the Armstrongs had was to have that same effect on her sisters. Jordan would be the next challenge.

CHAPTER TWELVE

BY THE TIME Sarah parked in front of Bell House on Sunday afternoon, she was exhausted, hungry and ready for her sister to arrive in Prospect. When she saw Rose's familiar note stuck to the door, she rested her head against the steering wheel and closed her eyes. Apparently, she was going to face Prue Armstrong in the Mercantile again and much sooner than she'd hoped.

Sarah's eagerly awaited backup had last texted from her lunch stop and wasn't expected to arrive until closer to sunset. That was assuming Jordan had less trouble following the GPS instructions than Sarah had on her drive to town.

At first, Sarah had been relieved that Jordan would be arriving late. She'd gone to Idaho Springs to meet with a real estate agent who'd agreed to talk with her about listing the Majestic for sale. Finding a Realtor who would take on a remote commercial property had meant more phone calls than Sarah expected, but she owed it to her sister to explore all their options. Even if one of the big developers who'd been pursuing Sadie was their final choice, Sarah didn't want to give up completely on the idea of finding buyers who could reopen the Majestic itself.

She'd finally gotten lucky with a referral for an agent who specialized in vacation homes and investment opportunities and who happened to be in town through the weekend.

To be sure that they could work together, Sarah had offered to drive to meet the agent and convinced her to extend her stay in the area for one more day. They'd made an appointment for Monday. Erin Chang would evaluate the lodge and the property for herself before heading back to Denver. Then they could iron out the rest of the details. For that, Wes would need to be involved. How hard would it be for him to navigate the business side of a real estate deal when he wanted to make the purchase himself?

She'd spent most of the day arguing every side of every option.

All silently in her head.

At least when Jordan got there, some of that thinking could spill out of her mouth.

"Get moving, Sarah. You can take a nap after you find Rose. That's incentive right there," she said in a falsely upbeat tone. Sarah sometimes tried to fake herself out, but it hardly ever worked. That didn't mean she would let anyone know about the heavy weight that settled on her shoulders as she walked back down the street.

At least it was a beautiful afternoon. Prospect's historic downtown covered the narrow valley formed by foothills which transitioned into soaring Rocky Mountain peaks. Everything was golden at this time of day, but the shadows were growing. The age of the town could be determined much like trees, by counting the rings of growth working out from the original town. More modern houses had been added as the population grew and changed.

As Sarah crossed the narrow side street in front of the Mercantile, she saw a park with a playground. Curious, she took the detour to get closer. Brightly colored swings and a tall slide in the shape of a rocket clustered near a pair of child-sized horses, which were made of finely crafted wood.

The rest of the park was green space. It was easy to imagine soccer practice and snowball fights taking place there. Enormous trees shaded the playground and the few picnic tables gathered at the opposite end of the grassy area. This was no new addition. Prospect had been tending this park for a long time. Picnic tables called her, but so did food. Sarah made a note to bring a lunch someday.

After she walked the entire park and ended up on a different side street, she realized she was on the other side of the Mercantile. Here, she saw a small medical clinic. The architecture made her think it had been built in the 1950s. The roof had an interesting curve, and the front wall was made of glass.

As she walked back to the entrance of the Mercantile, Sarah realized she'd never left the main street through town on her visits to Prospect. She'd just been a tourist. To understand how to live in Prospect, she had to branch out. There was more to the place than she knew.

When she pushed open the front door to the Mercantile, the stray thought that Wes might be inside flitted through her mind. Why? There was no real reason he would be except that his father ran it. Did she think he spent his time lounging against the counter, chitchatting? The urge to turn back around to peek through the window, in case it was true, was hard to ignore, but she pushed open the door to Handmade instead.

As the bells over the door jingled, Prue Armstrong glanced up from her seat behind a long table covered in fabric. "Good afternoon, Sarah. What a nice surprise."

Surprise? Maybe. Nice…

Sarah wiped her hands on her jeans and decided nothing good was going to come from holding a grudge.

And she was making progress. She was on a first-name basis.

"I've been out of town. I saw the note stuck to the door of Bell House, so I'm looking for Rose." Sarah wandered closer to the columbine embroidery pillow. She hadn't forgotten it since she'd made her first visit to Handmade.

"She ran over to the Ace to grab some pie for an afternoon snack." Prue had set down the large frame she was holding and drifted along silently behind Sarah.

"Do you mind if I wait?" Sarah asked with a speaking glance at the distance Prue had closed between the two of them.

"Of course not. I'm happy to have the company." Prue's expression was much warmer than their first introduction, but Sarah thought she might see concern in Prue's eyes. "Do you sew or quilt?"

"I've never learned to do either, but my mother used to do embroidery. She was an artist. She dabbled in everything." Sarah stopped in front of the columbine pillow and embroidery kits. "I saw this the first night and it reminded me of an apron she made. Sadie had planted columbines, different colors, around the lodge, and my mother loved how delicate they were. She gave the apron to Sadie, but every summer we came up, she'd wear it when she and Sadie baked together. The flowers weren't columbines, but in my memory, they were this same sort of periwinkle. My mother was never as creative a cook as Sadie, but she made the best pie crust." She hadn't thought of that in a long time. "Even Sadie said so."

Prue tilted her head up to look at the ceiling before saying, "Sadie would know. Nothing that woman ever made was a disappointment. I sure have missed her. I might have let my emotions about Sadie color how I welcomed you to town."

Surprised, Sarah met her gaze before picking up the pillow. Was that an apology? Something about Prue's attitude convinced her not to make a big deal out of it. Sarah waved her hand as if it was all water under the bridge.

"I wonder if I could embroider this. I'll need a souvenir of my time spent here." As Sarah watched Prue, she realized she'd landed on the perfect olive branch. "What do you think? Is it hard to learn?"

Prue's bottom lip poked out. "Aw, you're gonna get me, aren't you?"

Her irritation and amusement surprised a laugh from Sarah. "What?"

"There's a few surefire ways to get through to my soft side. First one's my boys, of course. I'm so proud of those troublemakers that it might as well be my Achilles heel. Another way? Ask to learn to make something in my store. The devil himself could come in and ask me to show him how to quilt, and I'd be in here sweating in the fire."

Sarah smiled and picked up the instructions. "Surely it's not as terrible as all that?"

Prue smiled back. "Of course it isn't, Sarah. I do like to exaggerate. It makes me a colorful person."

Since Sarah could hear her great-aunt saying something similar and in a matching exasperated tone, she immediately liked Prue better. "I don't want to hurt Prospect."

Prue gestured to Sarah to join her at the table in the center of the room. "I know, I know, but after nearly a lifetime here, I'd like to believe that I'm in tune with what this town needs. And I'm not wrong." She rolled her eyes. "Okay, I am almost never wrong. Ninety-nine times out of one hundred, I am correct, and it would be bad to have any smug developers coming in to wipe the Majestic clean off the map and build some atrocious eyesore that will attract a wild crowd."

Sarah took the seat Prue pointed at. "Weren't places like Prospect wild back in their heyday? Seems like it might be part of the tradition."

Prue narrowed her eyes. "Hmm, now, that is a point. Walt likes to mention a certain

Armstrong that was Robin Hood's biggest fan during the Great Depression, did a little liberatin' of funds from the wealthy folks who liked to spend time on Key Lake and redistribute as needed." She shrugged. "And Sullivan's Post burned down twice thanks to too many saloons in too small a space, before folks moved into the valley some and spread out. But now things are different in Prospect and it's a family place."

Sarah considered suggesting that the right kind of new development on the lake might do more to attract families than leaving the place empty, but she also didn't want to rock the boat that was floating along so easily. "Can you help me gather the materials for this, Prue? I should be able to follow the instructions from there." Probably. How hard could it be?

"Yes, ma'am, here's a hoop. You're gonna want to try stitching with it and without it, see what works best for you." She pulled out drawers that lined the walls and laid brightly colored hanks of thread against white fabric included in the kit. After tilting her head this way and that, eyes squinted critically,

Prue nodded. "I like these colors. What do you think?"

Sarah smoothed one hand down the threads. "Purple for the star petals." She checked the photo of the embroidery pattern. "White with a tinge of pink for the rounded petals and this gold for the center."

"There's a couple of different greens. You can try them to see which you like, or mix up the leaves and stems to add some more dimension." Prue placed a pack of needles on top and something shaped to go over the end of a finger. A leather thimble? Sarah had never used one of those. "This will get you started. If you don't like these, I've got options." Prue leaned against the table before straightening suddenly. "Oh, I just got these in. You have to have scissors." She hurried up to the counter and grabbed something before returning. "Aren't these beautiful?"

She spread out three pairs of scissors. The handles were decorated in the style of art masterpieces. "Is this *Starry Night*?" Sarah loved them. "And some Monet water lilies?"

"And the third pair is Picasso." Prue clasped her hands together. "The best thing about running my own shop is I can buy one of everything I like. Then, if it sells, I can buy a whole lot more."

"That is an excellent benefit." Sarah realized at that moment that she hadn't brought her purse with her. It was still in the car parked in front of Bell House.

"What is it? What's wrong?" Prue asked. "I also have Klimt and Jackson Pollock splatters."

"No, I love the van Gogh, but I don't have my purse with me." She put her hands on top of all the things Prue had gathered for her. "While you ring these up, I'll run get it."

Prue scoffed. "Listen, you can owe me. I hope this is the beginning of a bad habit right here. Even if you never finish this first embroidery. That's what keeps craft stores open, honey."

"Really? Thank you, Prue. I'll clear my tab before I leave town, I promise." Sarah didn't want to mention her short-term stay in Prospect, not when they were getting along.

"Nothing bonds us closer than shopping, spending and the promise of more, does it?" Prue asked. "Open up those instructions. I want to show you this website that has videos demonstrating how to do the different stitches."

Sarah didn't hesitate. After she'd quickly perused the instructions and written down the website Prue insisted she'd want when she was stitching late at night and needed answers that could not wait until normal business hours, she watched Prue work her own needle through some cloth at the next table. "That's not embroidery, is it?"

Prue shook her head. "No, it's this year's raffle quilt for the Western Days fundraiser. The binding is taking me forever, but we're almost done. I've got a small quilting group that meets every other week in the winter months. Normally, we're way ahead by now, but Rose took a vacation in the middle of last winter, so we're just catching up now." Prue raised her eyebrows at Sarah as if she thought Sarah would understand what any of that meant.

Then she opened up the rest of the quilt that had been carefully folded.

Sarah knew she was holding her breath as she stared at Prue's project, but it was almost impossible not to gasp when she saw how beautiful the quilt was. "That's amazing." She reached out to touch it before she realized what was happening and snatched her hand back.

"It won't bite, Sarah," Prue said with a glint in her eye. "We keep it covered to try to get it to the raffle without a stain or two. You can touch." She shifted it closer.

"What's this called?" Sarah asked as she draped the corner over her knee. "I recognize the mountains. Wow."

Prue looked disappointed. "Guess I'll have to tell Rose she was right about this one. We wanted something special this time to celebrate the hundredth Western Days festival. Isn't that something? I wanted to do the Colorado Beauty block." Prue traced the outline of a square. "But Rose said that was too simple." Prue rolled her eyes. "The woman can arrange fabric and color like nobody's business, but she has to remember that we all have lives. Anyway, she insisted we go all in, so we've got ninety blocks. Each one is assembled from four smaller blocks. I can't remember how many fabric combinations she used, mixing up the backgrounds to make this effect. There's a spreadsheet to keep it all straight and that is pushing my love of quilting to the maximum, if you understand."

Sarah nodded when Prue said *spreadsheet* as if what she meant to say was *unicorn* because that was how often she wanted to see one in her quilting.

"We wanted to raise a good chunk of money for the park." Prue motioned over her shoulder. "Got a small playground, but we want to build a gazebo and put up a statue for the miners who lost their lives in Prospect." She covered her chest with one hand. "I also think it would be real cute to build a train engine for the kids to clamber all over and for parents to take photos, but we'll have to see. I'd have my son build it, of course, but materials and landscaping…"

Sarah nodded. She knew all about the limits of a budget.

"I'm glad Rose isn't here yet. I need time to get my face straight before you tell her how pretty her design is." Prue sniffed.

"It's beautiful. I wish I were going to be here for Western Days. I would certainly enter to win." Sarah picked up the package of needles Prue had chosen for her and wondered if she'd ever be able to successfully thread the eye.

"You could always come back." Wes's mother was refolding the areas of the quilt she wasn't working on.

"Really? An invitation for a Hearst to return?" Sarah drawled, invisible fingers crossed that she wasn't reigniting hostilities.

Prue snorted. "We welcome everyone during Western Days. Town depends on the tourists that stay and play that weekend. I wish Sadie had been able to make it back home for Western Days." Prue studied Sarah over the top of her glasses. "She would have been a boost for all of us, for sure. We could have used her help."

"I was thinking about that when I walked around the lodge." Sarah licked her lips. Coming to terms with how she felt about Sadie's sacrifice of moving away from the home she loved so much for her family might take some time. "When I was in high school, my mother died. She was a huge part of the reason we came to Prospect in the summers. I remember her saying that marrying my dad was like hitting the jackpot. Inheriting a family member like Sadie was a prize, for sure. When we'd come, they'd spend all day in Sadie's kitchen, creating recipes and laughing. Bread and cakes." Sarah wished she could offer Prue some. Her mother's bread had been the equivalent of the quilt in her lap: something simple elevated to amazing. "Then my mother died in a car crash and my dad…" Sarah didn't want to go into the pain and confusion that had landed when her mother was gone. "He struggled. He decided to move us to LA for a fresh start, and we struggled harder there. Sadie followed us the next year. She always said it was necessary to have the career she dreamed of, but yesterday I realized it was more about looking out for us than her." The sting of tears surprised her. Controlling the tears was a battle she thought she'd won. "I wish she'd been able to come back here once she knew we were going to be okay. She never called any other place but Prospect home."

Prue sighed before squeezing Sarah's shoulder. "Both of those things could be true, Sarah. It was partly the career and partly her family, and it just made sense to move. Sadie's not here, but I expect she'd want you to let her speak for herself. No guilt. No worries. Her choices were her own. Did she ever strike you as a woman who let other people push her around?" Prue raised her eyebrows and they both laughed.

"No, she didn't." Sarah relaxed against her chair as she realized Prue was absolutely right. Whatever Sadie had done, she'd done it out of love and because it was what she wanted.

"Of course not," Prue smiled fondly. "I'll never forget the first time I met Sadie. She was doing a cooking class over at the Ace, and I was a newlywed, just moved to town after falling for a boy I had no sense in talking to. I wanted life in the city, and Walt Armstrong made it clear he was never meant for anything but the Rocking A. So, I had this starving husband. I needed help fast, and Sadie was teaching folks from the local church how to make a chocolate sheet cake. I horned in on the class at the last minute, and she welcomed me like I was a lost daughter. I can imagine being Sadie's niece means you know how sweet that welcome could be." Prue frowned. "No matter how many recipes I've experimented with over the years, Walt will still ask for that cake on every special occasion."

Sarah realized that this was what she'd

hoped to find on the way to Prospect, these memories. It surprised her that Prue was offering them to her.

"Thank you for sharing that. I do know how sweet it is. Missing her has been this fracture in my life. I'm not sure what I'll do when I go back to LA and try to sit at my desk at headquarters and know nothing will ever be the way it was." When she couldn't sleep at night, that was one of the things she worried about. Whatever was happening with Brooke and her husband in New York also occupied space. Convincing herself that Jordan was fine just like she'd promised she was took up time, too.

And missing her mother. She couldn't forget that, even if she'd never admit it to anyone.

Her father seemed content, but Sarah imagined he got lonely, too.

Sarah felt the pressure to take care of her family, and that pressure meant many nights her only wish was that her mother was there with her.

To take some of the weight of responsibility off Sarah's shoulders.

To hold Sarah close and promise her everything would work out in the end.

How was she ever going to manage keeping everything together now that Sadie was gone, too?

"Thank you for explaining how you missed Sadie. I've been so lucky to have her close for so long." Sarah rubbed her eyes. "My job was to think of ways to keep Sadie connected to all the people who loved her. New cooks, people who'd followed her from public access, the fans she made at appearances…there were so many people who wanted to be near her. I wish we'd carved out a space for Prospect, too. I know Sadie would have loved coming home."

Prue squeezed Sarah close, and it was a relief to relax into her hug. What a comfort it was to connect with someone else who understood the love and the loss. Refusing to cry took concentration.

"Well, if you decide you want to stay here in town, reopen the lodge yourself," Prue said slowly, "I know some young men who would love to help. They're good with construction, too. Maybe you've noticed a group of hand-

some cowboys? Or at least one in particular?"
Prue fluttered her eyelashes.

Sarah was glad for the distraction. The familiar weight of grief was settling around her
and it could be hard to brush off. Prue's teasing was the perfect antidote.

"Wes has been an amazing help to me. He
took time out of what has to be a busy schedule to saddle up Lady for me and ride over
to see the lodge and the remnants of Sullivan's Post."

When she glanced up from the shaky first
stitch she'd convinced herself to attempt,
Wes's mother's mouth was hanging open.
If anyone ever needed a model to illustrate
shock or gobsmacked, Sarah was certain Prue
could pose.

Then she realized what had to be causing
the trouble.

"I wasn't supposed to tell you that Wes let
me ride Lady, was I?" Had she screwed up
their lovely budding friendship already?

The loud snap of Prue's mouth shutting was
alarming, but Wes's mother's laughter helped
Sarah relax. If she'd been so surprised Wes
had loaned out her horse, she was getting over
it quickly.

"Lady is a sweet girl. I'm glad you had a chance to meet her." Prue picked up her needle again. "I didn't know you ride. How do you feel about kids?"

Sarah inhaled slowly while she tried to trace the path of the conversation. It had taken a hard left somewhere between borrowing Prue's horse and...kids? "Honestly, I haven't thought much about them at all."

A noncommittal hmmm was the only response.

Did she dare ask why?

"Well, the handsome cowboys here in Prospect..." Prue paused and waited for Sarah to look up. "All of them that I know, anyway, are hoping for families of their own, but families can come in a lot of different shapes and sizes, you know?"

Sarah understood that Prue was trying to communicate something important here.

But reading between the lines was not easy.

"Okay," Sarah said slowly, "I like families. My father and sisters are important to me, so I would say I understand that."

The urge to say more was clear on Prue's face, but before she could try again...without directly saying...whatever it was, the bells over the door rang. Rose walked in with a pie plate clutched in her hands and Wes following behind. "Guess who I found over at the Ace. He was in the mood for some pie, too." When Rose saw Sarah with all of her embroidery supplies spread out, she stopped in her tracks. "She's one of us."

Sarah had to laugh. The way Rose said it, they were all part of a secret society, possibly by invitation only or a birthright into the crafting world.

"Not quite yet, but I have high hopes." Prue held her hands out for the pie and everyone turned to stare at her. Sarah was almost certain Rose and Wes were silently asking themselves what had caused the change of heart. Sarah wasn't absolutely certain herself, but she was going to do her best to hold on to it.

"I came by the inn to find you, Rose, but instead, I started building my crafting habit." Sarah folded the fabric with the one line of stitching that was most definitely going to have to come out again as soon as she figured out how, and put everything in the bag Prue slid across the table. "My tab is already running."

"Ha." Prue chuckled. "I believe you're good for it."

Sarah met Wes's stare. He was bemused, too, but the way his eyes locked to hers as they communicated silently about Prue's change of heart made Sarah feel the warmth of connection again.

His eyes were dangerous. The last thing she should be doing was complicating an already complicated situation by allowing... attraction into the mix?

"Sarah, why don't you and Wes each take a piece of pie with you? Head on over to the B-and-B," Prue suggested as she hurried over to a small kitchenette with a coffeepot and a few plates stacked on top. "Wes can bring these back on his way out of town." Without waiting for any sign of agreement, Prue took the top of the pie plate off. "Oh, my, it's Dutch apple pie." Her tone was the same as saying "it's pure gold."

"This is one of Sadie's recipes, Sarah. I don't know if you've had it, but it has been on the menu at the Ace ever since I've been here. If Faye ever took it off, there would be picketers on the sidewalks demanding its return."

Sarah took the pie gratefully. Her hunger

had faded while she'd had the chance to talk one-on-one with her frenemy Prue, but it had since roared back to life.

"You children get going now. The porch swing will be nice this time of day—it's so breezy." Prue shooed them toward the door and before Sarah knew that she'd agreed to do it, she and Wes were slowly walking back toward Bell House.

CHAPTER THIRTEEN

"YOU WILL NOTICE if you spend much time around my mother that there are days when you have missing blocks of time." He pointed at the Mercantile. "You'll be able to remember walking into the Mercantile, and then you'll be seated in a porch swing with pie in your hand and you won't be able to remember the how, when or why."

Sarah grinned. Of all the paths she'd expected her day to take, not a one had ended up with Wes and pie after her first embroidery purchase and an impromptu lesson, so she could see his point. "I can live with that as long as I end up with pie."

His smile was sweet as he nodded. When they reached the swing, they both eased down to keep it steady. Then they both sighed at the cool breeze that floated across the porch.

"We are happy with our condition, aren't

we?" Wes asked. He tapped one boot on the porch to set the swing in motion.

"What do we have to complain about?" Sarah answered. They ate their desserts in comfortable silence. It was easy to sit there next to him as the sun sank behind the mountains.

"Busy day?" he asked.

Sarah stretched her arms to release the tension in her shoulder. "Yeah, I drove down to Idaho Springs to talk to a real estate agent. She specializes in mountain properties and vacation homes. I asked her to come see the lodge so we can talk about options."

He nodded. "Good."

"And I have a meeting set up with Platinum Partners in Denver. I hate that it's in Denver because I'd like to have you with me." Sarah had hesitated before agreeing to meet Henry Milbank there. If she had to describe her first impression of the property developer after a single phone call, one word came to mind: slick. Oily? Slippery? Something about his tone and oozing charm had her picturing a weasel.

On the verge of requiring Henry Milbank to come to Prospect so that Wes could back her, Sarah realized that she was placing too much value on her property manager/lawyer/

prospective buyer/closest neighbor/hot cowboy's opinion.

Wes's advice could not take precedence over Jordan and Brooke who were actual owners, and she'd told herself to get over it and agreed to the appointment. Jordan would go with her and they would have plenty of time to evaluate any offer because they needed Brooke on board. She could do this without Wes.

"I can review any paperwork you get, take my neighbor hat off and put my lawyer hat on," Wes said easily.

"You are good at both so far. I'm glad."

He stretched a long leg out and gave the swing another gentle push.

"I would like to ask one favor from you." Wes yanked his cowboy hat off and ran a hand through his hair.

Sarah nodded. "Of course."

He whistled. "Good thing I still have my lawyer hat on, because it's my duty to warn you about agreeing to things before you know the terms."

"I thought that was a cowboy hat, but good point." Sarah pushed with her foot to keep the swing going. "Better show me the fine print."

His rough chuckle was nice in the growing shadows of the porch.

"Before you make any decisions, please come back out to the ranch. One more time." Wes glanced at her. "There's a lot more than cattle business happening there, and it impacts… everything. It impacts my family, Prospect. I won't ask you to take anything less than the offer that suits you and your sisters, but I want to make sure you have the full picture."

Sarah wondered what he could be talking about.

"You know the five of us are the adopted sons of Walt and Prue. We all came from different backgrounds, some bad and some terrible. Coming to Prospect and the Rocking A changed us all for the better. I want to show you what it means to us today, what we're prepared to build and what we'll sacrifice to make it happen. It's my job, sort of. This means a lot to us."

Surprised at the urgency in his tone, Sarah turned to face him. Whatever he was about to say, it was important. What surprised her was how much she wanted to hear it.

WES HAD BEEN doing his best not to transmit any of the nerves that always accompanied any retelling of how he'd landed at the Rocking A. Anticipating the reactions he'd learned to expect made him avoid doing this any more often than he had to. Life in Prospect, where everyone knew all the history and gossip, meant he'd gotten out of the habit.

The fact that Sarah Hearst was seated next to him, her knee touching his leg as she shifted on the swing, made the telling both easier and harder. He wanted her to know.

But if her reaction disappointed him...

Well, that might be for the best. She would be leaving soon, and that might make it much easier to say goodbye.

"I hate talking about how I ended up in foster care," he murmured. Trusting her not to disappoint him was a big step.

While he hesitated, she watched him. "Mayor. Lawyer. Neighbor. Son. Big brother. It's a lot of hats, Wes."

She was right. Lately, the stress of balancing all his separate roles had started to pile up. When his brothers had been away from home, he and Matt had done fine in the old ranch house with his father. Now that Grant and Travis were both back and making plans to stay, Wes felt the pressure to make everything fit perfectly.

"You understand what it's like being the oldest," Wes said and waited for her to agree. Wind tossed a strand of blond hair across her lips and it was tempting to brush it away for her. Instead, he said, "I was the first one Walt and Prue brought to Prospect. How I ended up here…" *Just yank off the bandage, Wes.*

"My mother had been arrested in a drug bust and this time, the next-door neighbor who usually claimed me whenever police came around was missing, so the police officers called child services and I went into the system. I thought I was tough, but that scared me, like my whole world fell out from under my feet." He could feel the weight of Sarah's stare. No matter how many times he told it, this swell of emotion made it hard to breathe. He hated telling his story for this reason, but if he was going to make a case for selling to them, she had to know everything that was on the line.

"How old were you?" she asked. If she'd been any farther away, he wouldn't have heard her. But this close, seated hip to hip in

Bell House's old porch swing, her voice was low and sweet.

"Fourteen. Old enough to believe I could run away at any time and take care of myself. As long as I was in the city, I'd manage. I'd been doing that even before my mother was arrested the last time. That meant shoplifting food when I was hungry, pawning bicycles or small electronics I 'found' when I thought I could get away with it, petty crime. Walt and Prue had set up this place as a kind of group home specifically for kids who needed a new start. No families to go to. Some kind of trauma in their past. The most desperate kids, you know? I didn't realize it then, because I would have told everyone who listened that I didn't fit the profile. My dad never hit me. I never met him. My mom loved me, but not as much as she needed a fix. I'd been taking care of myself for…forever. Forget that—I'd been taking care of my mom forever. I spent a lot of time worrying about what she'd do without me in the early days, before she went to prison." He turned to face her. "I'm glad every single day I never decided to try to prove how capable I was of looking after myself.

"Coming to Prospect was hard. Being a fish out of water left me gasping for air in the early days. Eventually, getting five boys with messed-up backgrounds to coexist was a dangerous proposition, but Prue and Walt worked through it all, taking one day at a time."

Wes froze when Sarah reached over to take his hand. "I can't imagine. Losing my mom was hard, but I had so many people waiting to catch me when I stopped falling. Sadie was always there."

Falling. Her description matched his for how he'd felt in the early days. "Everything here was so normal. Walt and Prue were up in the morning to make breakfast and they said good-night to me when it was bedtime. Doing homework was a new thing, and I was not a fan at first but then I found history. I loved the barn and the horses and the quiet and the open pasture. Riding toward Key Lake or Larkspur Pass soothed all the sore spots in my soul." Wes realized how sappy that sounded about a second too late. "By the time Matt showed up, I was glad to step up as the world-weary older brother who has to show the kid the ropes. Walt and Prue preached college and excelling at all things, so I did, too."

Sarah moved closer. "Do you ever talk to your birth mother or…"

He was surprised she asked the question. Whenever he was forced to talk about his past, he knew people wanted more details about the drama and mess than the happy ending. Too often he had to shut down questions about how bad his "before" had been, and he hated that. Sarah was ready to find out who he was now.

"She wrote me letters from prison when she was attempting rehab." Over and over, she tried to get clean. "She died a couple of years after she got out. I was in law school, but I made the trip to see her. At that point, we might as well have been strangers from different planets."

Sarah squeezed his hand. "Lots of tangled emotions from that, I'd guess."

Relieved that he didn't hear judgment or curiosity for more of the details, Wes relaxed against the swing and nodded. "Yeah. Even now."

"I can't imagine how hard it is to talk about this. When people ask about my mother, I still get choked up and she's been gone for a long time."

They sat there quietly, the creaks of the swing, the whisper of the breeze and night sounds falling around them.

Wes was surprised at how peaceful he felt. When his mother had suggested appealing to Sarah's heartstrings, he'd resisted the urge. Remembering his past was a unique sort of ache at this point. It never quite went away and it was so hard to explain to someone who'd never experienced the same loss.

But Sarah was seated there next to him, her quiet acceptance easy after a lifetime of upbeat clichés about blessings in disguise or silver linings or how the light gets through the broken pieces or any of that. Those were meant to put a bandage over a wound so that the mess didn't bother other people.

"The ranch is important to my dad, of course. He's the latest in an uninterrupted line of Armstrongs who have made a home there. But then, also add the five of us." Wes had to explain how many hopes were tied to it, big dreams that needed space. "Are you close to your sisters?"

Sarah snorted. "Some days, yes. Other days, I'm sure they've been taken over by aliens who cannot be trying to blend in." Her crooked grin made it easier to sit there in his emotion, lightened the tension. "Brooke and Jordan…they never have gotten along. I spend a lot of time wishing my mother were here to deal with them so I don't have to, but… it's just me."

"What about your dad?" This wasn't a part of the heartstrings plan. Understanding Sarah and her sisters better would most likely mean coming to realize they needed to make the best decision for themselves…and he had a feeling theirs would be in direct opposition to the Armstrongs.

"My dad is…great. Very sweet, but he's always had this head-in-the-clouds approach to parenting." She tried to smile. "To life actually. I don't think he'll ever change, even if I get my hopes up that he'll be different. It was such a relief when Sadie followed us to LA. I was doing my best to keep the house running, but I didn't have it in me to mother my sisters. Now that Sadie's gone, I want to keep us together. I love them. I don't always understand them. And sometimes I want to shove them in a closet and not let them out like I did when I was nine."

Wes's chuckle surprised him. It was easy to

picture a much younger Sarah taking charge of her sisters.

"So you are close, then," he drawled before moving his arm to rest behind her shoulders. One easy tap of his boot had them swinging again.

"We are. I want to do the best for them, too." Sarah looked over at him. "This isn't going to work out for both of us, is it?"

Wes couldn't turn away from her. "It's hard to see how it could, but you and I are pretty smart. If anybody can do it, we can."

She rolled her eyes. "Good answer."

"The thing is, I want everything to work out for you, Sarah. I like you. I'm really glad the Hearsts returned to Prospect," he said.

Wes waited for the panic to hit. Admitting he was attracted to her was another big step for him.

Sarah shook her head. "I know it's not the best time to be thinking of a beloved relative when a handsome cowboy admits to liking you, but I swear I can hear Sadie laughing from her fluffy cloud. She always swore that smart women married cowboys." Sarah's grin faded. "I like you, too. Doesn't change the fact we have some serious questions to answer."

Wes squeezed her shoulder. "We can't give up yet. You'll go meet with Milbank to find out what his offer is. The real estate agent will give you some advice. I've got an offer for you. In the meantime, you'll continue winning over my mother and she and Rose will become your biggest fans. This will all work out."

Sarah wrinkled her nose. "If I'd known all I needed to do was ask her about embroidery, I would have done that on the first night."

"She does love her crafts," Wes drawled.

"And it doesn't hurt that she has five handsome sons that she's doing her best to get hitched." Sarah bumped his ribs with her elbow. "She offered me her handsome son who was good with construction to help out at the lodge."

Wes sighed. His mother was a menace. "What did you say to that?"

Sarah patted his hand. "Don't worry. I told her how helpful you'd already been."

Wes stared down at her hand as he worked through that. Should he tell Sarah that he was almost certain he hadn't been the son his mother was trying to match her to?

If he'd known he had to worry about both Clay and Matt, he might have given up completely. In the ranking of handsome sons, how far down the list did he fall?

Then he realized that whatever his mother thought, Sarah had assumed he was the handsome son.

And he immediately grew ten feet tall. It was a good feeling.

She was grinning at him, happy to be there in the conversation, but he knew the instant the feeling shifted between them. Her eyes dropped to his lips. A kiss was right there, shimmering in the air.

"One thing we haven't considered," Wes murmured as he studied her.

"What's that?" she asked.

"What if the Hearsts decided to make a go of the lodge itself? Stayed in town? Got to know their neighbors?" He waited for her to move away. With each beat of his heart, he moved closer, until she pressed her lips against his in a sweet kiss, the kind that makes a person wonder if they'd be happy doing the same thing a million more times. Their breaths mingled as she leaned back.

"I didn't mean to do that." She frowned. "Okay, that's a lie. I didn't sit down in this swing with the intention to do that, but…"

"Hey, I understand." Wes brushed the hair off her cheek this time, giving in to the urge to touch her skin.

Before he could ask her again if she'd given any thought into staying longer in Prospect, headlights swept over them as a car parked next to hers on the street. Neither one of them moved as a woman got out and brushed long brown hair over one shoulder. "Well, this is not what I expected, Sarah Elizabeth Hearst. Are you supposed to be out here with a gentleman caller at this time of night?"

Wes didn't recognize her, but he did know the teasing tone of a younger sibling giving a big sister or brother a hard time.

"That must be…"

"My sister Jordan," Sarah whispered. "She has always had the worst timing. That is why I pushed her into closets when I could."

Wes was laughing as he stood to acknowledge Jordan. "Hey there, Jordan. I'm Wes, a neighbor out at the lodge."

Her eyebrows rose. "Kissing neighbors? Is that a thing?"

Wes picked up the pie plates and nodded at Sarah. "Whenever you're ready to discuss offers, come by the ranch. Did you want me to meet with you and the real estate agent out at the lodge?"

Sarah elbowed her sister aside and moved closer to the steps. "Yes, I'd like you to hear what she has to say."

He was her lawyer and the man who knew the most about the property. Why did Sarah asking him to attend the meeting with the real estate agent stroke his ego? It was logical, but it made him feel even taller.

Wes nodded at Jordan before putting on his hat. "Good night, then." He watched Sarah as he stopped at the bottom of the steps but he didn't want to say goodbye.

She bit her lip and nodded. He was walking away when he heard furious whispers.

Unfortunately, he couldn't understand a single word they were saying. Was that a blessing? Wes wasn't sure. He was still considering the question when he walked back into Handmade with the empty plates. His mother and Rose had obviously been staring out the window. How did he know? When he walked in, they were studiously sewing, noses so close to the fabric that they could count individual threads.

"Thank you for the pie, Mom, Rose." He opted to go, deciding he'd make a quick escape and save himself an interrogation.

"Guess what she said," his mother sang as if she had the juiciest of secrets.

"Who?" he drawled, one hand locked on the door handle, escape within sight.

"I was telling her Clay was good with renovations, but I called him one of my handsome sons, and she thought I meant you. That you were my handsome son. She thinks you're handsome!" The way she crowed would have done a number on his self-esteem if he hadn't recently been kissed by a beautiful woman.

"From one to five, where do I fall on the list? I'm not the most handsome, so definitely not first but am I all the way at the bottom?" Wes held up a hand. "Don't answer that. I don't need to know."

His mother set down her needle. "Nonsense, every one of my boys is a one if that's the best rating, but you're handsome in different ways. That's not important. I'm saying Sarah thinks you're first and isn't that even better?"

It was. It was so much better.

Wes started to give his mother more flack over her surprise at Sarah choosing him over Matt or Clay, but then he realized that she wasn't saying anything about the kiss. Had they somehow missed that part of the evening? Whether they had or they hadn't, he didn't want to talk about it.

"Love you, Mom. Your conversation with Sarah helped, somehow, and we've both given her something to think about. The work continues tomorrow." She and Rose were doing a happy dance when he stepped outside.

As he climbed in his truck, he realized his smile was back. It might not leave his face for a while and there was no doubt in his mind where it came from.

The only worry he had was about what would happen when the reason for it left town again.

CHAPTER FOURTEEN

As SARAH TUGGED Jordan's suitcase up another step, Jordan stopped in front of the next frame on the wall. "Now, Rose, is this you as a baby? How adorable you were!" Jordan seemed content to ignore Sarah lugging a suitcase filled with what had to be bricks behind her as she questioned each new photo. On the one hand, Sarah was happy to see that Rose had warmed up, thanks to whatever Prue had said to her after Sarah and Wes left Handmade together with their pie.

But on the other hand, if she didn't get somewhere flat soon with Jordan's luggage, it was going to go tumbling back down to the first floor with a loud crash. The temptation to let go was already building.

Rose answered, "Yes, that's me. Youngest of six!" She propped her hands on her hips as if that was an accomplishment. Considering the trouble that sisters could be, Sarah realized it might be something to brag about. Rose and Jordan moved up a few stairs to the next frame, and Sarah labored to see the picture herself. She was not at all surprised to discover that Rose had three older sisters. No doubt at some point, they had been annoyed by her as much as Jordan was doing Sarah right now.

"I love these stories, Rose," Sarah said breathlessly as she braced herself against the banister, "but Jordan has packed enough shoes here for the whole town to borrow, so could I drop this in her room?"

Rose raised her hands. "Oh, my, of course, Sarah." She hurried up the last of the staircase and Jordan stuck her tongue out at Sarah before she followed.

Sarah glanced down at the gleaming wood floors at the bottom of the staircase and then at Jordan's suitcase. When she imagined the crash and damage to the floor and walls of Bell House, she set her jaw and finished yanking the suitcase up the stairs. Then she remembered her stroke of genius.

"Your sister insisted you'd want the largest room we have here at Bell House," Rose said uncertainly. "If you'd like something different, you can let me know, okay?"

Amazed at how the temperature of the reception had warmed with Jordan's arrival, Sarah paused to make sure she didn't miss any of Jordan's reaction. The wreath on her door was…fluffy. And very, very white. Almost like a wedding dress.

Rose opened the door and Jordan stepped inside. The room was large, yes. It was also clearly the B-and-B's version of a honeymoon suite, complete with white rugs, a romantic canopy bed draped with netting, a gorgeous fireplace and a large tub right in the center of the room. Nothing in it was heart shaped, so Sarah was disappointed, but it would do.

"Thank you, Rose. This is lovely." Jordan smiled. "I'm sure Sarah can answer any of my questions, but you've been a wonderful host."

Sarah also smiled as Rose passed. On her way out, Rose closed the door.

Then Sarah met Jordan's deadpan stare. "Is this a wedding suite? Did you choose it or did she?"

Letting go of the handle of Jordan's suitcase to watch it tip over and land with a satisfying thump was sweet.

"Never mind. I don't even need to ask. You did this to me." Jordan waved her hand dramatically at the bathtub.

Hauling up the suitcase had been hard work, but the payoff was nice. "I picked it based on my suspicion that the rooms here at Bell House are named after famous bells. I couldn't think of any other bells except the Liberty Bell, which is my room. I was dying to see inside more rooms. I took a shot and requested Wedding Bells. What's wrong? Does the theme give you ideas?" Sarah tried to keep an innocent, wide-eyed expression.

Jordan plopped down on the end of the beautiful bed. "Of the two of us, I'm the least likely to be picking wedding bells anytime soon."

Sarah rolled her eyes and flopped next to her. "Right, because I'm so busy with my packed social life."

"You." Jordan kicked off her shoes and scrambled around to sit facing Sarah. "You were kissing a cowboy!"

Oh, yeah, and she'd intended to avoid the subject of kissing the cowboy for as long as she could. Apparently that wasn't even fifteen minutes into Jordan's arrival.

"That was a surprise," Sarah muttered, determined to leave it at that. Jordan would keep pushing but she didn't have to answer anything she… "It was an amazing surprise."

Jordan immediately clapped her hands over her mouth to stifle the whoop she made. "As Sadie used to say, if I hadn't seen it with my own eyes, I'd have said you were lying like a rug."

Sarah scooted back to rest against the headboard. "Ha. No one would believe it, would they?"

Jordan made the "give me more" motion, her hands expressive as always. "Details. Dish. Tea. Spill."

What was there to say? Sarah couldn't explain what was happening to herself, much less to anyone else, and she'd lived it.

"He's been a tremendous help, answering questions. Yesterday we took a ride across the Rocking A to see the lodge." Sarah realized she hadn't mentioned any of this to her sister yet. "The Rocking A is the Majestic's neighbor. He was showing me the pastures and all the land that surrounds the lodge. It hasn't been developed at all."

Jordan's forehead wrinkled. "Did you go to

see the ghost town without me?" The way her voice rose at the end was proof of betrayal.

"I did, but we were riding horses, Jordan." Sarah held her hands out.

"Oh," Jordan said, "okay, then. I don't do horses."

Sarah had been counting on that to answer any complaints; it was nice when one of her strategies worked.

"How was it? The horse ride? I didn't think you did horses, either, anymore."

Sarah sighed. "It was amazing. A beautiful day. A beautiful horse."

"A beautiful man," Jordan said slyly, the corner of her mouth quirked up.

Jordan had eyes and they were working just fine. There was no need to agree or disagree with that statement, so Sarah moved on. "I hope that kiss doesn't make things awkward between us." More awkward. Wes was already so tangled up in the lodge decision that it didn't need any further awkwardness.

"I mean, falling in love with a neighbor seems perfect to me. Horses are terrifying, but a handsome cowboy to keep you safe would make it worthwhile," Jordan said.

Sarah shook her head. "Horses are lovely,

intelligent creatures. It's falling in love that's terrifying, Jordie."

Her sister grimaced. "This just got serious, but I cannot argue with that."

Sarah bit her lip as she considered unburdening her soul by dropping all of her thoughts about Wes Armstrong in Jordan's lap, but it was too soon for all that emotion to make sense. When they went back home, Wes would fade to a memory of something that could have been sweet if her life had been different.

"Let's trade rooms. You know I've always loved the Liberty Bell." Jordan poked her.

Sarah snorted. "No way. You don't love any bell any more than I do. You just want out of the romance suite."

"I do." Jordan stared up at the canopy. "It is pretty, I guess. I wonder if there's a dinner bell room? What would the decor be?"

Sarah nodded. "Figure out a way to ask Rose to show us all the rooms because I love these themes so much. She likes you."

"Yeah," Jordan drawled, "what's the story there? No one has ever accused me of being a people person. After the way you talked about the cold shoulders you were getting, I never expected Rose to be so friendly. You wanted to stay out at the run-down lodge instead of this perfectly lovely home."

Sarah wasn't sure she could explain it to Jordan when she was still trying to find answers herself. "I guess, when in doubt, bond over crafts. I spent some time over in Handmade and everything changed." Literally everything. Prue. Rose. Even Wes's kiss.

"Crafts?" Jordan asked, doubt clear on her face.

"The first night I was here, I had to interrupt a meeting to find Rose so I could check in here. It was at Wes's mother's store, Handmade. I saw this piece of embroidery. It was of columbines and it reminded me of the apron Mom made for Sadie." Sarah shrugged. "I couldn't get it out of my mind, so when I had to go back in today, I asked Prue how hard it would be to learn to embroider." She scrambled off the bed to grab the bag she'd dropped next to Jordan's suitcase. The rest was history and Jordan had already experienced the effects. No more words were necessary. Instead, she carefully spread the things Prue had gathered for her across the quilt on Jordan's bed. Fabric. Threads. Beautiful scissors.

Jordan rolled up on her knees to move closer. "I love that story. Let's see if we can find the apron when we go back to the lodge. You can take it home with you."

Sarah would have argued, because she didn't think she should be taking anything from the lodge until all three of them could go through what was left.

Then she realized how much she longed for the apron if they did find it and resolved to let Brooke and Jordan both have anything else they might want.

"Also, Wes's mother?" Jordan tilted her head to the side as she smoothed the hank of periwinkle thread. "Putting together the context clues, I'm assuming Wes is the hot-lipped cowboy on the porch. And his mother is the ringleader in town who was running the meeting the first night at her store, who turned Prospect into frostbite when she found out who you were, and now, on the basis of a shared love of needle and thread, has changed her tune?"

"Also horses," Sarah said. There was something about the way Prue had reacted when

Sarah had mentioned how much help Wes had given her that made her think there was another piece of the puzzle she hadn't quite figured out yet.

"I mean, that's a solid foundation you're building," Jordan said.

Sarah waited for her to add something else, but Jordan shook her head.

"What?" Sarah asked. It was never a good thing when bossy Jordan got quiet.

"Sadie was so amazing. The kind of person I wish I could be, you know?" Jordan said quietly. "What if she brought us here, not because she needed us to take care of this last piece of business, but because she was wrapping up loose ends herself?"

Sarah stretched out on her side and propped her head on her hand as she considered that. "That is a very Sadie thing to do, but I'm not following."

Jordan did as Sarah had done and stretched out. "As long as Sadie was around, I didn't worry, you know? It was like she was security in the world. Now I'm a little lost, no anchor."

Sarah nodded. She understood that perfectly. Sadie had become the glue they needed.

"What if she wanted you to come to Prospect to meet these cowboys? You were always the most like Sadie. What if she knew you were meant to be here with the horses and the barns and whatnot?"

"I'm the most like Sadie?" Sarah blurted in surprise before clapping a hand over her mouth at the volume. "Of the three of us, you could have been her no-nonsense twin and you know it. No one can cut through ridiculousness like Sadie Hearst and she taught *you* everything she knew."

Jordan pursed her lips. "This is valid. I accept this and appreciate the summary, but what I meant was loving the things that Sadie loved. You spent hours in the kitchen with her and Mom every summer. You went to school so you could work at the Cookie Queen Corporation with Sadie. You learned the business. I know you expanded the business because you can't help yourself." She paused. "When Mom died, you stepped up to make sure the rest of us were okay. Sadie did the same thing."

The sting of tears in her eyes surprised Sarah. Jordan had never said anything like this before.

She'd done her best to be strong for her sisters. Whatever happened, they'd get through it together. That was still true every single day. Crying because her heart was broken wouldn't help them at all, but Jordan being sweet was an emotional roller coaster.

"I don't have anything like Sadie's style." Sarah rubbed her nose.

Jordan shook her head. "That's Brooke's domain, for sure. The more sparkle, the better."

They both laughed.

"Two more things we know Sadie loved." Jordan held up a finger. "Prospect, her home town." She added another finger. "And cowboys."

Sarah rolled her eyes.

"It stands to reason that Sadie thought you should take another look at a cowboy, you know?" Jordan said with a grin.

"Do you believe that Sadie was preoccupied with matchmaking when she was drawing up her will?" Even as the words were coming out of her mouth, she realized it fit Sadie to a *T*.

Jordan snickered. "You didn't even get the question out before you realized how likely that was, did you?"

"Upend my life to bring me here to…fall

in love?" Sarah said as she stood. "That is a Sadie-worthy scheme, for sure."

"Uh-huh. What would scare me, if I were in your shoes…boots, is that Sadie's plans almost always worked. If you haven't yet asked yourself if you're prepared to turn your whole life upside down, we should probably get you away from Prospect and away from the cowboy ASAP." Jordan yawned. "Now, let's talk about what's really important. What's for dinner?"

Sarah desperately wanted to ask if it wasn't too soon to be contemplating such drastic life changes but she was afraid Jordan would say it was believable that a woman might be ready to upend her whole world after less than a week. Her gut told her Sadie would have jumped without hesitation.

Easier to think about dinner.

"Well, not too many choices here in town. There's the Ace High." Sarah held her arms out. "Ta da. The end. And as far as I can tell, they serve whatever the chef wants to make that night, so you have to be ready to eat what they set in front of you."

Jordan wrinkled her nose. "Or?"

"Or go hungry? Get in the car and drive

somewhere else?" Sarah covered her cheeks with her hands. "Actually cook something?" They both gasped as if it was the horror story that kept them up at night.

"If we were hoping to open a business," Jordan said slowly, "one could say there are several opportunities right here at the Majestic. I would think a restaurant with a limited but reliable menu might attract neighbors as well as visitors from nearby towns."

Sarah crossed her arms over her chest. "Do we want to open a business, Jordan?" It wouldn't surprise her if Jordan was already building it in her head. She'd wanted to be in business for herself her whole life.

"Just saying." Jordan smiled brightly. "If we can't find a single buyer for this place, maybe we have another option."

Sarah nodded. "Well, if that's how you want it to go, you better be coming up with a business plan. Finding a buyer won't be difficult."

Jordan's smile faded. "Really?"

Sarah nodded. "Choosing between the options we have is the only challenge now." The thought of having to make that decision was bringing her down. "Change clothes if you want to, and then meet me downstairs. Let's see what the Ace is serving first. From there, we'll organize our night."

Sarah closed the door to Jordan's room and did a little dance at the rustle of thick white tulle that exploded from the puffy wreath. As she let herself into the staid Liberty Room, she realized that whatever she and her sisters decided, everything would change. She'd never seriously considered reopening the Majestic, but apparently Jordan had.

If she had to guess Brooke's preference, it would be sell and pocket the cash. She and her husband had wasted no time and left for New York two days after he'd finished law school. They were a part of the political scene there with big plans for the future.

Finding her way back to Prospect would be nearly impossible for Brooke.

But Jordan was thinking of future economic opportunities, which suggested she hadn't quite made up her mind.

As she remembered the feeling of swinging beside Wes, Sarah wondered if she was ready to cut all ties with Prospect.

Reopening the lodge would be huge and would take money none of them had on hand, even with their promised inheritance from Sadie.

It didn't make sense to struggle to hold on to a place they hadn't visited in years.

Sadie had always been the draw to the lodge.

After dinner, when she was alone, she'd have to spend some time figuring out why her heart had started racing when Jordan suggested a practical future for them all here in Prospect.

CHAPTER FIFTEEN

WES UNDERSTOOD HE'D miscalculated almost immediately as he trotted down the steps toward his truck on Monday afternoon. Travis was the first to spot him and let out a wolf whistle. That attracted Grant's attention from inside the paddock he was using to train a filly they'd named Starla because of the star-shaped white blaze centered between her ears. Grant was covered in dirt, suggesting that his newest project was giving him a run for his money. Wes hated that he'd missed the show.

"Well, now, if it isn't Wesley Armstrong, Esquire," Grant drawled.

"The tie is too much, isn't it?" Wes muttered as he ran one hand down the silk tie he'd put on at the last minute. For some reason, it hadn't bothered him that Sarah had only met him as a cowboy. For this meeting with the real estate agent and Sarah's sister,

Wes had wanted to make it clear that he had another side.

"Are you headed for a job interview?" Travis asked.

"Nope, over to the lodge. Sarah has a Realtor coming to advise her on how she might sell the place." Wes shoved a hand in his pocket. The pocket belonged to ironed khakis, not jeans. As if putting on the costume of a small-town lawyer might improve his chances of being taken seriously or something.

Travis tilted his chin. "Have you set up our day? The one where we put on the full show for her to convince her to give us a good deal?"

"No, I'd like Clay to be here, too. He can address how the ranch will need to expand to make room for the kids and how we'll do it frugally." Wes rubbed his forehead. "What I can't wrap my head around is why any of us think this will matter. We wouldn't try this silly maneuver with any other business deal, would we?"

Grant rested his forearms on the fence. "We might, if Mom told us to."

Wes felt better when Travis nodded in agreement. He would do anything for Prue and Walt, even waste his time and Sarah's. It seemed his brothers agreed with that tactic.

"Will you both be around on Wednesday?" Wes asked. "Maybe that will work for Sarah and her sister."

They nodded so he went to climb into the truck.

On the short drive over to the lodge, Wes surveyed the pastures on either side of the road. Years of being empty of cattle meant tall grass and some holes in the fence that would need repairs, but if he could convince Sarah to sell this back to his family, he could definitely add heads to the herd. Grant's nest egg could be used for that, even if no one in the family wanted to spend it to buy land. If fortune turned and Grant needed cash quickly, cows could be sold easily.

He slowed the truck around the largest pothole and made a mental note to ask Sarah if she wanted him to hire a road grader to come out and smooth the thing out. It had been an unnecessary expense when he was the only one checking on the lodge, but if there was about to be traffic in the form of potential buyers, it would help the sale of the place.

When he realized that was the last thing

he wanted to do, make the lodge seem like a better bargain, Wes wanted to bang his head on the steering wheel. It was such a roller coaster to be on Sarah's side at one point of the conversation, and then realize he'd slid across the table from her as a buyer instead.

He had to do the right thing…but for which Wes?

As he pulled up next to Sarah's rental car, he realized the only thing he could evaluate objectively was what would be best for Sarah and her sisters in this situation. She'd be better off if the road was repaired, so he should do that. There were funds in the lodge's account to cover it. Easy enough to do, no matter who ended up owning the place.

"Wes," Sarah said as she got out of her car, "this is Erin. She handles vacation properties outside of Denver." He could feel the weight of Sarah's stare as she took in the tie and the khakis while he shook the real estate agent's hand and accepted the business card she held out to him. It was hard to read Sarah's expression but he decided she was impressed. That was the reaction he wanted.

"I'm the lawyer here in Prospect who has been managing the lodge since Sadie closed it down." Wes fidgeted with his tie and realized Sarah's sister stood to the side, waiting patiently to be acknowledged. "Nice to see you, Jordan." He offered her his hand to shake.

"The cowboy turned lawyer," Jordan said in a not so un-business-like tone. "We've already met, but it's nice to have the official introduction."

He nodded and refused to think about the kiss on Bell House's front porch, not while Jordan was studying him so closely.

"Jordan and I haven't explored much of the lodge," Sarah said while she stared hard at her sister. Wes noticed Jordan mimed zipping her lips and wondered what the real story was. "We're anxious to see the rooms."

Sarah unlocked the door and led them inside. When Jordan nudged his arm to hand him a flashlight, Wes was almost certain that they had to have spent more time inside than they were letting on. It was gloomy but nothing had been disturbed in the large lobby that would have been a place to check in and gather to meet friends when the lodge was open. It had been a no-frills kind of place, so the furniture was sparse, and the overarching theme was wood. Wood on the floors, walls, ceiling.

"So," the real estate agent said as she twirled in a slow circle. "Good shape for what it is, but I'm sure I don't have to tell you that the options for this room as it is are limited."

"Most folks would take one look around and be ready to check right out." Jordan turned to her sister. "Do you remember it being like this? So...woody?"

Sarah grimaced. "Yes, but I think some sunshine, a good clean to get rid of the cobwebs and dust and Sadie beaming at you from the front door would change the atmosphere in a heartbeat." She took a few steps. "Wasn't there a big rug in the center? Oval? Reds and yellows? A braided rug?"

"You're right! It was much more cheerful than this. We'll have to add color," Jordan said.

Making plans like that? Was Sarah's sister on board for a future at the lodge?

The agent shone a light up at a dark corner of the ceiling. "I'm not sure, but you might have a leak or some damage. A roofing contractor should get up there to check it out. Before we finalize any listing price, we'll have to have a real inspection done to get an estimate of the repairs we'd need to keep the lodge usable. If they're too extensive, I'd suggest selling this at the value of the land. Anyone who buys the place would most likely want to start from scratch here."

"Knock it down," Jordan said flatly.

Erin nodded.

Wes wasn't sure whether Jordan and Sarah were ready to hear that, but the look they exchanged made him think they weren't fully committed to losing the building itself, at least, not at this point.

"Let's open one of the rooms," Jordan said as if the agent hadn't given them the easiest, fastest way to sell the place. If they priced it for the value of the land, they didn't have to worry about repairs or what shape the building was in. They could remove whatever they wanted, list it and sign the paperwork from LA. He would show any potential buyers around, but most everyone would quickly see the merit in the land and lake access alone. Wealthy Denver or Colorado Springs buyers or anyone who wanted a secluded place to build a lakefront luxury home would find the perfect spot here with just a bit of demolition required.

Instead of arguing, Sarah nodded enthusiastically. As he brought up the rear, Wes experienced a prickling sensation along his nape. Was someone else in the building? He shone his light along the opposite hallway that led to the dining room and restaurant, but couldn't see anyone.

When he joined them in the guest room, Wes could see they were studying another spot on the ceiling. Definitely needed work on the roof if the building was going to be saved. That wouldn't be cheap.

"Don't know how long the leak has been here, but it got the carpet and this couch for sure," Sarah said. The nightstands and round table in front of the window were in good shape, and the mattresses were dusty but stain-free.

The real estate agent stood in the doorway to the small bathroom. "You might be able to salvage some investment here if you want to sell these fixtures as a lot only. They are out-of-date but in decent shape. Still, I don't know how much it would cost you to remove these. You might have to spend more than you'd make reselling them."

Her tone was purely business, numbers cascading through her brain and out her mouth like a human calculator. In the gloom, it was hard to see the impact on Sarah or Jordan, but they decided to keep the inspection going.

"Was it twenty guest rooms total?" Jordan asked and Sarah nodded.

"I imagine they're in roughly the same shape." The real estate agent pointed to a hallway that led behind the lobby. "What's this?"

Sarah stopped. "That's the family quarters, where Sadie and her parents lived until her mother and father moved down to Denver and she took over running the lodge by herself." She wrapped her arm over Jordan's shoulders. "This was Sadie's place."

The agent paused. "Should we skip this part of the tour?"

Jordan shook her head. "No, I'd like to see what shape it's in."

Wes followed silently behind them. He'd never been in this spot, where he had to go back to a loved one's place after they were gone, but it couldn't be easy, even if Sadie herself hadn't returned for years.

Sarah found the right key to unlock the door, and he watched her shoulders rise as she took a deep breath. Then the door was opened and it was like stepping back in time. It was clear that Sadie had made a home here. The first room was an open space containing the kitchen with a large island and living room. Furniture was covered with dust sheets, but there were still shelves of books and frames on the wall. When she'd left, Sadie had planned to come back. Life had turned out differently, but her stamp remained.

The agent obviously realized that now was not the time to explain how little value the room held unless someone included senti- mental value and Erin certainly did not. She moved to stand silently next to the boarded- up window that looked out over the back of the lodge, a green expanse that would match the view from Wes's office window. It was too bad they couldn't let that light in right now.

Wes wasn't sure how the room had existed before Sadie took over, but it was clear that the woman who had lived here had loved two things: her family and her kitchen.

"Do you remember that summer we were

roped into helping with the renovation Sadie had started?" Jordan asked. "She wanted the kitchen she deserved."

"That was the only time you spent any time in this kitchen at all, as I remember it. You swung that hammer like your life depended on it," Sarah said as she wiped dust off a wide family portrait.

"I enjoy knocking things down, for sure," Jordan murmured.

In the frame, Wes could see a large group of people gathered in front of the lake with Sadie at the center. There were three girls kneeling right in front of her. That had to be Sarah and her sisters. When Sarah stepped away, Wes moved closer. It was easy to see Sarah in the lanky teenager who had wrapped her arms over a girl on each side of her. Same gorgeous smile. Today, she had the same ponytail, too.

"Step away from the childhood photos, sir. I do not want to have to disappear you to contain the evidence." Jordan motioned him away. "What an awkward phase."

"You were adorable." Sarah immediately disagreed. "Mean, but still very cute."

Jordan nodded. "Sadie said the same thing."

The real estate agent checked her watch. "I'm sure there are so many things that you'll need to pack up. We'll have to discuss how quickly you want to list and how much time you'll need to clear the property."

Sarah glanced up from a row of cookbooks that lined the counter as if she'd forgotten that the woman was still with them. "Right."

"Look," Jordan said softly as she held out an apron. It was a checkered pattern, yellow and white, with a white band at the top. The whole piece had dulled with age, but he could see blue flowers worked across the stitching. "We found it." Jordan slipped it off the hook on the wall and handed it to Sarah.

"Yeah, we found it." Sarah spread the material out over her arm. "Do you think Brooke would want it?"

Jordan snorted and then immediately followed up with a sneeze. "Are you kidding? Vintage she might go for, but never in an apron." She squeezed Sarah's hand. "Take it. Please. I bet we can find someone to help us clean it up."

Sarah nodded and folded the apron carefully. Wes wanted to know more about why it was so special to her.

Jordan had moved back toward the hallway. "There's no need to check out the bedrooms." She turned to Sarah. "Right?"

Wes rested his hips against the counter. If they wanted to touch every one of Sadie's things, he was happy to stay right where he was. They deserved the time they needed.

Sarah cleared her throat. "Right. We don't need to keep Wes and Erin here while we walk down Memory Lane. We can come back later."

Jordan nodded before holding up one finger. "We definitely have to find out whatever it is that's in the restaurant kitchen."

Sarah immediately agreed. "Right. One more stop and then we'll head to the lake."

"Whatever it is that's in the restaurant kitchen…" Wes frowned over the strange phrasing as he followed the women through the lobby. When they made it across the restaurant to the swinging doors that led to the kitchen, both Sarah and Jordan peered through the windows into the back. What could they see? It was as shadowed and dark as all the rooms they'd explored so far.

They communicated something with a brief look before shoving the swinging doors open. Wes peered from his spot in the dining room, watching their lights scan quickly over the empty kitchen. When the sisters were satisfied, they moved inside and the agent followed. Wes wanted to know the answer to the puzzle of whatever it was they were hoping to find. Or more accurately, what they were afraid to find?

"Surely Sadie packed up everything she could take from the kitchen," Jordan murmured.

The lodge had had a well-run commercial kitchen as far as Wes could tell. Industrial shelving lined the walls and held plates, glasses and silverware. The pantry was open, but most of the shelves there were empty. The freezer that took up a chunk of real estate was closed, locked. Since the electricity hadn't been on in years, whatever was inside would be…not good.

"We aren't opening that, are we?" Sarah asked her sister.

"No, you aren't." Wes wasn't about to allow that to happen on his watch. If he had to, he'd hire a hazmat crew from Denver to come in and clear it before anyone he liked attempted it.

"I'm almost certain it's empty." Sarah bit

her lip. "If Sadie had closed the kitchen down, it would be." She sniffed loudly, took a step closer to the freezer and did it again. "I don't smell a horror story inside."

No one was in a rush to take a chance and verify that, though.

"No, I think I smell…" Jordan frowned. "Vanilla? And I don't see anything that could have made that crash we heard."

The way she jerked when Sarah poked her side told Wes that neither he nor the real estate agent were supposed to know about this crash. How would two women who'd never been inside the kitchen since they'd returned to Prospect have heard a crash anyway?

When Sarah met his stare, they both knew the story was incomplete and that she'd have to finish it for him. Later. When they didn't have an audience.

"Should we head down to the lake?" Jordan asked brightly. "I haven't been there yet."

Jordan led the real estate agent away and Wes stuck with Sarah as she made sure everything was carefully locked up. They wandered out into the grounds of the lodge afterward. "Want to head to the lake?" he asked, content to follow her lead.

Sarah shook her head. "No, I don't want to hear much more about what has value and what doesn't." She brushed the apron draped across her arm absentmindedly.

Wes thought he understood what she meant. "It's never the things that mean the most, is it?"

"Sadie's apartment back there..." Sarah waved a hand in front of her face. Tears? Did that mean tears? Wes immediately felt the urge to do something but he had no idea what would help. "I wasn't exactly ready for that."

Instead of saying something silly that only filled in the air between them and did nothing to make her feel any better, Wes put his arm around her shoulders. "I imagine it's kind of bittersweet. You want to remember her, but then you can't escape the reality that she won't be here with you again."

Sarah gulped and nodded. "Right."

They watched Jordan point out something for Erin at the marina that had been shuttered not too long after the lodge closed. Without the lodge, there were fewer boaters on this area of the lake, but Wes was certain the real estate agent could estimate an amount for the equipment left behind. The dock itself would be valuable to anyone who built here, even if the slips available were more suited to a commercial enterprise than to a luxury home.

"Want to tell me about the crash? In the kitchen?" He bent down to catch her stare. "The one you and Jordan had definitely not been in since you came back to Prospect."

Her lips twitched. "Okay, so…" She tipped her head back and took deep breaths of the clear air. Wes was glad to see the amusement on her face. Whatever grief she carried with her, he had to believe that Sadie would have wanted that chased away.

"The day I came out to the ranch to get the paperwork," she glanced up at him through her eyelashes, "I drove over here. Jordan called as I was getting out of the car, so I put her on video and we made it as far as the dining room." She motioned as if they could see inside the room. "There's a spot where there are some photos and news clippings about Sadie. I was reading those when there was this…crash, like metal bowls falling off the counter or…" She hesitated. "I'm not sure, but I didn't hang around to investigate, you know?"

Wes crossed his arms over his chest as he pictured what his own reaction might have been.

"No way, no how was I going in there alone. I believe the technical term for my retreat was a 'skedaddle.'" Sarah slashed a hand across her throat. "I ran back to the car and locked myself inside. Jordan had no idea what was going on, but we agreed we weren't going in a second time without backup."

Wes forced himself to frown at her even as hearing her say "skedaddle" made it nearly impossible. Watching her think was entertaining, as it involved every muscle in her face, arms and legs. Sarah paced and pointed to punctuate her main ideas.

"Don't you think your backup today should have been informed about this possible intruder?" Wes crossed his arms across his chest.

She patted his arm. "I wasn't worried as long as you were with us."

As if he had to be comforted! He tried not to smile.

"To Jordan's point, I didn't see anything metal like that stacked up in the kitchen or what might have fallen." Sarah frowned. "Did you?"

Wes replayed his scan of the room. "No, but it was dark in there. Maybe we missed it?"

She nodded. "Okay, when it comes time to clear out the place…however we decide that should be done, we'll need to uncover the windows and get the electricity back on. Then we'll need to hire a team of guys to move that freezer to some undisclosed place where it will never be opened again."

Wes couldn't argue with her plan. "Think that's where the crash came from?"

She bit her lip. "It sounded too loud to be muffled by that much insulation and closed doors and… I'm sure Sadie had the thing thoroughly cleaned out, too. I had imagined spoiled food, but the way Sadie harped on about safety, it's probably clean enough to perform surgery in there."

Wes nodded. That made sense. He still wasn't planning to be the volunteer who verified that.

Even if his presence was enough to make Sarah feel safe enough to face the unknown. Her faith had him feeling pretty invincible.

"What do you think might have caused that

crash?" she asked with a grimace. "It's some kind of critter, isn't it? A raccoon? A possum?"

As dark as it had been in the kitchen, it could have been a bear, but Wes wasn't going to say that. "When you're ready, we'll turn the utilities on and bring in a moving team to help you pack. Make sure they're slow, too. That way, if you have to run out of there, you won't be last."

She pursed her lips as if considering his words. "Good plan."

"I'm much more than backup, Sarah." He tapped his forehead. "Brains and brawn, see?"

"You forgot good-looking," she added and then gasped. "Are you blushing?" She tilted his hat back and he knew he was busted. It didn't bother him much because she wrapped her arms around his middle and squeezed, her laughter floating around them.

"You did that on purpose, didn't you? To rattle me." Wes laughed at how delighted she was by his reaction.

"Maybe." Sarah stepped back before he was ready to let her go.

They were grinning at each other when Jordan and Erin returned to the lodge.

The way her sister stared him down, Wes was pretty sure Jordan had some thoughts about him and Sarah spending time alone together. They weren't positive, either.

"I want to go back to my office and run the numbers, explore the possible scenarios," the agent said, "but my first answer would be to continue with the idea to sell this as a lot. The acreage is larger than it has to be for a nice luxury estate, but the lake is a sure selling point. The marina should be sold off separately as a commercial property. I don't do as much of that, but I work with someone who can help if you decide to go that way." Erin scribbled notes as she spoke. "The lodge will come down, but you won't be responsible for that."

"Under your plan to sell the lot as is and the marina separately," Jordan asked, "what are you thinking this would list for?"

The agent tapped numbers into the calculator in her binder. "Conservatively? If you were to list everything together for a quick sale, I'd say...one million, easily. At least." She shrugged. "We could raise that, of course, with a few different tactics to reach a different level of buyer, someone who has more money to spend on a place this large, but you'll end up holding everything longer and paying more in taxes."

Wes had expected to hear worse than a million, but there was absolutely no way they could find funds like that in the Rocking A's finances. Loans…maybe, but every rancher who'd been in the business for a minute understood the risk involved with taking out a loan on the land they owned free and clear. Was it worth that risk to gain back the acreage that had been sold off?

"And you don't think there's any way we could find someone who'd be interested in running a fishing lodge outside the tiny town of Prospect?" Sarah asked. The resignation in her tone bothered Wes.

The agent looked doubtful. "I wouldn't say it's impossible, but you're shrinking down the pool of buyers so much that the odds might be the same as being struck by lightning. You'd have to find the right buyer at exactly the right time." She faced Sarah. "And there's no guarantee that whoever bought the place would leave it as it is. If you sell, you lose control over what happens to your great-aunt's lodge no matter which way you go."

Sarah nodded. "Right. Of course."

Erin pointed at her car. "I'll be going then. I want to ask some questions about the marina and I'll see what other agents in my office think about selling to someone looking for a lodge to run. Then I'll put together something formal. Email it to you this week?"

Sarah nodded and they waved as the agent slid into her car and drove away.

Then the three of them were left there in silence.

"Did you tell him about the serial killer in the kitchen?" Jordan asked.

"She told me about an unspecified crash in the kitchen," Wes drawled. "That's what we're going with at this time."

"Smart. Definitely better for the listing, too." Jordan nodded before asking Sarah, "What's next?"

Wes knew exactly how Sarah was feeling in that moment. He'd stood there in front of one or more of his brothers before when they needed an answer. He wasn't sure what she thought about the agent's words, but she'd be doing her best to present a confident manner to her little sister.

"Tomorrow we're going to Denver. We'll

meet with Henry Milbank. He's the most insistent of the developers." Sarah shrugged. "Then we've got one more potential buyer to talk to, and we can...decide."

Jordan frowned but she didn't ask any questions about the other buyer. Sarah smiled up at him, but some of the glow was missing.

Wes was certain they both understood that a million dollars for Sadie's property was the low end of the offers that would be coming in. Sarah had to know why that would be out of his reach, too.

Neither Sarah nor Jordan seemed comfortable with the promise of the lodge being torn down and turned into a luxury vacation home. It wasn't time to give up yet.

CHAPTER SIXTEEN

SARAH WAS STILL considering everything the real estate agent had said when she and Jordan loaded up her rental car to make the trip to Denver. They'd both dressed for business, but Sarah was already regretting her pants choice and she'd removed the scarf that she'd tied around her neck as the perfect accessory less than three minutes into the drive.

"Is it the country air?" Jordan asked as she fidgeted with the sleeve of her jacket. "That makes clothes that fit perfectly last week pinch like a torture device?"

"No idea, but we might have miscalculated." She dodged the arm Jordan flung out to wriggle out of her jacket. "If we show up half-dressed, we're going to present a much different picture than dangerously effective negotiators."

"Can't sit here in that for the whole drive.

Can't do it." Jordan settled back in her seat with a happy sigh. "Better."

Sarah hadn't been excited about the extra drive to Denver, but it was more fun with Jordan along. "Have you come to any new conclusions after a good night of rest and the stellar breakfast Rose set up this morning?"

Jordan pointed her finger in the air. "You know, that might be why my clothes belong to someone else, someone thinner, this morning. Rose's breakfast spread. Pancakes and waffles? Iconic choice and Rose was so excited to show us that photo album. Her family pictures belong in a museum. So much history." She stared out the window for a long moment. "No new conclusions about what to do with the Majestic. In the back of my mind, I expected the agent to say everything she did, though. It makes sense that the building isn't the selling point and the repairs required to reopen would present a challenge to finding someone who wants to run it as a fishing lodge. That sure doesn't make it any easier to contemplate life after the Majestic, birthplace of Sadie Hearst, the Colorado Cookie Queen, is gone. In my head, it'll always be there. It doesn't change."

Sarah fidgeted with the visor as she considered that. The same vision had ping-ponged back and forth in her head, keeping her awake long after the excellent pasta dinner from Ace High should have knocked her out.

"Doesn't seem like the world should go on spinning as usual after something that big, does it?" Sarah asked quietly.

Jordan shook her head. "Here's my dream. Someone else buys the lodge, renovates and reopens it. Years later, we come back and catalog all the differences, small improvements, but the shape of this life that Sadie lived would still be there."

Sarah inhaled slowly. "Yeah." Selling the land to someone who would make good use of it was okay with her, but that had been the problem that kept stopping her in her tracks. Once the sale was done and the lodge was gone, it would be gone forever for them. No going back.

"We shouldn't hurry into any decision," Sarah said slowly, finding her way as she went. "Really, what is the rush?" She'd seen the taxes, and assuming they had to cover the bill for as long as they held on to the property, it would be an expense, but it wasn't astronomical. It would take a while to wipe out the portion of funds they received from the sale of Sadie's other properties.

"You have a better idea than I do of how much delaying will cost. If you think we can buy some time to… I don't know. Resign ourselves to selling? Is that what we'd be doing if we put this off? Because why put off doing what we're going to end up doing eventually?" Jordan rubbed her forehead. "And then there's Brooke and whatever is happening with her right now."

"Have you talked to her lately?" Sarah asked.

"This morning before the sun came up," Jordan replied. "She called me and asked me how to change a tire. She'd gone down to her parking spot to get something out of her car and noticed the tire was flat. Over the phone, she wanted me to teach her to change it." She raised her eyebrows. "Does that sound like Brooke? Or me, for that matter?"

Sarah slowed down to navigate a steep curve as she considered that. Did it? "Why didn't she call Dad?"

"Or her husband?" Jordan said immediately.

Loudly.

It was a good point. Paul should have been first on the call list as he was a few floors away from the underground parking. Theoretically, anyway.

Were they having more serious trouble than even Sarah had already considered?

"Or whatever expensive concierge service that takes care of parking and all the other annoyances of highfalutin living?" Jordan added. "It was weird."

It *was* weird.

"Were you able to help her?" Sarah asked. Of the two of them, Brooke had made the right call. Jordan had dogged every single one of their father's steps growing up. If anyone had ever learned to change a tire, it would be her.

"I didn't have a chance. I asked her to switch me over to video so I could see what we were working with, but she refused." Jordan frowned at Sarah. "That's even weirder, isn't it?"

"She said there was no way she could hold the phone and work on the tire, anyway. Then she hurried to end the call so she could phone for assistance." Jordan stretched. "Something strange is going on, but I can't figure out what it is. If she needed us, she'd tell us, right? Skip all this secrecy and come out with it?"

Sarah considered the question as she drove. "I don't know. I wonder if she's feeling disconnected. We're together in LA, and she's all the way across the country. She wants us to think things are fine, no matter what."

Jordan grunted. "Who made that decision? New York has been her dream ever since Sadie took her to her first Broadway show."

That was true. Sarah had missed the New York trip because she'd been touring colleges, but Brooke had not stopped talking about the wonder of her first Broadway musical for weeks. *The Lion King* had made an impact on the youngest Hearst sister, and from that point on, when anyone asked her what she was going to be when she grew up, the career would change, but the place never did.

"When we get back from Denver, let's call her. We can update her on everything we know and get a sense of how things are with her." Sarah wasn't sure it was enough, but it felt better to have some kind of plan in place.

"I know she wants to sell. But before we do that, she needs to come here, to see it one last time." Jordan sounded sad, although she made a good point. If they sold, it would be Brooke's last chance to say goodbye to Sadie, too.

"We'll all say goodbye together."

They were quiet as Sarah navigated the turns that took them back down into the city. At one point, she put on the radio and they sang along with the country music that Brooke would have hated. Just before Sarah had to get serious with the GPS directions to Platinum Partners' office, her phone rang. The car display showed her cousin's name.

"What does Michael want? He made it clear that neither you nor your job were needed at Cookie Queen central," Jordan muttered. "Ignore it. What's he going to do?"

Fire me. But he was probably going to do that anyway.

Sarah punched the button on the car's steering wheel to answer. "Hello, Michael. How are you?"

Her cousin cleared his throat. He had a habit of doing that. "Good, good. I need you back for an informal board meeting on Friday. Where are you now?"

Sarah raised her eyebrows at Jordan who immediately straightened in her seat, ready to fight. "Jordan and I are in the car in Denver. We're on the way to meet with someone who is interested in purchasing Sadie's property. Friday won't be possible." If they decided to delay selling, it might be possible to head back to LA for a bit, but she didn't want to commit to that.

Not with him.

"You'll have to come home and then go back if you're still working through the sale. This board meeting isn't optional," he said firmly.

The snotty face Jordan made as she mouthed, "optional" was funny when it was aimed at someone else instead of Sarah.

"What's it about, Michael?" Sarah asked as she pulled over into a parking lot. She needed her phone for GPS directions, not bossy orders from her cousin.

"Plans for your job. Also, Howard Marshall has questions regarding Sadie's personal property that dovetail with similar issues I'm having here at headquarters. I have an idea on how to handle everything, but I don't want to make a move without your involvement. Your father insisted and the more I think about it, the more convinced I am that he's right." Michael cleared his throat again.

Sarah stared hard through the windshield at the convenience store at the front of the parking lot as she thought.

If her father believed she needed to be there, she did.

Sadie's reputation had always been the focus of Sarah's job for Cookie Queen, handling Sadie's fans and requests for appearances as well as evaluating any opportunities that didn't fit with the core of the business. That definitely extended to her legacy. The lawyer's questions made her think this was something Sadie hadn't considered or planned for, and she definitely wanted to be there to represent her.

"Fine. I'll be there. At ten o'clock as usual?" Sarah asked.

"Good. Yes. We'll see you then." Michael hung up the phone before Sarah could ask for any more info. Luckily, she could pick her father's brain if she needed ammunition before the board meeting. Sarah waited to make sure the GPS was ready to direct her to the developer's office before she pulled out into traffic.

"That seems to be a vote for slowing down

on the sale." Jordan was fussing with her jacket, smoothing out the sleeves as she prepared to put it back on. "We could meet with this developer today, and then your other potential buyer tomorrow before we return to LA. We could do the road trip back together."

Sarah tapped the steering wheel. "Except I need to drop off the rental car in Denver. I'll be flying home."

Jordan thumped her head with her palm. "I forgot about the car."

"If you could force yourself on to an airplane, we could fly back together and leave your car here." Sarah steered into the large parking deck that the GPS directed her to, took the ticket and headed underground to find an empty spot.

"And have no car? In LA?" Jordan said it as if Sarah had suggested she could live on the moon without a space suit. It would be tough to navigate LA without a car but not completely impossible. "Fine. I'll make the long drive back alone. All by myself. A single, vulnerable woman without a big sister on hand to protect her from the dangers of this world."

"It was always the plan, Jordan." Sarah had

to employ her big sister voice because they were headed into an argument.

Jordan sighed. "Right. Forgive me for thinking things are more fun when you're around." She hopped out of the car and was slinging on her jacket before Sarah could respond. When they were both outside the vehicle and fully dressed in all the items they'd removed for comfort during the drive, Sarah hugged Jordan tightly.

"I agree. I've loved having you around. We need to make more time to be together in LA." Sarah waited for Jordan to nod. It took longer than she expected but she didn't have time to dig to the bottom of whatever that was. She held her arms out. "How do I look?"

"Powerful. Strong," Jordan immediately answered before following her. "How do I look?"

"Tough. Mean," Sarah said. "Nobody better mess with us."

They both straightened their shoulders and headed for the lobby of the tall office building that housed Platinum Partners. As soon as they got off the elevator, Sarah realized that this was no small operation. There were architectural drawings displayed in the foyer.

"Is that the new casino they built on the Strip in Las Vegas?" Jordan asked. "Took them like fifteen years to buy the land and knock down existing places. I saw a news story about the historical society or someone protesting. Did you know there was a historical society in Las Vegas?"

They stopped in front of one showing the facade, a looming tower of impersonal glass that would have been unremarkable in any major downtown in the world. Did that work on the Vegas Strip, the home of remarkable as a style and a way of life?

Sarah wasn't an architecture student, but she would have guessed that it didn't fit the aesthetic.

"She's a beauty, right? That is Cosmos." A man wearing an extremely well-tailored suit stepped out of frosted doors leading to the offices. "Sarah Hearst? And Jordan?" He asked as he offered his hand to shake. "That's our newest gem, all modern amenities, smart programming and spacious rooms above two floors of gambling action. We're pretty proud of how it turned out, a destination casino prepared for the future."

Sarah met Jordan's stare and urged her sister not to offer an honest opinion. They didn't need to start off the interview with their prospective buyer holding a grudge.

When Henry Milbank cocked his arms out to the side as if he were preparing to escort them formally down the grand staircase to meet the queen, Sarah carefully did not meet Jordan's eyes again as she slipped her hand into the crook of his elbow. If she'd felt overdressed on the drive down, she definitely wondered if she should have gone for evening attire at this point.

Then she realized she was being…too much. He was a salesperson. Big gestures were a part of his DNA. She and Jordan would have something to cuss and discuss on the way home.

If she preferred Wes's quiet chivalry and the way he and his brothers held their hands out to provide guidance without touching women they didn't know…well, not everyone was going to be Wes Armstrong, were they?

"I hope your drive down from Prospect was nice, not too much traffic on those twisty roads." Henry waited until they were seated and slid icy glasses of water in front of each of them. Platinum Partners might not have the view of LA that Howard Marshall enjoyed, but this boardroom would give Sadie's LA lawyers a run for their money. Everything was hushed, as if thick carpet and expensive furniture were soaking up anything that might not want to be heard.

"It was a wonderful day for a drive. I'm enjoying this time relearning Colorado. We lived in Denver until I was a teenager. Moving to LA was hard, but it has become home. Being back here reminds me of everything I loved about the air and the sunlight." Sarah realized she was talking too much when Jordan raised her eyebrows. "Thank you for meeting with us today. As you know, we've inherited this lodge property outside of Prospect…"

"And now you're ready to sell. I told Sadie this day would come." He held up his hands, a gold pinkie ring flashing. "Not that I can blame her. We grow older. We get set in our ways and it's harder to imagine changing anything, even something that you haven't seen in years." He smiled. "Am I right?"

Set in her ways? Sadie?

Before Jordan could illuminate him on exactly what she thought about that, which Sarah was certain would not be positive, she said, "Wes Armstrong told me you'd been the most persistent buyer, so I'd love to hear what you have planned for the spot. Is Platinum Partners looking for a fishing resort?" Of course, they weren't. If she'd had any doubts, seeing the drawings of their other developments answered them.

"Or are we talking about a new housing development, lake homes for people who don't mind a nice drive in the mountains?" Jordan asked. Her voice was tight, but Sarah wasn't sure Henry would understand that he'd overstepped his bounds and Jordan had started ticking. Unless Sarah defused the situation, Jordan would go off with a loud bang soon. No one insulted Sadie Hearst, and calling her old would have been a high insult to their great-aunt if she were in the room.

"No, even better," he said as he pulled out two glossy folders. Across the front, Sarah read, Prospect Pass Resort and Casino.

Jordan didn't even pick up the folder. "Casino? You're planning to open a casino on Sadie's land?"

Sarah gripped her sister's hand. There was no reason to get upset at the idea, was there? Hadn't they spent the last few days telling themselves over and over that once they sold, they'd have no control over what happened next?

"It will depend on whether we can get all the licensing straightened out, but that spot seems ideal for a destination casino. It's this new idea we've been kicking around for years now. We're developing one in Montana, too, but basically it works like this." Henry clasped his hands together. "We're going to build a nice conference center adjacent to the hotel. We want to have about five hundred rooms, so we can host some midsize conferences there. We're also going to put in cabins, luxury, high-end, for couples who'd like to spend quality time together and also enjoy the lake, the restaurant, the casino." He frowned. "We go back and forth on a spa. Some folks are really into that."

Sarah had heard enough, but a voice in her head was still shouting to give this a chance. Her future and her sisters' could be riding on it. He pointed at the table to the right of his desk. "Here's what we've got going in Montana. The acreage is larger than what we'll pick up on Key Lake, but there's no water access, no marina. Now, if we have all that, too, we could buy up more space in Prospect and add the spa there. I'm not sure what the town will allow, as far as knocking down any of the older facades remaining there, but creating a fresh, modern storefront would be perfect. We're working with a few partners who are planning restaurants after we get the casino open in Montana. We expect to do the same in Prospect. It's a beautiful building, isn't it?"

Sarah stared hard at the glittering towers they were proposing. If she was counting right, the towers would each rise about ten stories, with the other buildings spreading out from there.

From twenty simple rooms in a fishing lodge to five hundred rooms arranged in towers.

On Sadie's land.

How would they make that work?

What would they destroy while they were building it? Prospect itself framed a two-lane road which became thinner and less maintained until it ended in the rutted mess of the lane up to the Majestic.

They'd have to build better, wider roads, pave over pasture for parking…

If Platinum Partners had tried to come

up with something as far away from Sadie's lodge as possible, they'd succeeded. "It's…" Sarah bit her lip as she tried to find the right word.

"Never going to work," Jordan said. "This is all wrong for the site. You'd have to remove all the trees, cover all the pasture. This would ruin everything that makes that spot special."

"What do we need pasture for?" he asked. "We aren't going to be a dude ranch. I guess if we wanted to attract families, we would do something…outdoorsy, but this won't be that kind of place." He grimaced. "What Sadie had here is special. Finding a place like this without a lot of development already or competition to make succeeding there harder? It's too rare. Hidden gem doesn't even begin to cover it. That's why I would not take her no for an answer."

Henry's eyes had a telling gleam. "Now, I have an idea how much it's going to cost to get this deal done, likely two or three times what you were expecting to earn from the sale, if I had to guess."

Sarah knew her lack of a poker face had betrayed her when Henry winked. "Let me guess. You met with a real estate agent who is thinking of selling this off for a vacation home lot. Roughly two million is her best guess?" He didn't wait for Sarah to confirm or deny but pointed back at the folders he'd prepared. "Inside you will see an offer for four million dollars. Immediately. No inspection. No loans required to come through or be verified. We will work on the titles, sign the papers and you and your sisters will be millionaires. Less than thirty days, I'd guess." He stretched back in his comfortable chair, smug certainty on his face. "No one's going to beat that offer. I promise you."

Sarah tapped her fingers against the folder.

He was right. That amount was far beyond what they'd expected.

It was in the range of too good to be true.

It would change their lives forever to have that amount of money at their disposal.

"What's the catch?" Jordan asked. She didn't even pretend to be interested in the offer.

He shrugged innocently. "No catch. We're excited about this purchase and we'd like to move quickly."

She crossed her arms over her chest.

Instead of ignoring her, which might have been the best option, Henry sighed. "Okay, we haven't completed the impact study yet. There could be some damage to the local environment, and if that's the case, I would expect there to be a big fuss by the people in town or local environmental groups. I'm thinking that once we draw attention back to Key Lake, there will be a few people determined to protect it. Everyone knows it's special."

Thinking of the crystal waters and the way she and her sisters had played in the lake without a single concern, Sarah knew Henry was right.

And if Prue Armstrong had any say in the matter, the stink caused by these plans would spread far and wide. Imagining Sadie's reaction to such a proposal was easy. Her great-aunt would have ripped his offer to pieces and given him an earful while she did it.

"We always factor in the fines we'll have to pay for any damage we cause in our profit-and-loss estimation." Henry waved an unconcerned hand. "If we do this fast, though, you'll be back in LA and far away from the noise by the time it starts. We are used to handling these kinds of protests, so it's not pertinent to our decision."

So, destroying the environment or the neighborhood around a new development was business as usual for Platinum Partners.

Sarah knew that there was no way they could accept this offer. No way. Sadie, if she were still around, would be incensed at the idea that they would even consider it.

"Have a lot of experience ruining places, do you?" Jordan said as she rose slowly.

"Bringing jobs to the area. Encouraging the development of restaurants and other amenities that will draw tourists and even people who might want to settle down in Prospect. You know what that means? More tax revenue, better schools and so many other benefits." Henry was counting things on the fingers of his left hand. It was clear he'd given this same answer often enough to have it committed to memory.

"All without any say by the people who are living there." Sarah stood and picked up the folder. Jordan was already headed to the door, her opinion clear.

"Thank you for your time, Henry. I'll take this. I want my lawyers to review it before we decide, but I'll make sure to give you a call in the next few weeks." Sarah nodded and followed Jordan.

Henry must have seen his chances dying on the vine. "Is it the size of the offer? It's generous already."

Sarah met Jordan's stare. Her sister didn't have to say a thing. "I don't believe there is a dollar amount that would make this the right agreement for us, but we'll discuss it with our lawyers. My sister Brooke is in New York, so she couldn't be here today. As the third owner, she'll have some direction on what we do, but anyone who knew Sadie Hearst would understand that this is the wrong decision to honor her legacy."

Confusion wrinkled his smooth forehead. "But Sadie's gone. Her legacy is whatever it will be, right? Wouldn't she want you to make the right choices for your lives now?"

Okay, so that was not a terrible point.

"Sadie raised us. There's no way our legacies aren't tangled together." Jordan yanked the door open on an amazing exit line and marched toward the elevators.

Sarah considered stopping to shake Henry's hand in the accepted manner of all disappointing business discussions, but she could see

Sadie in her mind, telling her she didn't have to make friends with rattlesnakes. Instead, she handed back the folder. "On second thought, we won't need this."

When the elevator doors closed between them and frowning Henry, Jordan said, "Good choice. We aren't taking that offer."

"Not even if Brooke is all in?" Sarah asked as she watched the numbers over the door light up on the way to the ground floor.

"Not even then." Jordan crossed her arms firmly. "If it's money she needs, she can have my share of the settlement of Sadie's assets and give me her vote."

"I doubt that will come anywhere close to four million, Jordan," Sarah said.

"I never said we were going to tell Brooke that part of the offer. Brooke doesn't need to know how many designer outfits she's missing out on by rejecting it."

Jordan narrowed her eyes at Sarah. Was that a warning? Probably. But she had to know there was no way Sarah was going to keep it a secret, either. As long as Brooke understood how terrible this decision would be, it would all work out.

CHAPTER SEVENTEEN

WES'S COMMITMENT TO fully support the heart-strings plan had led him to require every single member of the family to report to the ranch for the breakfast meeting he'd set. Sarah had called to explain she'd need to leave Prospect sooner than expected and he'd leaped into action. Now that they were all here, even Clay, who had arrived at sunrise, crammed into the tiny ranch kitchen, he was having second thoughts.

When his mother smacked Matt's hand away from the bacon she was piling up to serve, he decided he'd gone into third and fourth thoughts.

"When Sarah and Jordan get here, try not to overwhelm them. Let me do the speaking. Until then, we can go in turns around the table, get a refresher course in the manners Mom tried to teach us." Wes caught and held each of his brother's stares while nodding meaningfully. He got a solid nod in return from each one. Then he addressed his mother and father. "I don't know what to say to you two. I…" He wasn't sure how to tell them to act. They'd never listen to his directions, anyway.

"Your show, son. We'll follow your lead," his father drawled before reaching behind Prue's back to grab some bacon.

His mother inhaled slowly, deliberately. "I remember why I quit cooking for you boys. It's chaos and not in a fun way." She set the spatula she'd been smacking hands with down on the counter and moved to pour two mugs of coffee. "Go greet your visitors. I hear them pulling up."

Wes wiped his hands on his jeans and hurried to the front door. Today, he'd fallen back to ranch wear. No more ties for at least another fiscal quarter, thank you.

When the Hearst sisters walked up the stairs, he said, "Thank you for coming. I don't know whether apologizing in advance for my family will help or hurt, but I feel it's the right thing to do." Dressing like himself had been the right decision. Sarah and Jordan would fit right in around the table in their jeans. No one watching from the outside would understand this was a business meeting, one with a lot of money hanging in the balance, but he was happy everyone involved was on the same page.

Jordan touched his shoulder slightly to urge him to step aside. "You forget we come from a large family, too. We've done worse, I bet."

Sarah's smile as she stopped in front of him was sweet. He'd missed it.

"She's right, although I wouldn't have warned you. We're hard-hitting negotiators here." She reached for his hand and squeezed. "Don't worry. We are friends." She waited for him to agree. "Right?"

Friends who had kissed on the porch swing at Bell House and then…never discussed it again?

It was definitely the wrong time to get into that.

Wes nodded and followed them toward the kitchen but Jordan stopped in front of the long parade of family pictures. "Did you force your parents to take down the embarrassing elementary school photos, the ones where your front teeth had fallen out and your cowlick refused to behave, or did you spring forth, completely handsomely formed like this?" She moved slowly down the line of pictures.

Wes frowned as he tried to work out the right answer to that. "We were all adopted. As teenagers?"

Did that answer her question? Had it been a question?

"Oh," Jordan said quietly. Was there a touch of blush in her cheeks? "I didn't know that. Sorry for the snark there."

"She never apologizes for snark," Sarah whispered loudly and clapped her hand over her mouth when Jordan stuck her tongue out.

"That's because there's no need to apologize to sisters, Sarah," Jordan said. She froze in front of one of the photos, but Wes wasn't able to see which of them had caught her attention. When she focused on Wes again, he and Sarah exchanged a glance.

"You okay, Jordan?" Sarah patted her sister's back.

"He's the other buyer—this is a visit to the other buyer, not a visit to the lawyer," Jordan said in a victorious tone. "And the family he's apologizing for, it's every single brother, isn't it? Are they all here somewhere?"

Wes considered the way the question was

worded but couldn't figure out where the trap was, so he said, "Yep. We've got breakfast on the table." Then he motioned them toward the kitchen.

He and Sarah watched Jordan stare at the wood beams overhead. Wes wasn't sure but he thought her lips were moving. He couldn't make out the words. Was she praying or…?

Then she straightened her shoulders and muttered, "Let's get this over with."

Sarah shot him a confused stare but followed her sister. Wes was happy to see that everyone had seated themselves politely at the table. His brothers were farthest away from the head of the table where he, Sarah and Jordan would sit with Prue and Walt forming a nice barrier between the company and his brothers.

"Sarah and Jordan, let me introduce you." Wes pointed as he went. "My parents, Prue and Walt. Then you have Grant, Travis, Matt and Clay."

Each brother waved a hand until he got to Clay. Instead of waving, he said, "Hey, Jordan, long time, no see."

First, Wes turned to Sarah to see if she had any clue. The slight shake of her head told him she was lost, too. They both looked at Jordan.

"Hey, Clay." She hurried to pull her chair out and take a seat, blushing and furiously ignoring how the rest of the family was enjoying the unexpected drama between her and Clay.

Wes cleared his throat. "Okay, well…" He pulled Sarah's chair out and waited until she was seated. "I wanted to discuss our plans for the ranch. We have an offer prepared for you, but I want to make sure you understand why it is what it is. We won't be able to match even the conservative number the real estate agent threw out. I expect her final number to be higher." He rubbed his forehead. "And I'm certain Platinum Partners' offer was even higher."

Jordan put her napkin in her lap. "Not that we need to worry about that. We won't be taking his offer."

"Well, we can't exactly toss it out right now." Sarah licked her lips. "You're right. It's an amazing offer, but we haven't spoken to Brooke about it yet. And it has serious problems. Jordan has concerns, and I can't say I blame her."

Wes watched the way Sarah was concentrating on Prue and wondered again what they'd talked about the afternoon he'd found Sarah attempting embroidery in Handmade. Why hadn't he asked for more information?

"Okay, well, I've put together our all-in best offer. We can't go any higher, no matter what the top number might be. But first, let's eat. Business is better on a full stomach." Wes motioned at his mother to get her to start passing plates around.

"Now who taught you that, Wes?" his father drawled as he took a fluffy biscuit out of the basket passing in front of him.

"You did. Taught me everything I know about business." Wes smiled at Sarah to show her this was all normal, perfectly fine. The conversation was stilted. Neither Jordan nor Clay contributed anything to it. She stared hard at her plate, even as she cleared it, and Wes wasn't sure Clay ever took his eyes off her face.

At some point, yelling at his brother for not giving him the whole history of his relationship with the Hearsts, whatever it turned out to be, would have to hit the top of his to-do list.

But not today.

"Travis, you start. Tell the Hearsts about your plan to foster kids here at the ranch." Wes relaxed in his chair as both Sarah and Jordan gave his brother their full attention.

"The five of us had our lives changed when we landed here at the Rocking A with Walt and Prue. Whatever our lives were before, after that, we had a real family, a strong community, work that yielded rewards, and the potential to do things we couldn't ever imagine before. I joined the army. We have an actual rodeo star at the table. And the rest? They made it to college, law school, veterinary school. It was Prue and Walt that gave us that chance." Travis rubbed a hand over his lips. Wes could tell his brother was nervous. He didn't make speeches, and they wouldn't see him for days after this while he recovered, but Travis knew it mattered.

And an Armstrong could do anything it took when it mattered.

"More than that, this place made me okay again. I grew up bouncing around and forcing myself to fit safely in whatever space I was offered. I had to, to protect myself. For a long time, I struggled with that, but here I had both space and time. There were wide open pasture and sunlight and so much more. I want to offer that same chance of hope, of potential. I want a new generation of kids at the Rocking A to have what we did. No one will understand them better than us." Travis fidgeted with his collar while he worked out the next part of the speech.

Sarah touched Wes's hand. He wasn't sure what it meant, but he was happy to tangle their fingers together.

"To do that, we have to make changes. I've spoken with the agency that will certify us as a foster home, and there are hurdles. The easiest of those hurdles is to make renovations to this house." Travis motioned with his head. "There haven't been any since we moved in, and you can tell it. For us, it's fine. No need to invest the time or money, but for a kid... we have to update a lot. Now that Grant and I have moved back home, place is bursting at the seams anyway. We need to add on separate living quarters for Dad, at the minimum, reconfigure the rooms we've got and add on at least one more bedroom. Clay here can design it all and organize the renovations for us."

Clay crossed his arms over his chest. "I'm ready to get started."

"We had planned to build a couple of cabins to give Grant more room and then to set Matt up with a real veterinary office closer to the highway for visits from town," Wes added, "but we're going to put those ideas on hold for now."

"I'll see about a place in Prospect, divide my time up between there, making all my house calls and here with the Rocking A's livestock," Matt said with a wave, "burn up the road in between."

"I'm going to take some time off from my construction company in Colorado Springs, come home to work on the renovations myself to keep the costs low," Clay said. "We've prioritized the list in terms of need and impact, and built a tight budget based around that."

Wes opened his laptop so that Sarah could see the small slideshow he'd built.

"Those are the plans we're placing on hold to pull funds for the purchase of Sadie's land. Additionally, I want to increase the herd size now that Grant is home, because that's what keeps the ranch in business. More hands can mean more business, but for that we need more pasture. We can do that eventually if we incorporate Sadie's pasture. Buying Sadie's land back restores the Rocking A to what the original Armstrongs worked. But this is Travis's dream. Nothing matters more than that to any of us now." Wes knew it was on the tip of Travis's tongue to protest because he hated to be at the center of things. But no one at the table doubted how much it mattered to every one of the Armstrongs that they continue the endeavor Prue and Walt started.

"So, here's where we began," Wes said, as he showed Sarah and Jordan the best number he could free up by putting things on hold and selling what he could without jeopardizing the ranch itself. "Five hundred thousand dollars." Which was nothing to get excited about but then he had to add the bad news. "Less ten percent which we've set aside for Clay's initial renovations to meet the agency's minimum standards. I'm proposing a large lump-sum payment of three hundred thousand dollars, followed by scheduled payments, including interest over the course of the next five years to reach the full amount."

It wasn't enough. Everyone at the table knew it, but he'd promised to do the best he

could to show the Hearsts that Sadie's property had more value than just the financial
one. Wes was comfortable they could meet
the demands of this offer without jeopardizing the stock and other promises and guaran-
tees they'd made. If Grant decided to spend
any of his nest egg on more cattle, they might
be able to accelerate the payments, but this
proposal was steady, reasonable.

This was the way he would do business.

But he knew how far off the mark they
were when he saw Sarah's face. She immediately attempted to cover up what was most
likely dismay with a confident smile.

Jordan slumped in her seat. "I was hoping
for something to make this decision easier.
That's not it."

Sarah added, "I appreciate you explaining
everything that's happening here at the Rocking A. That does matter." Wes watched her
nod to his mother as if they were communicating on a deeper level. "You asked me how I
feel about kids. I understand. I know what this
decision could mean." Then she turned to face
him. "Would you email me your outline? Jordan and I are calling Brooke to discuss our options this afternoon before we return to LA."

She shrugged. "I don't know that we'll have an answer immediately." But it was possible. Wes had a hunch that they expected Brooke to have firm opinions, and even now, he could see that Jordan wasn't in favor of selling to his family at such a loss.

He had never had high hopes, so why was he struggling now?

Wes nodded his agreement. "I'll walk you to the car, then, and we'll wait for a decision or direction on what you'd like me to do next as the property manager." Clay stood at the same time Wes moved back from the table. Were they about to find out what might be between his brother and Jordan?

"Jordan, I'd love to catch up." Clay waited for her to stand and followed behind her. "Let me show you the barn."

Wes waited for Jordan to argue. Hadn't Sarah said her sister was not a fan of horses? Instead, Jordan spoke generally in the direction of everyone around the table and avoided Clay's corner altogether. "It was a lovely breakfast. Thank you for the invitation."

Sarah raised her eyebrows as her sister left the kitchen, presumably for the barn, Clay two steps behind. Whatever was going on between them, she was in the dark, too.

"Yes, thank you, everyone." Sarah went to go, but his mother said, "I hope you'll stop in to say goodbye before you leave town, Sarah. At Handmade?"

Sarah pointed at her. "Yes, ma'am, I'll be in to make good on my tab before I take off. I found the apron I was telling you about, the one my mom made for Sadie. I thought you might like to see it." She spoke a little uncertainly. Wes wondered if his mother made her nervous. Probably so. Prue Armstrong made him nervous now and again.

"Of course I would. I don't know how long it will be before I see you again, so I don't want to miss my chance to wish you luck." Prue stood and moved around the table to wrap her arms around Sarah in a hug. "It was good to remember Sadie with you."

"It really was," Sarah agreed. He recalled her saying something about expecting to find Sadie again in Prospect. He was glad his mother had helped with that. "Well, then…" Her voice trailed off. There wasn't anything to add.

Sarah waved before heading for the front

door. When they stepped out into the shade of the yard, she paused and stared up at the blue sky and inhaled slowly. "Today I want to cry because your mother was nice to me. What is that about?"

"It's usually the other way around—us driving my mother to tears. No wonder she was so sad to see you go," Wes drawled.

Her giggles eased some of the tight tension in his chest.

"You still think I'm the handsome one, right? Of all the Armstrongs? When I realized you had me in first place, I floated for days."

Watching her delight slowly fade reminded him that he'd failed his family.

If he was reading her correctly, Sarah had hoped she might be able to swing the sale his way, too.

"I wish this was all happening at a different time. A year. Even six months from now. Things would be easier. I can't ask Travis to wait. He needs this. Since he's come home from the army, he's been focused on his goal. It's so important." Wes tangled his fingers through hers and pulled her closer. When she stepped up next to him and rested her head in the center of his chest, he felt the rightness settle in deep.

"Four million dollars, Wes," Sarah said as he held her tight. "Can you imagine saying no to that?"

It would be tough.

"But we're going to do it. Say no. Platinum Partners would destroy this whole town and the Majestic." She leaned away from him. "I have no idea what Brooke will say or do, but we can't let that happen. Jordan and I agree on that."

Wes brushed the hair away from her eyes. "Makes it harder to say no to the reasonable real estate agent's plan, though, doesn't it? Closer to two million, after everything is all said and done and parceled out, is a good compromise."

She didn't agree but she didn't have to. The sadness on her face confirmed it.

"I can't believe how depressed I am to be going back to LA." She traced a fingertip over his forehead. "I only planned to be here for the weekend, and would return home with an easy, clear decision."

"Trying to erase some of my worries?" he

asked and closed his eyes to commit the feeling of her skin against his to memory.

"I wish I could. After this morning, I understand even better how much weight you're carrying, for your family, for Prospect. It's too much. Are you still going to be our property manager?" Sarah wrinkled her nose.

"You mean after you dash all my family's hopes and dreams?" Wes asked and chuckled at the grimace on her face. "Sure. I don't think there are any hard feelings here."

"If that's true, the Armstrongs are better people than the Hearsts would be in the same position." Sarah stood on her tiptoes to press another kiss to his lips. They paused there, together in the moment. Wes didn't want her to go.

Wes wrapped his arm around her waist to hold her close. "I expect we're much the same. We want to do the best for our families, Hearsts and Armstrongs alike."

Sarah squeezed him tight before she stepped back. "Okay. I'll hit the road to Denver to catch my flight. I'll talk to you as soon as I know our decision and when we'll be back in Prospect."

He held her hand tightly but whatever he might have said was lost when Jordan stormed out of the barn, stomping like she had a burr under her saddle. "Stop kissing. We need to go." She climbed into the passenger seat, slammed the car door and yanked her seat belt on.

Sarah inhaled slowly and exhaled loudly. Wes was familiar with the feeling.

"I'll see what I can find out from Clay. You do the same with Jordan. We'll compare notes. Surely, we can write the whole story from there," Wes murmured before winking at Sarah.

She gave him a thumbs-up. "This is good. I like it." She groaned as she added, "I can't believe how much I hate saying goodbye to you, Wes."

Stay. Don't go. Let's go for a ride.

He wanted the right words, but they didn't come.

"She's not the boss of me. Jordan. It's important to remind them of who is first," Sarah said as she slipped her arms over his shoulders. "Will you kiss me again?"

What he wanted was the quiet, private porch swing.

What he had was the front yard with an audience of who-knew-how-many watching.

Wes studied her face, her dark eyes, the splash of pink across her nose and the tops of her cheeks. A loud car honk made them both jerk.

"Your sister's kind of…a lot," Wes said.

"You have no idea. I will kill her after I use her vote to shoot down Platinum's offer," Sarah vowed.

Wes was smiling as he pressed his lips to hers and none of that was important anymore. The place fell away. The audience disappeared. All that mattered was Sarah.

Who fit perfectly against him.

Until she moved slowly away, her fingers trailing down his arm until she straightened her shoulders and headed for the car. Sarah waved before she drove off, and a weight settled across his shoulders.

He understood what she meant about saying goodbye.

It was hard.

But not as hard as it would be when Sarah left for the last time.

When she returned to Prospect to wrap up listing the property, it would be her final visit. There would be nothing to bring her back.

CHAPTER EIGHTEEN

SARAH WAS EXHAUSTED when she dropped her luggage inside her front door after a long trip home to LA. The emotional swings from angry arguing to worried searching for different solutions to confused, sad and really sad bouts of tears had taken their toll.

After she and Jordan had left the Rocking A, they'd argued all the way back to Prospect about who Clay Armstrong was to Jordan, why Sarah had been kissing Wes in front of the whole world again and whether or not to tell Brooke every detail about the offers or to make the decision and inform her about it later.

In the end, Sarah had learned nothing about Clay, but she had threatened to offer him Jordan's phone number if her sister didn't stop giving her so much grief about Wes. She and Jordan had barely agreed to disagree about what to tell Brooke. They'd postponed their plan to schedule an update until after the board meeting since it might have some impact on their decision.

Instead of exploring Prospect, she and Jordan had plopped down on opposite ends of the B-and-B's porch swing with their laptops. Sarah had decided to go through her work email before she had to show up at headquarters. Jordan had been playing solitaire and building an inspiration board of what looked like braided rugs and quilts that might work on hotel beds when she thought Sarah couldn't see over her shoulder.

If they were speaking to each other in anything other than mean glares at that point, Sarah would have asked if Jordan was killing time or was she getting serious about a plan to reopen the lodge.

Picking out decor was one thing, the fun thing. Figuring out how to pay for it? Was Jordan even considering that?

Luckily, dinner at the Ace High was excellent, and they hadn't needed conversation other than yum.

The next morning, Sarah had been relieved when she'd stopped in at Handmade to pay for her purchases. Prue had hugged her again, as if it was hard to say goodbye.

Jordan had hugged her hard, too, but had refused to say anything other than "be careful on the way home" before she'd loaded her suitcase in the rented car and turned toward Denver.

And if that didn't capture life with a younger sister in a nutshell, what did?

Sarah half leaned, half squatted on her suitcase and pulled out her phone to find the family group text. She typed *I'm home* and hit Send because the rule was they let each other know when they made it home safely, no matter how mad they might be about anything else.

Jordan replied with a thumbs-up. The end. Sarah went straight for her bed and collapsed back on the mattress. She had approximately one million things to do before heading into the Cookie Queen headquarters in the morning, but at this point, she was too tired to move.

Or too sad.

Possibly both tired and sad.

Before she knew it was happening, she was asleep. Sarah woke up as the sun was rising. She grimaced at the clothes she left Prospect in, all wrinkled after a drive to Denver, circling the airport twice to return the rental, a delayed flight, a race through her connecting airport, two jammed flights and almost ten hours of sleep.

She dropped her clothes in a pile as she stepped into a hot shower. She'd consider burning them later.

Then she realized she had never gotten any scoop from her father about this meeting she was crashing.

As she soaped her hair, she called him and put him on the speaker. When he answered, she said, "Hey, Dad, yes, I'm in the shower, but I need any information you can give me about this meeting." She tilted her head back to rinse the shampoo out of her hair.

"The queen of multitasking. It's weird, Sarah, but I don't see any hope of changing you at this point. Good trip to Prospect?"

This was why she hadn't waited until she was showered, dressed and fully caffeinated. He could never come straight to the point. He had the Hearst manner of winding up to tell a story instead.

"It was good. We have a few options, but only one that makes perfect sense. I think we'll end up listing for sale as a vacation home lot on Key Lake." No matter how she evaluated the choices, that plan came out on top when she considered everyone involved.

"You don't sound pleased." Her father had always paid as much attention to her voice as her words.

"No matter what we do, we're losing Sadie. It's hard to be content with that." Sarah turned off the water and grabbed her fluffy towel. It was the last clean one. Laundry was swiftly becoming priority one.

"Yeah," her dad said. "Well, that's connected to the reason Michael wants you at the board meeting. Sadie's office, her home, the headquarters, they all have so many pieces of memorabilia that Sadie loved, you know? She earmarked certain pieces for each of us, but there's still so much more to…"

When he trailed off, Sarah asked, "Dispose of? Is that what Michael wants me to do? Approve dumping Sadie's stuff?" Because she was never going to do that. Sarah surveyed her two-bedroom condo and realized immediately there would be no way to house Sadie's things from Prospect there, much less whatever it was Michael wanted moved out. "No, I won't authorize that. The corporation will need to rent space or something. I'll go through everything and…" And what?

Could she find museums that might like some of Sadie's items?

"Exactly what he wants to discuss. It's a good sign he invited you," her dad said.

Invitation? That wasn't how Sarah remembered it, but arguing the point now didn't make much sense.

"Okay, I'm glad to know some of the background. I'll see if I can find reasonable warehouse space somewhere close to the headquarters before the board meeting. We can clear her house, the apartment and the lodge, move everything there to evaluate what to do next."

Her father agreed. "I knew you'd figure it out. You never disappoint."

Sarah closed her eyes as she wondered if that was true. Never disappointed? On the things that mattered most to her, she couldn't find the answers that made her happy.

"I'll see you later, Dad. I'm going to go in early, see what Michael has done to my office." Sarah ended the call and moved to her closet. She was going to dress the part, just as she had to go see Platinum Partners. Michael might be family, but they were not usually on the same side of an issue.

She pulled out three different dresses, tried them on, tossed them all on the bed and then decided on her favorite navy suit. Sadie had always told her she was wearing her firing suit when she'd worn it to work.

When she walked into the lobby of the Cookie Queen Corporation, Sarah was happy she'd put on her business armor. It seemed Michael was moving quickly to give the whole place a facelift. Fresh paint had covered up the red-and-white-checked Welcome greeting that covered the wall behind the reception desk. Everything was stark white.

Mandy the receptionist said, "Good morning, Sarah. It's nice to have you back."

Sarah pointed at the bare wall. "What's going on here?"

Mandy motioned over her shoulder. "The plan is to put a portrait of Sadie there with a history of the company and then smaller shots of the current board of directors." She shrugged. "According to the company email, the goal with any renovations is to pay homage to the history of the company while com-

municating clearly the goals for the future."
She recited it from memory as if she'd had
plenty of opportunity to get the wording
down correctly.

She hadn't made it that far down in her
inbox, so she was glad she had Mandy's recap
before the meeting.

"Thanks, Mandy." Sarah considered that as
she waited for the elevator. It was a good goal,
honestly. The place could use an update and it
wasn't a bad time to do that as long as it was
done carefully. Sadie's employees were loyal
because she was one of the few bosses in the
world who meant it when she said she viewed
them as family. She'd made personal loans to
more than one employee, never missed send-
ing a gift for a birth or flowers for a funeral.

When Sarah stepped off the elevator in
front of her office, she realized she approved
of Michael's decision. That was new.

Then she opened the door to her office, a
small but comfortable little spot that was superior to the cubicle she'd moved out of by
virtue of the door. It wasn't spacious but it
was quiet.

And today, the door banged hard on something that made it necessary for Sarah to

shimmy in the small opening before turning on the light.

That something? The absolutely immense painting of Sadie's beloved mountains. It had come down from Sadie's office, traveled through her lawyer's conference room and then been squeezed into Sarah's office when she wasn't around to object.

This was the Michael she was used to. It was nice to return to comfortable footing.

With the painting wedged into the remaining space beside her desk, getting behind it to reach her computer meant sliding across the top.

The pile of mail she bumped into teetered but Sarah managed to catch it before it toppled below where it would never have been seen again. That was until the building was disassembled and the painting thereby removed from her office.

"This is fine. Sadie, if this was what you wanted for me, I guess this is fine." Sarah bit her lip as she waited for her laptop to boot up. "You could have made my job secure, but no. Instead, I work in a storage closet."

Sarah angrily spread the mail out on her desk, slapping junk mail in one pile, misdirected mail in another, things she'd need to respond to in a third, and tried to calm down. When she saw a lumpy envelope from Sadie's lawyers, she grabbed it out of the stack. Was this the letter Sadie had promised? Maybe there was more here to explain why Sadie had left her job hanging like this.

The card that Sarah pulled from the envelope was pure Sadie. It was a picture of a grinning horse with the question "Why is it hard to talk to a racehorse?" Sarah felt the sting of tears as she opened the card and read, "They don't hang around furlong." The joke was so bad and so Sadie that she had to giggle even as the tears slipped down her cheeks.

The piece of paper that slipped out carried the scent that would always remind her of Sadie. It was a mix of vanilla and a clean, sunny floral.

Sarah set the thumb drive that also landed on her desk aside. When she opened the letter, it was another emotional pinch to see her great-aunt's bold, scrawling cursive. Every note Sadie ever wrote might as well have been an autograph. It had flair and style. This note was also short and sweet. "Sarah, stop crying and put the thumb drive in your computer, my beautiful girl."

"Even when she's gone, she's still bossy," Sarah muttered as she followed directions. When the file appeared on-screen, Sarah clicked on it to play. What did she want Sadie to tell her?

Two things, really.

First, what she expected Sarah to do with the rest of her life, since it did not appear to be working at the Cookie Queen.

Second, what she wanted to happen with the lodge.

Sarah had a feeling neither one was contained in Sadie's message.

"I bet you didn't expect us to meet again this way, did you, sweet Sarah?" Sadie asked with a twinkle in her eyes. This message had been taped at the same time as the video they'd watched in the lawyer's office. Sadie was in bed, propped up, but she was still herself. Strong. Funny. Slightly annoying in the way that the most beloved relatives can be. "I know you are dying to ask questions. You always were the one who needed to know more. Jordan would shoot off like a bucking bronco soon as the gate opened. Brooke had to be coaxed, prodded and pushed to get her in motion, but you liked to go slow and steady, an easy walk instead of a gallop. This thing with the lodge is a puzzle, isn't it?" Sadie sipped some water. "I can't tell you the answer, but it relates to the other burning question. If you want to stay here and work the rest of your life, do that. You have everything you need to make it happen. Smarts. Respect of your co-workers. Everything I know I passed along." Sadie fluffed her hair. "You don't have to thank me for that part. We both know it ain't nothing to toot my horn about, but the fact is you can do more. If you want to."

Sarah leaned forward. She didn't want this to end, even if Sadie had nothing else to say.

"I loved having you with me, working by my side. I never could stand to be too far away from you girls, not when I knew how much you needed me. In my mind, if I was there, I could keep you safe." Sadie rolled her eyes. "Although that Jordan tested all my powers of persuasion, didn't she? Leaving you three behind is difficult. This is the only way it could be accomplished." She cleared her throat. "Please, have a real good visit in Prospect. I was me there, more me than I have ever been. It's a place that makes that possible, lots of space and air and light, like we're all plants and we grow better there. I tried to give the whole world a piece of that through the power of the TV." She wrinkled her nose. "I'm a grandiose old woman, ain't I? And I bet you're scribblin' notes down, determined to carry forth my orders. I loved that about you even while it was as annoying as a horsefly in June. You three have the Majestic, not because I need you to determine what happens to it, but because I think that lodge can determine what happens for you." On the video, Sadie waved at someone. "Nurse is here to give me a painkiller and just in time. Humble and heartfelt has come over me when I wanted ornery and bossy. I haven't answered anything, have I? I didn't intend to." She waggled her eyebrows. "But if I can pull any strings from up above to send a handsome cowboy across your path to further muddy up the waters of your future, I'm going to do it. I expect you to display my picture in a prominent place at the wedding." Her grin was contagious. "In the meantime, make sure to tell the cousins you got your own personalized video. It's good to foster competition now and then." She pressed her hand to her mouth and blew Sarah a kiss. "Love you more than the mountains, sweet Sarah."

She was waving and talking to whoever was recording when the video ended.

Sarah brushed tears off her cheeks and tried not to sniff loudly enough to disturb her coworkers. A glance out of the corner of her eye reminded her of the painted mountains that were looming over her desk and the laughter felt good, the perfect chaser for the bittersweet shot of love and loss of Sadie's recorded message.

The ding of the alarm on her phone warned her she had ten minutes to clear up her tears, reapply some makeup and make it to the board meeting. Whatever Michael wanted, Sarah knew that Sadie would expect her to be bossy and ornery in her stead. She could do that.

So when she walked into the executive conference room, Sarah was prepared. She hugged her uncles and her father, shook hands with Wil and then patted Michael on the back. "You've been busy." Satisfied that her comments could be construed as either praise or a threat, Sarah took her seat and clicked her pen. "Who are we missing?"

Michael glanced around the room. "No one. This is an informal meeting of the board to discuss options. Once we've decided, I'll have something formal drafted up to send out to the company, a press release if necessary, that kind of thing." He pointed at a stack of printouts in the center of the table. Sarah took one off the top and passed it to her father. "This is a partial inventory of items that Howard Marshall is requesting direction on. You can see that the list runs the gamut, from small appliances to paintings with no real resale value, files Sadie kept of recipe development for her books, old photos with celebrities who appeared on her shows." He held his hand out. "A lifetime of things all related to Sadie. Her true assets were carefully distributed and marked for sale or gift, but there's so much more here."

The list made her think of the embroidered apron Jordan had encouraged her to take from the kitchen at the Majestic. It had no "true" value but was priceless to her.

"The absolutely enormous painting crammed

into my office… Is it on the list?" Sarah asked as she flipped through the pages.

"No," Michael said, "but it had to go… somewhere. All this stuff has to go somewhere."

Sarah nodded. "Right. And you have a proposal, I'm guessing. That instead of working here at the Cookie Queen, I take over all the stuff and I put it somewhere…else, out of your way."

Michael straightened his tie. "Yes, in a manner of speaking, but I had an idea for a permanent display of mementos. You may not have seen the email I sent out regarding our new aesthetic. It will impact our decor here as well as our brand identity. We're going to honor our past but move forward to a future Sadie would have wanted." He tapped the list. "These celebrity photos? I can see a display of those here. We need a curator to evaluate what fits the level of display, things that speak to the Cookie Queen's history. That's what I want you to do for us. Take this project, curate the items and make it worthy of Sadie." He sighed. "We both know how I feel about your 'job' as customer relations director. Not a real thing. Marketing? Sales? Those are real things." He cleared his throat. "But no one knew Sadie better than you. This position can make a significant difference for the company and for Sadie's family."

Sarah glanced at her father who was watching her, and then at the others around the table.

She met Michael's stare. He was sitting in Sadie's usual spot, and instead of his normal suspicious expression, he was earnest. Or was it hopeful? It was alarming to see the change on his face.

"You are the perfect person for this, Sarah. Please say yes. We'll give you a budget and control over the design of the space we set aside for it…" He sighed. "I'm not sure about that yet, where we'll fit it. We may need a separate location constructed, but we'll do that under your direction. And pay you a salary. And you can take whatever time you need to get the lodge sale finalized."

When the silence grew too loud, Sarah realized she was going to have to say something here.

But what?

She was going to have to fight through the rising excitement and unusual, growing love and gratitude for her oldest cousin, to come up with something.

"In Prospect, I was searching for Sadie. But the Majestic is weathered and the grounds nothing like what she would have allowed. It was heartbreaking. I wanted to sell it, get back in the car, come home and try to not think about it anymore." Sarah fiddled with the corners of the printouts in front of her. "Then I went inside and saw this display of photos, posters, newspaper clippings from when Sadie's cookbooks hit the bestseller list. I found an apron Mom made for Sadie. I talked with folks who knew her. They shared impact she'd had on them, even women who learned to bake thanks to Sadie and one who served a recipe of Sadie's on her menu at the restaurant."

Where was she going with this? Sarah was picking her way through the overgrown path as she talked.

"Obviously, I want to do this, Michael. I get it that this isn't your…forte?" Sarah said and realized she sounded a bit like Sadie at that point. When her father laughed, she felt stronger.

"Good." Michael relaxed against his seat.

"First item I need you to take care of is find a giant warehouse. We need to start clearing the LA house quickly. Howard has a buyer who's interested, but the offer is pending on how soon they can move in."

Sarah sniffed, crossed her arms over her chest and tried to channel Sadie. A plan was slowly forming in her mind. "One moment." Sarah scribbled a nonsense note on the paper in front of her to buy time. "Would the company be prepared to pay a lease, a fee for space rental, if I could suggest an alternate location for the perfect Cookie Queen *museum*?"

"Do you mean in Prospect?" Michael asked, a frown wrinkling his brow. "We need it closer."

Sarah nodded. She'd expected him to say that. "We'll do that too, exactly what you want here, with displays that fit the new and improved headquarters, that tell the story, but we both know we're talking about a fraction of the things Sadie collected over a lifetime. There are also all her taped shows and cookbooks and apparel and so many things. What if we had a showcase for all of that?" Sarah was spitballing, the words coming out of her mouth almost as soon as they formed in her brain.

"Are you reopening the Majestic as a museum?" her father asked. "It could work beautifully there."

"If we do, will you come visit?" Sarah knew it would be hard for him to return. He'd face the loss of both Sadie and his wife there.

"I'll book my room now." He clasped her hand under the table. "It has been too long since I've been to the mountains."

Michael's mouth was quirked on one side. Was it a grin? The beginnings of one?

"I don't know if it's the time away, but I can see the great Sadie Hearst in you right now." He nodded. "Yes, we'll pay for a lease to house Cookie Queen memorabilia at the lodge if you decide to keep it and it works. I want the best room at the grand reopening. Don't put me next to the lobby. When we stayed there in the summer, fishermen woke me up before sunrise tromping on those old wood floors." Michael waited for her to agree. "I don't know that another space in Prospect itself fits as well. If you decide to sell the Majestic, you and I can agree on where we build something to honor Sadie. We will cover the rent to store items that do not fit there or here but may be worked into rotating displays. You'll be the director."

Sarah could feel something bubbling up in her soul, the kind of lightness that she'd always associated with the joy of Sadie's warm welcomes. This was the purpose she'd been missing all along.

Sarah clicked her pen again. "I have other ideas I'd like to pitch at some point, things I believe will fit in with the new Cookie Queen's direction."

Michael raised a brow. "Like?"

The ideas were percolating under the surface, but it was too soon to share them.

First, she needed to convince her sisters that renovating the Majestic was the right thing to do.

Jordan was already teetering on the edge. Brooke might need a push.

That reminded her of how Sadie had described them all so perfectly.

"Let's finalize the details for this partnership. That will give us the foundation for the next step." Sarah realized that she had definitely zigged when the whole world expected her to zag, a page right out of Sadie Hearst's playbook. Her father, Michael, the board... they expected her to accept their offer gratefully, not negotiate for concessions.

Her sisters expected her to agree to sell the lodge. Instead, she was tying her whole future to holding on to it.

And Wes Armstrong, his family and her neighbors in Prospect expected the Hearsts to leave again.

Sarah wasn't sure what would happen when people learned that she had more Sadie in her than she'd previously shown, but she was up to the challenge.

CHAPTER NINETEEN

WES SADDLED UP Arrow before the sun had completely cleared the ridge of the mountains and rode out in time to avoid meeting his brothers on Saturday morning. He'd spent every minute since Grant had moved back in refereeing arguments and he needed space to restore his nerves. Immediately.

Under normal circumstances, his brothers got along well enough. For many years, they'd been scattered here and there, leaving him, his father and Matt to negotiate the ranch house's limited space. Now? It was like a herd of bulls had been shut up in a china shop. Clay was in town and determined to start demolition today on the wall they planned to knock through to add on a space for their father.

Probably because he needed to hit something and wanted to make the hole in the wall count.

Travis hadn't uttered more than three words after their meeting with the Hearsts. Eventually, Wes was going to have to address that issue.

Wes inhaled slowly as Arrow shook his head. "Sorry. I don't need to be taking my bad mood out on you."

Arrow nodded once but that was all he had to say on the matter, and Wes appreciated that. His horse was always a good listener. "What do you think? Mountains or lake?"

Wes waited to see which way Arrow would go. Nine times out of ten, the answer was lake, but today the horse continued up the rise that would lead to Larkspur Pass. From there, Wes could turn back and see the Rocking A spread out below or he could face forward and pretend he was the only man on earth. Today the choice was easy. Arrow knew the destination well and headed for his favorite shady patch of grass. Wes slid out of the saddle and tied the horse's halter to the sturdy Rocky Mountain maple situated next to one of Wes's favorite thinking spots, a rounded outcropping perfectly shaped to hold a seated cowboy.

Wes pulled his hat off so the breeze stirred

his hair as he scanned the pasture below. Cattle were following the movement of the sun as they grazed. He could see splashes of pink from the shrubby wax currant blooms scattered around the green grass. It was peaceful. Quiet.

But his mind kept turning.

Wes's biggest issue?

What to do about missing Sarah Hearst as much as he did.

It surprised him. She hadn't been there long enough for him to miss her like this.

Every time that thought tumbled through his brain, it was swiftly followed by a worse one: he was going to have months, years to get over that because her next visit would also be her last.

On the day she'd traveled to LA, he hadn't been able to sleep because he didn't know that she'd made it home safely.

She'd mentioned the board meeting was on Friday and that was why she had to go back to California, so on Friday afternoon he'd stopped more than once and wondered what it might mean to Sarah and her future. Thinking about her future led right into worrying about his own without her.

He'd battled the urge to demand answers when he saw Jordan in the Ace High on Friday night. In the end, he'd sat at a different table and watched her scroll through her phone until she'd glared at him and snapped, "Are you going to lurk every time I come into town?"

If he hadn't had years of practice dealing with the scourge of younger siblings, Wes might have lost his temper. Instead, he smiled. His brothers always got nervous when he flipped the script. It had to work with sisters, too. "I'm surprised you're still in Prospect. Is Sarah on her way back?" It was the only thing that made sense, that Jordan was staying because they were moving quickly to settle the Majestic. He'd been happy and sad at the same time that Sarah would be in town soon.

Jordan had shrugged. "Probably. She's postponed our decision about the lodge until she's arrived."

The answer only raised more questions but Wes hadn't pursued any of them.

After a long moment, Jordan got up and moved over to slide into the booth across from him. "If you like her, do something about it. Speak up. Ask her to stay or something. Please."

Reading her expression wasn't easy, but Wes thought she was trying to encourage him.

To do what? That was even less clear. Then he'd made the mistake of asking what her history was with Clay, and Jordan had marched up to pay her bill and escape the Ace High before he could follow.

Thus, the ride to his thinking spot along with his adviser Arrow.

Wes rested against the rock and stretched out his legs to stare up at the sky, brilliantly blue with wispy clouds drifting past. If he asked Sarah to stay, shouldn't he have a plan for what came next?

Didn't he always have a plan?

He'd just closed his eyes when his phone rang. "The most important feature of my thinking spot, that cell coverage is so spotty, lets me down when I need it most," he muttered as he dug in his shirt pocket to retrieve his phone. When he saw Sarah's name, he jerked upright and dropped the phone in his hurry to answer the call.

His hello was breathless and when she

didn't immediately answer, he was afraid the call had disconnected that quickly. "Sarah?"

"Hey, am I catching you at a bad time?" she asked. He could hear hesitation in her voice.

"No, of course not. I'm available for you any time you need me." He squeezed his eyes shut again. "To call me, I mean."

In the silence between them, he pictured the small frown on her forehead that appeared when she was thinking hard. "I was surprised I have cell reception. I rode up to Larkspur Pass this morning."

"Already? I guess you have to work from sunup to sundown to get all those hats on, don't you?" Sarah said. He thought he heard a smile in her voice. "I don't want to keep you from your...rustling? Herding? What should I call it?"

Wes stared down at his boots comfortably crossed at the ankles and Arrow who had moved closer to the stand of trees to lazily scratch an itch. "Let's go with work and leave it at that." He shook his head. "How are you? How did the board meeting go?" He forced himself to stop at the two questions. They covered the most important topics.

"I'm good. Everything went better than I

expected. My cousin offered me a new job for the Cookie Queen corporation and I think I'm going to take it. I haven't told Jordan that yet, so if you run into her, please keep that between you and me, okay?"

Wes nodded and realized she couldn't see that. "Sure. Of course. Congratulations." He rubbed his chest at the sudden ache that appeared. Continuing her career for the Cookie Queen would mean living in LA. What could he offer her that would ever make Prospect a viable alternative?

"Thanks. I'm so excited by this plan that I have, but I need one piece from you before I present it to Brooke and Jordan. Do you have time to draw up another offer for us to consider?" Sarah asked.

Wes knew he'd have time to mourn the Hearsts selling off their only reason to return to Prospect later. Sarah was all business. He could be, too. "I can, but nothing has changed on our end."

"Right," Sarah said, "I get that, but I had an idea. You said you wanted all of the land, but what you need is the pasture. That's the key to expanding the herd. You don't need the marina or the run-down lodge or even the land it sits on. Can you take a look at the acreage that hasn't been developed, whatever is still pasture, and draw up a proposal to split it that way?"

Wes sat up and propped his elbow on his knee as he considered her question. "Sure. I can do that. That should make it easier for the real estate agent to list it, too." And his family might be able to cobble together the purchase price without the extended payment period. It would mean Sarah and her sisters would have an immediate infusion of cash while they waited for the marina and the lodge to sell.

"I want to make sure that the sale happens with an agreement that grants right-of-way access from the highway to the Majestic in perpetuity because whoever owns the lodge will need to cross that pasture, so can you put on your lawyer hat and draw that up for me?" Sarah added. "I'm not sure about the terms on how to determine the upkeep on common use areas like the lane that both properties would use, but I bet you've handled that before."

He had. It was completely common when negotiating pasture sales.

"Sure thing." Wes realized she'd handed

him a load of work, but he was energized by it all. He and his family had thought the door was shut on a possible purchase. Maybe it had, but Sarah was opening a window and holding her hand out for him to climb through.

"Good. I have a few things to take care of here in LA, but I'm going to be in Prospect next week. This time, I'm driving, so it'll take a bit longer. Thursday? Could we meet on Thursday? At your office. Bring Clay if he's around. I'll drag Jordan along. It will be interesting, if nothing else," Sarah said, drawling the last part theatrically. "I haven't gotten a single bit of gossip from her, although that might be because we're just now back on speaking terms."

Wes realized he was hearing a new side of her on this phone call.

She was confident. He could detect excitement bubbling under the surface, too.

This job offer had made a positive change for her.

It was hard to be upset about it, even if it meant there was no way she'd leave LA for good now.

"Clay will be happy for the chance to sit down for a minute. He and Grant started work on the extension for my dad's new quarters and every day I'm afraid they're going to turn their hammers on each other. He's not saying much of anything right now. I'm scared to ask him about Jordan." Wes smiled as she laughed. It was nice to be able to do that, entertain Sarah.

"I've missed you," she said softly.

Everything stopped, even his breathing, while Wes absorbed that.

"Yeah. I regretted not asking you to call me when you made it home. I was worried. Then I almost called you half a dozen times on Friday to ask about the board meeting. That's silly, right?"

"No. I love it. I'm the worrier on my family's group chat. When people don't check in, I chase them down. It would be nice to have someone worrying about me..."

Wes pressed his phone harder to his ear as her voice trailed off. When he understood she wasn't going to add anything, he realized she was exactly where he was, even miles away. They wanted more but didn't know how to get there.

He wasn't leaving the Rocking A.

And now, she wasn't leaving LA.

"I'm glad I'll see you soon," Wes said. What else was there to add?

"Me, too." Sarah sighed. "Okay, I'll get back to packing things and tying up loose ends." He thought she was about to tell him goodbye but then seemed to change her mind. "Oh, I forgot an important piece, Wes. This offer, for the pasture, it needs to be fair market value. Nothing less. If you need ten years to pay it off, that's fine. We will carry it for that long, but I can't ask Jordan and Brooke to accept less than the land is worth, you know? I can make that work for both the Hearsts and the Armstrongs."

Wes realized Sarah might not wear as many different hats as he did but her mind was always focused on the problem, finding a solution or a compromise or a way through.

They shared that trait.

It was nice to share that burden, too.

"Got it. And Sarah…" Wes rolled his shoulders as most of his tension disappeared. "If you think of anything else you need…or you want to talk, please call me."

He hoped she understood he meant anything, anything at all.

"I'll see you soon," Sarah said softly and hung up the phone.

Wes stared hard at his phone while he inhaled slowly and then let it all go.

"Arrow, I believe this place has worked magic again. Are you ready to head back home and into the chaos?"

His horse snorted and shook his head.

It was an honest answer. Arrow could be trusted to tell the truth above all things.

"Too bad, friend, we have important work to do, but we'll go nice and slow." He untied the horse and ran a hand along his neck. In the saddle, Wes realized his mood had improved due to a single phone call. To celebrate, he said, "Let's take the scenic route down by the lake."

Arrow followed his directions. It was sweet to ride across the ranch where he'd come alive as a boy and understand that the next generation was going to enjoy this same space, the view, the sweet air, and, if they were lucky, horses as good as Arrow.

Whatever happened with Sarah would happen, and he might be sad about it, but the Rocking A would be there for him.

And for Grant and Clay, who were yelling

over the whine of a saw when he rode into the paddock near the barn. His mother was frowning as he and Arrow trotted toward her. "I can't tell whether to break it up or sell tickets," she said as she waved with the digital camera in her hand. "Good thing I'm taking photos, not video."

Wes glanced at the pretty quilt that was strategically draped across the top of the nearest fence. She was bending and twisting and shooting from different angles. He guessed sometimes the mountains were the backdrop and sometimes the barn. "What are you doing?"

She straightened. "Taking pictures. What are you doing?"

Wes wondered if he could move permanently to his quiet rock in Larkspur Pass. "What are the photos for?" he asked slowly, patiently.

"Advertisements for Western Days. This is the raffle quilt. Matt will put all this off to the last minute, so I'm going to work up a poster and image for social media. We need the festival to be big this year, for the anniversary." She pointed to the left. "Move over this way and tell Arrow to hang his head over the railing so I can get y'all into the picture. If you'd turn that frown right side up, it might be a nice shot to have." She blinked up at him as she waited.

Tell Arrow to hang his head over the railing. The urge to grumble about her orders was hard to resist but he did as she asked. And Arrow, being smarter than the average horse, must have taken modeling classes at some point in his past because he hit his mark on the first try. His mother launched into paparazzi-style photography, most likely trying to get his good side.

"Okay. I'm done." She let the camera dangle around her neck and moved closer to hug Arrow. "Good job."

Wes didn't thank her. She wasn't speaking to him.

Arrow whiffled and then moved back as Grant yelled something at Clay that was indistinguishable, thank goodness.

"I was in such a good mood on my way here," Wes murmured. "Now I remember why I left in the first place."

His mother fluffed her hair, completely unconcerned by the chaos. That had to be because she could leave at any time. "What had sweetened your mood?"

"Sarah called," Wes said and realized his error immediately as his mother's gaze homed in on him like a raptor with prey. "She wants me to draw up a new proposal for the pasture only and a legal agreement to share the lane up to the Majestic. I guess she's moving forward with selling the land in parcels instead of one lot."

His mother nodded. "Okay. I suppose that's not horrible, a rich new neighbor who stirs things up in town a few times a year and otherwise leaves us alone. Much better than a loud, bustling casino." She shuddered as if Prospect had dodged a grim fate there.

Walt stepped up to prop his elbows on the fence. "What's got you all stirred up, Prue?"

"Wes and Sarah are going to find a way to get us the pasture back, even if we can't get the whole parcel."

"Think we can afford it?" his father asked. He and his dad had the best understanding of the ranch's financial situation. It made sense he'd be worried.

"Yep. Sarah is going to make sure our offer works." Wes slid out of the saddle.

"We trust her that far?" Walt asked slyly, glancing at Prue out of the corner of his eye.

Prue tangled her arm through his. "We do. Sarah is our kind of people. Family matters to her."

Wes met his father's stare but neither one of them brought up her chilly reception on Sarah's arrival.

"Like that Jordan, too. She seems like a firecracker. I do love me a good firecracker." Walt waggled his eyebrows at his ex-wife.

"The girl barely said three sentences at that breakfast meeting. How do you know?" his mother asked slowly.

Wes was glad she asked. He wanted to know the answer. Or he thought he did. He had failed miserably at dragging any details out of Clay.

"Came into the hardware store. Bought some tools. We jawed about the weather and the town, you know, making conversation." Walt shrugged as if it was nothing out of the ordinary.

"Tools." Prue frowned. "Like a hammer?"

His father nodded.

Then Wes and his mother exchanged a

look, because why would Jordan, who was staying at the B-and-B, need a hammer?

Before Wes could ask that, Walt turned, pulling Prue along with him. "Come see my new palace. If these boys don't kill each other first, it will be nice."

Wes said to Arrow, "I'll solve the Jordan mystery another day. Today is about spreadsheets." And he did love a good spreadsheet. Arrow was not a fan. The horse moved toward the barn, ready for a brush, a stall, some food and a lot of water.

Wes hoped he could sneak into his office and get the door closed before any of his brothers spotted him. He wanted to spend time thinking about the future, not breaking up arguments.

Sarah had managed to find a compromise.

If he thought about it hard enough, there might be a way to solve his and Sarah's other problems, too.

CHAPTER TWENTY

THE SECOND TIME Sarah drove into Prospect after the sun sank below the ridge of mountains, she was exhausted, but that fatigue was accompanied by relief, as if she'd made it home again. So much of the two-day drive was monotony, and it had left her plenty of time to think. And this time, she knew where she was going to lay her head and sleep for approximately twelve hours. Jordan had reserved a room for her at Bell House when Sarah had called to let her know she was on the way.

"Come get my suitcase, little sister," Sarah said as Jordan answered her phone. "I'm back."

Jordan squealed and hung up the phone.

Stretching her legs felt good as she opened the SUV hatch. Jordan skidded to a stop next to her and, midhug, exclaimed, "What is that?"

Sarah grabbed her sister, squeezed her hard

and then handed her a suitcase to carry. "That is artwork. Don't you recognize it?"

"Artwork," Jordan repeated but Sarah didn't hear her catching on.

"Sadie's favorite painting in the world was stuffed inside my office when I made it in to work." Sarah shut the hatch and then turned to go up the steps to the porch. "I decided to toss it into the car with me and drive it across state lines."

Jordan had followed behind, grunting under the weight of Sarah's bag which may or may not have included an extra pair of shoes or three that she'd packed specifically for the trip. "Why are you chauffeuring around a painting?"

"I didn't have anywhere else to put it," Sarah said. She shrugged and opened the door to Bell House before motioning Jordan ahead of her. Instead of being forced to track down Rose at the Mercantile, Sarah found her and Prue Armstrong nursing cups of coffee at the kitchen table.

"We expected you to arrive sooner," Prue said, "but I couldn't leave without saying hello."

Sarah hadn't expected an audience. Her

plan wasn't fully formed yet. She still needed her sisters to sign on, but she knew Wes had shared her idea to sell the pasture with his mother. Her warm welcome gave it away. Now she had to make this sale happen or else risk another cooling off from Prue.

If everything went the way she wanted it to, she and Prue needed to get along.

Because she and Wes were going to be spending time together.

"It's always nice when family comes home, isn't it?" Prue asked before taking a sip.

Jordan frowned. "I mean, always? I don't know if I can cosign that, but I'm happy to have her back."

Sarah met Prue's stare. She wanted to ask about whose family Prue meant. Was she including Sarah in the Prospect family now?

Prue nodded and patted Sarah's arm and then Jordan's on her way out of Bell House. "Oh, I am happy, too. And I bet I can name a cowboy who isn't sleeping tonight, excited like it's Christmas Eve. I believe I'll go give him a ring, to test my theory." Prue was gone before Sarah could stop her.

She hoped Wes's mother was right and that he was still awake.

It was nice to imagine Wes waiting up until he knew she'd made it safely home.

"Jordan picked a new room for you," Rose said. "She explained how much you love the themes." She slid a key ring across the counter. "Silver's the room right next to Jordan's, too."

"You can't beat the location," Jordan said as she blinked innocently.

Sarah knew that payback was going to be swift. Whatever room Jordan had chosen for her, it would be an adventure. The problem with playing pranks on her sisters was the escalation. The return volley was always bigger and louder.

"Lead the way." Sarah pulled out her phone as she trailed Jordan. When Brooke answered, she said, "Is it too late to talk, baby sister? I got hung up in LA, so it's taken a while to cover the last leg of the trip. That's why I'm only just calling now." She handed Jordan the key and braced herself as her sister swung the door open to reveal Silver.

As in "Silver Bells."

Or even "Jingle Bells."

Sarah realized she'd guessed the theme correctly on her first night at the B-and-B, but she hadn't thought far enough ahead to keep her sister from reserving it for her.

The wreath on the door to Silver jangled loudly. How did the visitors stand it when Bell House was at capacity?

How would Jordan stand it when Sarah made four or five unnecessary trips in the middle of the night?

From the evil grin on her sister's face, it was clear she hadn't anticipated that.

As a good big sister, Sarah resolved not to give her any advance notice, either.

She heard Brooke repeating her name, so Sarah returned her attention to the call. "Sorry, Brooke, what did you say?"

Brooke sighed heavily. "I don't sleep a lot lately. This is fine. I can't believe you've put off this discussion this long, but if we have to have it at midnight, let's do it."

"Okay, I asked Jordan to discuss our options with you. Did she?" She raised an eyebrow at Jordan who nodded broadly and rolled her eyes before scrambling behind the Christmas tree. Sarah noted a beautiful old fireplace, stockings hung from the mantel, of course. Jordan's chortling as blinking lights blazed was amusing, even if the glare from the tree was not. Sarah switched Brooke to video and carefully propped her phone on the nightstand so her sister could absorb the full effect.

"What in the Christmas-in-July-but-really-September is going on in your room?" Brooke asked. "We can't talk business until you explain how you time traveled to December."

Her sister's concern was valid. "Bell House's owner enjoys a good theme, apparently. The name of the room? Silver. The theme? Christmas explosion, I guess." Sarah grabbed the pillows that tumbled when Jordan plopped down on the mattress next to her.

"I picked this for Sarah after she had Rose put me in the honeymoon suite. *Wedding bells*. It's all bells, all the time here."

They watched Brooke process that. It took about as long as Sarah expected.

Eventually, Brooke shook her head. "I may need to come back to this when I have had some rest. Let's discuss the lodge. That's got to be easier."

"Tell me what you know," Sarah answered. It wasn't that she didn't trust Jordan to tell their younger sister everything, but she really didn't.

"Platinum's offer was four million dollars,

but there's no way in the world we could accept that." Brooke brushed her bangs off her forehead. Sarah could tell she really was exhausted. Was the latest political campaign doing this to her?

"Right." Jordan squashed beside Sarah to get on camera. "We both know that Sadie would never allow Key Lake to be used for that. I didn't even have to convince Brooke to say no."

Sarah waited for her youngest sister to snap about Jordan's know-it-all tone or bossiness, but it didn't come.

That was another sign that Brooke wasn't herself.

"So that leaves us with the real estate agent." Brooke yawned before covering her mouth with her hand. "I say break it up into pieces to be sure we get the best offers. That gives us more control over who moves in, too."

Since that had been the case Sarah wanted to make, she was relieved. Suspicious, but relieved.

She stared at a confused-looking Jordan who raised both hands. "What?"

The ache across Sarah's shoulders flared as she realized she was going to have to get to the bottom of whatever Jordan had done to pull the strings she wanted pulled. Her innocent look was the truest sign that she was up to something.

But first, Sarah was going to secure the sale of the pasture to the Armstrongs.

"I called Wes this weekend and asked him to put together his best offer for just the pasture." Sarah watched Brooke closely. "Did Jordan explain to you that the Armstrongs want to buy Sadie's land back? I want them to have the pasture for their cows."

"Because she's in love with a cowboy," Jordan said slowly before poking Sarah's leg.

"Stop that." Sarah smacked her hand. "I'm not in love. I'm in…like."

"Kissing. That kind of like," Brooke said, "doesn't come along every day. Jordan says the cowboy is cute. And a good guy. I believe *salt of the earth* was the term she used."

"Salt of the earth?" Sarah repeated. She would have said that applied to old men, weathered by the elements, boring and…old.

"What's wrong with that? Noble and good. Come on—it was a compliment," she said.

Noble and good definitely fit Wes Armstrong. It probably applied, even if she and Wes were young and definitely not boring.

"There's an entire gaggle of them, Brooke." Jordan shook her head. "If I hadn't seen it with my own eyes, I wouldn't have believed it, but I'm also certain that the kissing has something to do with the large painting residing inside Sarah's SUV. I haven't connected the dots yet, but I am intrigued."

Sarah hadn't figured to get into the hazy plan forming for a small but noteworthy museum for Sadie's memorabilia.

Perhaps she should have considered that before hauling Sadie's mountains to Colorado.

Brooke leaned back against her pillows. She was alone. Was Paul away somewhere? "Jordan and I had to stop talking because we were shouting about which of the other options was best. Before that starts again, I gotta know more about how Sadie's artwork fits in."

"It's a bunch of small pieces that don't quite snap together. The board meeting. Michael offered me a position as the curator of Sadie's memorabilia. He wants to have displays at the Cookie Queen, but there's entirely too

much from Sadie's life to fit at the business."
Sarah tangled her fingers together. This made
her nervous. A space devoted to Sadie? Even
Sadie would think that was over the top. But
if anyone could support Sarah's plan to find
her own way in Prospect, it was her sisters.
"So, I'm going to create a place here in Prospect. If we keep the lodge…" She hadn't fully
committed to the idea yet because her sisters
had their own goals for this inheritance.

"Or when we sell it…" Brooke leaned forward. "What are we going to do with a fishing lodge? I'm across the country, Sarah, and
Jordan has got a busy career. You can't do this
on your own." She frowned. "What am I saying? Of course, you can, but do you want to?
Don't let Jordan talk you into it. You know
how she is."

"What does *that* mean?" Jordan asked in a
challenging tone.

Sarah wanted to wade in to stop the storm
before the clouds started swirling, but it was
too late. "What I mean is you are so enthusiastic about your next inspiration, Jordie.
You've always been that way. Full speed
ahead, dragging me and Sarah behind you.
Then what happens?"

Sarah knew the answer but she'd never been able to call Jordan on it. Brooke was the one up to bat.

"With you, it gets hard or boring or something shinier catches your attention, and then Sarah or I or both of us sometimes finish up while you skip along unbothered." Brooke tapped her fingers along the nightstand as if they were happily skipping along. "You have a good career. Don't torpedo that for something that sounds fun now but is really going to be difficult when you get into the middle of the mess." Brooke pointed through the screen at her. "If Sarah is stuck there in the mountains in a money pit while you return to LA in three months, you and I are going to fight."

Jordan was suspiciously quiet in the face of Brooke's righteous speech. There should be pushback at this point. That meant there was something she and Brooke didn't know. "What, Jordan? What aren't you telling us?"

"A couple of things to consider here." Jordan fussed with invisible strings on the beautiful red-and-green quilt spread across the foot of the bed and didn't meet her eyes. "About that career."

Sarah crossed her arms over her chest. A

quick check of her phone showed Brooke had struck the matching pose on her end.

"My boss vetoed my vacation request to come to Prospect and help out." Jordan wrinkled her nose. "So I quit. I won't be going back to that job."

Jordan held up her hands at the dire sounds Sarah and Brooke made. "What else could I do? You needed me here." She sniffed and studied the quilt pattern as if it held important answers.

"And you don't think things through. You never have. You leap and expect someone to make a soft landing for you," Brooke muttered. "You didn't like working there, so you seized the chance to...not work there."

Sarah inhaled and exhaled to get her nerves settled.

"The silver lining is that I have plenty of time to help out here in Prospect. Absolutely nothing is holding me in LA now." Jordan met Sarah's stare, ready to hear whatever she might say.

Brooke was absolutely correct. This was the way Jordan operated. She followed her instincts and her heart. She shot right out of the gate as Sadie said.

But Prospect had saved Jordan once.

The worry in the pit of Sarah's stomach for her middle sister untangled for the first time in a long time. Jordan had been sent to Prospect as a teenager to get her life back on track. What if being in the unique little town worked its magic again and was what Jordan needed to find her future?

At the thought, it was so easy to picture Sadie's beautiful, happy face in her mind.

"What's the other thing," Brooke demanded from her screen. "You said two. Drop that shoe now."

Jordan grimaced. "I already started on the renovations." She squeezed her eyes shut. "Not a lot. I swear! I didn't go inside the place because there's still the problem with whatever is squatting in the kitchen, but I was bored."

Those words sent a shiver down Sarah's spine. Jordan and "I was bored" usually led to trouble.

"What did you do?" Sarah asked calmly.

Jordan shrugged. "I took the boards off the windows along the front. The ones not covered over with hedges."

Sarah waited. That didn't really seem so bad.

"I broke one of the windows, but I'll fix it." Jordan smiled brightly.

All things considered, that still didn't seem terrible, so Sarah nodded.

"Any other revelations you'd like to drop in the middle of the night?" Brooke asked.

Jordan shook her head.

"Okay, I support this sale to the neighbors. If they can use the pasture and pay a fair price, I want to do that. Jordan mentioned our reputation could use some repair in Prospect. Maybe that will help." Brooke rubbed her eyes. "What else do we have to decide tonight? I still think selling the rest is the right way to go."

Jordan bit her lip. "Could we agree to a trial period? We list it and see what kind of offers we get. In the meantime, I work on the renovations? I can make a difference. Maybe there's still a chance to keep the Majestic going."

Sarah met Jordan's pleading stare and then turned to Brooke. "There's no reason we have to say no now. Dusting cobwebs could keep her away from creating more catastrophe elsewhere."

Brooke raised her hands in surrender. "Sounds

terrible. Go for it. We list it and then we evaluate any serious offers together."

"You need to come back to the lodge before any sale is final. It could be your last chance to see the place." Jordan had scooted closer to the phone.

"If I can, I will." Brooke smiled. "Don't break anything else, Jordie. Call me after you guys meet with the handsome cowboy."

"I'll let you know about the offer," Sarah said.

"And I'll tell you about all the kissing," Jordan sang as Sarah picked up her phone.

"Love you, Brooke. I hope you're taking care of yourself." Sarah waited. Sometimes Brooke opened up if she gave her enough space.

"Love you, too, Sarah. Watch out for yourself, okay? If Prospect is where you want to be, then that changes everything." Brooke wrinkled her nose. "Don't tell Jordan I said that, though."

"Too late. I heard you," Jordan said.

Brooke was laughing as she hung up.

Jordan jumped up and started straightening the quilt.

"You quit your job. Without a single worry."

Sarah rubbed her forehead, amazed again at Jordan's fearlessness.

"I'm fired up by the possibilities of the Majestic," Jordan said. "I can see how it all works for you and me, for Brooke, for the Armstrongs and the town."

Sarah lunged for her sister and landed on top of her to hug her tightly while Jordan giggled. "Yeah? Can you see a shop with Sadie's cookbooks and Western shirts for sale while episodes of her TV show play in the background, Sadie Hearst, the Colorado Cookie Queen, with her famous friends?"

Jordan pretended to fluff the pillows. "I can. We'll need to expand so we can run the cooking class retreats that I'd like to start with the famous chef we're going to recruit."

Sarah considered that. "Sadie would love that."

"I know," Jordan said softy as she rested her head against Sarah's shoulder.

Suddenly, it dawned on Sarah that what she was feeling was content, relaxed. She stared up at the blinking light cast on the ceiling by the Christmas tree.

In September.

In Prospect.

Even that was starting to make sense to her.

Sarah might not be able to see the future yet, but she was starting to trust that it was going to work out.

CHAPTER TWENTY-ONE

"WOULD YOU QUIT PACING?" Clay muttered the second time Wes passed by him as he marched over the bridge above the stream that ran in front of Prospect Lodge. "The real estate agent keeps shooting worried looks at us while she pretends to take a phone call."

Wes knew his brother was right, but he was ready to see Sarah.

He'd been restless that day in the barn when she made her first trip out to the Rocking A, but he hadn't really known anything about her then.

Just the fact that he'd be face-to-face with her was enough for the anticipation to bubble up inside him.

Today, he knew so much and he'd missed her greatly, so the eagerness had doubled.

Would it always be like that? The more time he spent with Sarah, the worse he'd miss her when she was gone, and the harder it would be to wait to see her again?

If so, he was doomed.

He had arrived at Prospect Lodge early, and he'd explained patiently to Clay that it was because he was the property manager so he should open up the doors before everyone else got there. It was good they'd arrived ahead of the others. It gave them time to cover the broken window. He'd been surprised to see the exposed windows on the restaurant, but his brother had somehow been prepared with the drill and screws needed to reattach the plywood. When things were calmer, he was going to get to the bottom of it, but Clay's muttered "Jordan" had been a significant clue.

Erin Chang had been the next person to show. They'd made small talk about the weather until she excused herself to make a supposed phone call.

The rumble of tires…

That had to be Sarah.

Clay clamped a hand over his shoulder. "Do not run out into the parking lot. She'll cry if she hits you and I don't trust you not to chase the bumper like a stray right now."

Wes shook his brother's hand away but realized Clay might have a point. "Is that Jordan I see?"

Watching Clay clamp his mouth shut in response made him feel better, more in the know. Whatever had happened between them, it had been epic.

As the women got out, Sarah called, "Hey, Wes, can you help me with something?"

He and Clay followed her to the back of the SUV she'd been driving. Sarah opened the trunk.

"This painting needs to go inside. For now, let's put it in the lobby somewhere." Sarah smiled at Clay, so he stepped forward to slide it out carefully. Jordan moved around to take the other end and they managed to agree to carry it inside without exchanging a word.

Wes wanted to say something clever, but every thought was blown away like a wish made on a dandelion when Sarah wrapped her arms around his neck and pressed her lips to his. "I've missed you. I don't like being so far away."

Relief settled into his bones. There was no way she'd missed him as intensely as he had her, but she still fit perfectly.

"It took me forever to get back to Prospect. I'm glad to be home." Sarah ran a hand down his tie. "I'm guessing you're a lawyer today. No khakis this time."

He shook his head, but over and over, he heard her saying *home* in his mind.

"Home is LA. Where your job is," he said when he could make words flow again.

She jerked back. "Is that an order?" Her frown was intense. "Because let me tell you, I have been pulling strings on enough tangles to make a new quilt..." She waved her hands. "Okay, the analogy doesn't work, but it's a lot of strings is what I'm saying."

Wes tilted his head to the side. "Strings for what? You got the promotion. You were excited about it. I know. I remember the sound of my heart busting into a million pieces. That job is with the Cookie Queen in LA."

Sarah blinked. "All true but that last part. It's in Prospect if I want it to be in Prospect. If you want it to be in Prospect." She huffed out a breath. "There's this guy there that I'm totally falling for and I moved some mountains to have the time to finish that properly."

He knew the grin on his face was silly. That didn't mean he was in any hurry to chase it away. "Is it me? Am I the lucky guy?"

Sarah narrowed her eyes at him in what he

guessed was intended to be a mean glare. "At some point, put on the mayor hat and walk me through whether we can convince your mother to agree with my plan to open a Sadie Hearst museum here. That was the job offer; take all of Sadie's memorabilia, her recipe files, her TV shows, all of that and put something together for the headquarters in LA to show her history, and bring the rest here and make sure Sadie's legacy is preserved."

Wes yanked his hat off and held it as he pulled her close. "You tell me what I need to do to make it happen."

"You took off your lawyer hat. We need to negotiate an agreement on the pasture first," Sarah said, one corner of her mouth curling slowly.

"I'll put it back on, but now I'm just Wes." He rested his head against hers. "I'll do whatever it takes to get you here to Prospect."

She stepped back. "Let's go talk real estate before my sister figures out how to honk another horn."

Wes was laughing as he followed her inside. The painting was leaning against the long check-in counter.

"It fits behind here," Jordan said. "I'll get a ladder and hang it up this week."

"Not by yourself. And cleaning this place will stir up some dust. Better cover it until it's time," Clay stated matter-of-factly.

Even from his spot in the doorway, Wes could see Jordan's spine snap straight.

Angry whispers drifted across the lobby and Wes thought he heard something about Clay already having to board up a window thanks to her. But Sarah said loudly, "Erin, thank you for coming. I'm hoping you can take a look at the Armstrongs' offer and assure me and my sisters that it's fair market value."

They spread the paperwork over the counter and everyone was silent as the real estate agent flipped through the stack of documents Wes handed her. Eventually, she shook her head. "No, it is not fair market value."

Sarah blinked. "Uh, yes it is."

Wes smiled at her immediate defense.

"No," Erin replied, "it's actually somewhere between five and ten percent above what I'd calculated as a fair price."

Sarah exhaled slowly.

"The only odd thing that I see, which…"

Erin hesitated. "Well, in most cases, the bank carries the risk of default of payments, but Wes has offered you a large lump sum at signing and then payments with interest. It's an unusual structure."

"That's why we're paying a little over the average price per acre, as a premium for financing the loan. It should cover the carrying cost of any taxes on the land." Wes ran his hand under Sarah's hair to her nape and rubbed the tension there. He could see the worry melting from her face.

"It's a good offer. I can't speak to the easement contract Wes has drawn up, but these additional items offered as in-kind trade…" Erin laughed. "Really different, but I'm guessing they're going to be popular."

Sarah frowned as she tugged the papers closer to read. "'In addition to the aforementioned monetary payments, the Rocking A Ranch offers the services of Wesley Armstrong as land management agent without additional compensation for the period of the loan.'" Wes watched her nod.

She continued, "'In the event that the Hearsts need advisement for renovation construction or design during the same period, Clayton Armstrong will work as a consultant and assist with booking necessary tradespersons to be wholly compensated by the Hearsts and waive his hourly fee." Jordan rolled her eyes at that, but Sarah raised her eyebrows at Wes. "Interesting." He nodded. He'd thrown everything including the kitchen sink into this agreement, determined to make sure Sarah Hearst knew he'd do what it took to keep her here. He'd expected convincing them to make a go of the lodge would be a long shot, but it seemed the odds were improving.

"I'd advise against spending any time or money on renovations if we're moving forward with a listing," Erin said firmly. "I understand your concerns about the demolition of your great-aunt's lodge, but when this sells, the new owner will rebuild. I'm certain."

Sarah studied Jordan and then said, "Three months. We're going to list it while Jordan sorts through the ideas she has for the place. The three of us will seriously consider any offers that come in." She turned to Wes. "That should give me time to work through the items that come into the warehouse near headquarters to see how much space we need here. If the spot for Sadie's showcase isn't going to be the lodge, it will be in Prospect. You can help me find the right place, somewhere with a lurid history that Sadie would love?"

He tapped his hat. "I can make that happen."

"And at the end of three months?" Erin asked.

"We'll regroup." Sarah returned to reading the list of addenda. "Matt Armstrong will provide investigative and relocation services for any animal found to be cohabiting in the lodge while the Hearsts are in residence." Sarah's lips twitched. "What if it's not an animal? What if it's human or paranormal?" She widened her eyes.

Wes pretended to think that over. "Matt's really better with animals, but he could probably handle ghostbusting, too. He's not here, so I'll volunteer him for that as well."

Sarah's chuckle was sweet. "He should have shown up for the meeting."

Erin frowned. "Are you saying the place is haunted?" She brushed hair behind one ear. "Badly enough that I need to include it in the listing for the lodge or…"

Sarah looked sheepish. "Nope. No ghost."

Jordan murmured, "Not confirmed, anyway."

Wes laughed. Whatever happened with the lodge, whether they reopened it or sold it, the Hearsts were going to be fun to watch.

"Now, this is only for me," Sarah said as she glanced at him. "Grant Armstrong will select, train and stable a mare in the Rocking A barns for the personal use of any Hearst in Prospect." She placed a hand over her heart. "But I'm the only Hearst that rides."

He nodded. "I'm hoping that will be a regular occurrence. There's so much more to see. I can't wait to show you."

Sarah met his stare and it was impossible to look away.

"Do we have a deal?" he asked softly.

Sarah nodded before moving closer to kiss him. They had to find a better time and better place, but at this point, he was thrilled to have her back in his arms.

And somehow, they were going to make more time.

That had been his concern. He'd fallen hard and fast.

This agreement would give him the days and months to make sure she tumbled right after him.

Wes didn't step back when he heard Jordan say, "The kissing is a lot."

Clay added, "Poor guy doesn't realize he fell right into Prue Armstrong's trap."

Wes grinned at Sarah. "He's right. She told me to swoop you up as soon as you rolled into town." He almost copied the motion his mother made but he didn't want to let go of Sarah.

"Yeah?" Sarah asked. "Before she knew who I was."

"And because she was afraid I wouldn't stand a chance if you saw one of my handsomer brothers first." Wes held her close, loving how she felt in his arms.

"Little did she know we were already tangled up in the strategies of Sadie Hearst, the Colorado Cookie Queen." Sarah laughed.

"Do you think Sadie has any other surprises in store for the Hearsts and the Armstrongs?" Wes asked.

Sarah motioned with her head toward Jordan and Clay, who had moved over to the broken window to discuss the damage. "Sadie is just getting started."

* * * * *

*Don't miss the next charming
installment of the new miniseries,*
The Fortunes of Prospect, *from
acclaimed author Cheryl Harper and
Harlequin Heartwarming—coming soon!*

Get 4 FREE REWARDS!

We'll send you 2 FREE Books plus 2 FREE Mystery Gifts.

FREE Value Over **$20**

Both the **Love Inspired®** and **Love Inspired® Suspense** series feature compelling novels filled with inspirational romance, faith, forgiveness and hope.

YES! Please send me 2 FREE novels from the Love Inspired or Love Inspired Suspense series and my 2 FREE gifts (gifts are worth about $10 retail). After receiving them, if I don't wish to receive any more books, I can return the shipping statement marked "cancel." If I don't cancel, I will receive 6 brand-new Love Inspired Larger-Print books or Love Inspired Suspense Larger-Print books every month and be billed just $6.49 each in the U.S. or $6.74 each in Canada. That is a savings of at least 16% off the cover price. It's quite a bargain! Shipping and handling is just 50¢ per book in the U.S. and $1.25 per book in Canada.* I understand that accepting the 2 free books and gifts places me under no obligation to buy anything. I can always return a shipment and cancel at any time by calling the number below. The free books and gifts are mine to keep no matter what I decide.

Choose one: ☐ **Love Inspired**
Larger-Print
(122/322 IDN GRHK)

☐ **Love Inspired Suspense**
Larger-Print
(107/307 IDN GRHK)

Name (please print)

Address   Apt. #

City   State/Province   Zip/Postal Code

Email: Please check this box ☐ if you would like to receive newsletters and promotional emails from Harlequin Enterprises ULC and its affiliates. You can unsubscribe anytime.

Mail to the Harlequin Reader Service:
IN U.S.A.: P.O. Box 1341, Buffalo, NY 14240-8531
IN CANADA: P.O. Box 603, Fort Erie, Ontario L2A 5X3

Want to try 2 free books from another series! Call 1-800-873-8635 or visit www.ReaderService.com.

LIRLIS22R3

Get 4 FREE REWARDS!

We'll send you 2 FREE Books plus 2 FREE Mystery Gifts.

FREE
Value Over
$20

Both the **Harlequin® Special Edition** and **Harlequin® Heartwarming™** series feature compelling novels filled with stories of love and strength where the bonds of friendship, family and community unite.

YES! Please send me 2 FREE novels from the Harlequin Special Edition or Harlequin Heartwarming series and my 2 FREE gifts (gifts are worth about $10 retail). After receiving them, if I don't wish to receive any more books, I can return the shipping statement marked "cancel." If I don't cancel, I will receive 6 brand-new Harlequin Special Edition books every month and be billed just $5.49 each in the U.S. or $6.24 each in Canada, a savings of at least 12% off the cover price, or 4 brand-new Harlequin Heartwarming Larger-Print books every month and be billed just $6.24 each in the U.S. or $6.74 each in Canada, a savings of at least 19% off the cover price. It's quite a bargain! Shipping and handling is just 50¢ per book in the U.S. and $1.25 per book in Canada.* I understand that accepting the 2 free books and gifts places me under no obligation to buy anything. I can always return a shipment and cancel at any time by calling the number below. The free books and gifts are mine to keep no matter what I decide.

Choose one: ☐ **Harlequin Special Edition**   ☐ **Harlequin Heartwarming**
(235/335 HDN GRJV)   **Larger-Print**
(161/361 HDN GRJV)

Name (please print)

Address   Apt. #

City   State/Province   Zip/Postal Code

Email: Please check this box ☐ if you would like to receive newsletters and promotional emails from Harlequin Enterprises ULC and its affiliates. You can unsubscribe anytime.

Mail to the **Harlequin Reader Service:**
IN U.S.A.: P.O. Box 1341, Buffalo, NY 14240-8531
IN CANADA: P.O. Box 603, Fort Erie, Ontario L2A 5X3

Want to try 2 free books from another series! Call 1-800-873-8635 or visit www.ReaderService.com.

*Terms and prices subject to change without notice. Prices do not include sales taxes, which will be charged (if applicable) based on your state or country of residence. Canadian residents will be charged applicable taxes. Offer not valid in Quebec. This offer is limited to one order per household. Books received may not be as shown. Not valid for current subscribers to the Harlequin Special Edition or Harlequin Heartwarming series. All orders subject to approval. Credit or debit balances in a customer's account(s) may be offset by any other outstanding balance owed by or to the customer. Please allow 4 to 6 weeks for delivery. Offer available while quantities last.

Your Privacy—Your information is being collected by Harlequin Enterprises ULC, operating as Harlequin Reader Service. For a complete summary of the information we collect, how we use this information and to whom it is disclosed, please visit our privacy notice located at corporate.harlequin.com/privacy-notice. From time to time we may also exchange your personal information with reputable third parties. If you wish to opt out of this sharing of your personal information, please visit readerservice.com/consumerschoice or call 1-800-873-8635. **Notice to California Residents**—Under California law, you have specific rights to control and access your data. For more information on these rights and how to exercise them, visit corporate.harlequin.com/california-privacy.

HSEHW22R3

THE NORA ROBERTS COLLECTION

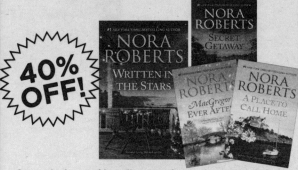

40% OFF!

Get to the heart of happily-ever-after in these Nora Roberts classics! Immerse yourself in the beauty of love by picking up this incredible collection written by, legendary author, Nora Roberts!

YES! Please send me the **Nora Roberts Collection**. Each book in this collection is 40% off the retail price! There are a total of 4 shipments in this collection. The shipments are yours for the low, members-only discount price of $23.96 U.S./$31.16 CDN. each, plus $1.99 U.S./$4.99 CDN. for shipping and handling. If I do not cancel, I will continue to receive four books a month for three months. I'll pay just $23.96 U.S./$31.16 CDN., plus $1.99 U.S./$4.99 CDN. for shipping and handling per shipment.* I can always return a shipment and cancel at any time.

☐ 274 2595   ☐ 474 2595

Name (please print)

Address   Apt. #

City   State/Province   Zip/Postal Code

Mail to the Harlequin Reader Service:
IN U.S.A.: P.O. Box 1341, Buffalo, NY 14240-8531
IN CANADA: P.O. Box 603, Fort Erie, Ontario L2A 5X3

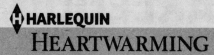
#463 HER AMISH COUNTRY VALENTINE
The Butternut Amish B&B • by Patricia Johns

Advertising exec Jill Wickey knows all about appearance versus reality. So why does she keep wishing that spending time with carpenter Thom Miller—her fake date for a wedding in Amish country—could be the start of something real?

#464 A COWBOY WORTH WAITING FOR
The Cowboy Academy • by Melinda Curtis

Ronnie Pickett is creating a matchmaking service for rodeo folks—but to be successful, she needs a high-profile competitor as a client. Former champ Wade Keller is perfect...but could he be perfect for her?

#465 A COUNTRY PROPOSAL
Cupid's Crossing • by Kim Findlay

Jordan's farm is the only security he's ever had. So when big-city chef—and first love—Delaney returns home with suggestions for revamping it, Jordan isn't happy. But Delaney has a few good ideas...about the two of them!

#466 A BABY ON HIS DOORSTEP
Kansas Cowboys • by Leigh Riker

Veterinarian Max Crane didn't expect to find a baby on his porch—or for former librarian Rachel Whittaker to accept the job caring for his daughter. Now, most unexpectedly of all, they are starting to feel like a family...

HARLEQUIN
PLUS

Try the best multimedia subscription service for romance readers like you!

Read, Watch and Play.

Experience the easiest way to get the romance content you crave.

Start your **FREE TRIAL** at
<u>www.harlequinplus.com/freetrial</u>.